FORBIDDEN BY DESTINY

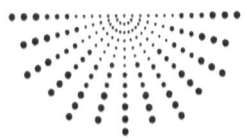

NEGEEN PAPEHN

CITY OWL
PRESS

FORBIDDEN BY DESTINY
Forbidden Love, Book 2

CITY OWL PRESS
www.cityowlpress.com

Cover Design by Mibl Art and Tina Moss. All stock photos licensed appropriately.

Edited by Amanda Roberts.

For information on subsidiary rights, please contact the publisher at info@cityowlpress.com.

Print Edition ISBN: 978-1-949090-22-2

Digital Edition ISBN: 978-1-949090-21-5

Printed in the United States of America

PRAISE FOR NEGEEN PAPEHN

"Forbidden by Faith shows how family, love, and faith can collide, even in this modern age." – *Romance Author, A. K. Leigh*

"Forbidden by Faith is a New Adult coming of age story with several twists, giving us a modern Romeo and Juliet tale where religion, culture, and class prejudice act as the hurdles for our lovers to overcome." – *Romance Author, Katie O' Sullivan*

"A heartfelt immigrant love story." – *Publisher's Weekly*

"Rich in culture, this first book in the Forbidden Love series immediately draws the reader in to this modern take on a familiar star-crossed lovers tale. The chemistry between Sara and Maziar sparks white hot immediately and every interaction sizzles." – *InD'tale*

"Nothing is better than this feeling, when you read the first pages of a book and you just know it will consume you. What I love the most about Papehn is the fact that you can tell that each of the books of this series is written with passion and that it's not just another book to sell to eager readers. Her stories are never predictable, she writes about heavy subjects and it's not always easy to read but it's also never gratuitous, everything on her characters journeys happen for a reason." – *Alyssa of LoveLysBooks*

"Ms. Papehn is a wonderful storyteller! I was immediately caught up in the lives of her characters. In Forbidden by Destiny, the heroine, Leyla, might be of Iranian descent but her story belongs to all women." – *Carrie Nichols, Author of The Small-Town Sweethearts series*

"This book goes far beyond being a romance novel...it covers a range of experiences women might have and treats them in a compassionate, loving, healing way. You're going to want to read this book, I guarantee it, and then you'll want to pass it along to a friend, a sister, or a mother." – *Diane Byington, Author of Who She Is*

For my parents
Thank you for always making me feel magical

CHAPTER ONE

I bounce back and forth on my toes. I have no idea what's taking him so long, but I wish he'd hurry up. I just want to get this over with.

Fidgeting uncomfortably before the steel gray door, I notice the sunny day, a light breeze bustling through the neighboring trees. I'm on the second floor of the apartment building, which gives me a direct view of the leaves. They're bright green against the backdrop of the blue sky. A squirrel jumps across the branches, an unidentifiable seed between his teeth.

It's cool out, despite the sun, and I pull my sweater in a bit tighter around my waist. I push my red hair off my shoulder, annoyed at how it clashes against the dark blue material, making it look more orange than usual. I worry that my proximity to the ocean is turning the curls into a frizzy poof as I stand here. The dreaded Persian girl hair—never a dull moment.

Why am I so nervous? I didn't break up with him—Sara did.

When Sara asked me to get her things from the apartment, I couldn't say no. She's been in the hospital with Maziar every day since the accident. She claims she can't leave him, but I know she just doesn't want to face Ben. She's not good at confrontation, especially when she's just torn his heart out from his chest after promising him forever. I don't blame Ben for hating her. I just hope I don't get stuck in the crossfire.

I'm standing in front of his door after a two-hour drive, wondering why I agreed to do this. I should have told her to send her brother. I imagine that exchange would at least be quick, if not painless.

The metal apartment numbers are gold, clashing against the gray. What an odd color choice. The paint's chipping off, no doubt from the dampness of the ocean breeze and longtime sun exposure. I have the urge to reach out and flick off a dried piece, when the door swings open.

Ben stands towering in the frame. His six-foot height dwarfs my small five-foot-two stature. The sun is glaring in his direction, reflecting a strange haze around him, almost as if he's glowing. For a moment, he reminds me of an angel painted on the ceiling of the Sistine Chapel. His crystal blue eyes sharpen the image. Wrinkles fan out prominently from their edges as he scowls at me. There are dark circles framing his lids. He looks exhausted and there's an edge to him, like he's ready for a fight. I don't blame him for directing it at me. Currently, I'm Sara's stand-in.

"Hey, Ben."

"Hi, Leyla." We stand frozen in an awkward staring contest. "Come in," he finally says.

He pushes the door wider, taking a step back, giving me space to enter. I can smell his aftershave, it's mingled with the scent of soap, and his hair's wet. He's in a pair of blue sweats and a crisp white T-shirt. His phoenix tattoo is visible on his arm, the outline of its tail and wings stark against his golden skin. *I've always loved that tattoo.*

The warmth of his gaze warns me that I'm staring. He's watching me closely. A puzzled expression transforms into a pull at the corner of his lips as he suppresses a smile. *What am I doing?* I shake my head, trying to dislodge my thoughts. *I'm here to get my best friend's things, not gawk at her ex-boyfriend.*

"You want something to drink?" he asks, catching me off-guard.

"Um, sure." I stumble over my words, having expected him to throw the boxes, and me, out of the door instantly.

"I have Coke or water."

"I'll take a Coke, please."

"Coming right up." I catch him laughing as he turns toward the kitchen door.

I'm mortified. *How long was I checking him out? And why does he seem to find that amusing?* Thank goodness there's a wall separating us, so he can't see the red I'm sure is creeping up my neck. These are the times I wish I had the classic Iranian olive tone instead of my strange milky-white skin. I'm a real Persian anomaly. My sister likes to tell me I'm adopted.

When he comes back to the living room, I'm sitting on his dark gray couch drawing circles with the edge of my fingertip into the fabric, waiting. I can hear the ice cubes clinking against the side of the glass when he hands me the cup, another reminder of the unbearable awkwardness surrounding us. He crosses the room and takes a seat. The plush blue chair he's sitting in makes his already intense eyes glow. I fidget beneath his gaze.

"Is there a lot of stuff I have to take back?" I ask, trying to cut through the silence. I can't take it.

I feel his energy shift at the indirect mention of Sara. His expression becomes somber with the weight of the past few weeks. It pushes down on us, suffocating me with its heavy and desperate makeup as it sucks the air out of the room. Despite my not mentioning her name, the damage is done. I instantly regret speaking, wishing I were content to stay in the uncomfortable quiet of a few moments ago.

"There's a bit," he says, pointing with his chin toward the front door.

His eyebrows are pinched together emphasizing his deep scowl. I can imagine how difficult the past week has been for him. He'd thought he was going to start a life with Sara; they were practically engaged. But instead, she dropped him at the first sight of her past. That's rough.

By the door, there's a stack of about ten large cardboard boxes with Sara's name written on them. Each letter is carefully shaped with his impeccable penmanship, the only order in the sea of chaos.

"Oh. That's more than I expected," I mumble.

"I'll help you get them into your car." Always the gentleman.

He exhales slowly, and it becomes obvious the fight has left him. I can see it in the way his shoulders are hunched forward, the way his elbows rest limply on the armrests. I can see how tired he is in the droopiness of his eyes. When he looks back toward me, the blue of his irises has dulled. I imagine when I leave with Sara's belongings, it somehow solidifies the end of their relationship.

Suddenly the heat of irritation courses through my veins. Unexpectedly, it's directed toward Sara and the state she's reduced him to. *He doesn't deserve this.*

Ben and I were friends. It was inevitable with all the time we spent together in Sara's presence. When she broke up with him, I dropped him without a second thought. The situation was complicated and convoluted and I took the easy way out. Now, as I watch this broken man before me, I wish I had been a better friend to him.

"Have you had lunch yet?" I ask. He looks at me as if I'm speaking a foreign language. "You know, have you had any food?" I jokingly make the gesture of putting something into my mouth. He smiles and it feels like a little win.

"No, I haven't. I've been dealing with boxes all day."

"Let's go get some food," I say. "It's beautiful outside. The sunshine will do us some good."

He looks at me thoughtfully, not quick to agree to this sudden outing. I'm sure he's sizing me up, trying to figure out if I'm friend or foe. After how I treated him, how could he possibly think I'm safe? Plus, Sara's my best friend, making me guilty by association.

"Come on," I insist.

I don't really know what I'm doing exactly, just that I can't take the idea that he's so hurt. He's nothing like the fun, carefree Ben I'm used to. This fractured version of him is depressing, and I suddenly have the urge to save him.

"Okay, let me change," he finally consents. Then he gets up and leaves the room

My nerves are on edge, making me feel sick. Am I betraying Sara by spending time with Ben? It's not like she hates him. She just doesn't love him like she loves Maziar. Would she be upset if we get some food? I mean, we both need to eat. And it's not like we're going out on a date or anything.

Ben steps back into the living room five minutes later. He's changed out of his sweats into a pair of khaki shorts to go with his white T-shirt. He's thrown on a baseball cap, "Stanford" written across the front for his alma mater. Wisps of his dirty-blond hair curl out from beneath the edges like the hair on a little boy's head. I find it endearing.

"Ready?" he asks, grabbing his keys. "I'll drive."

A smile spreads across my face as he holds the door open for me. My stomach flips in response, throwing me off balance. I'm not supposed to feel this giddy, but I try to ignore it, telling myself that I'm just being nice and finding a way to take his mind off of the breakup. Any decent person would do the same. Nonetheless, when he places his hand on the small of my back turning me toward his car, a shiver runs through my body, leaving a cluster of goosebumps in its wake.

Fifteen minutes later, we're walking across State Street looking for a place to eat. The options are plentiful, so we decide to make a lap before we commit to a location. He's standing a few inches away from me. Our fingers accidentally brush against each other when I take a step too close. A current rushes up my arm at the contact. He doesn't mention it, just takes a half-step farther away, breaking the connection. The disappointment that follows is jarring. What an odd reaction; I'm not supposed to care.

I'm making small talk, asking about the food at one place and the beer at another. As I continue to ramble, the tension eases out of Ben's shoulders and his gait becomes more casual. He's smiling more readily now; it reaches the edges of his eyes and sets his dimples deep on either side of his face. He even manages to laugh, the sound fanning out from the center of his chest like a blooming flower. It's infectious, causing a flutter beneath my ribcage.

We settle on a small deli, taking a table in the far corner. The seats are white and plastic, the tablecloth checkered like we're at a picnic. He takes my order, then steps up to the counter to place it while I hold our spot. I can't help but notice the outline of his back, the muscles tight and taut beneath his shirt. I can distinctly see their shapes, tracing them with my eyes. I know I shouldn't be looking at Ben this way—he's Sara's ex—but I can't help it. He's a handsome man. I've always thought so.

I'm still staring when he turns back toward our table, a plastic number on the end of a metal rod in his hand. Our eyes lock and I suddenly can't breathe. I have to look away as he makes his way over, worried he can see the strange effect he's having on me. When he sits down, I notice the receipt in his hand.

"Did you pay already?" I ask.

"Yeah," he says.

"How much do I owe you?"

"Nothing," he replies.

"You didn't need to pay for me, Ben," I protest.

"I know."

There's a confidence about his chivalry that's so attractive. He isn't flirting with me. It's obvious that in his world, paying when he's with a girl is just the way things are. He seems clueless to how much of a gentleman he actually is, making it that much more appealing.

He's staring at me funny, then reaches his hand out and grabs one of my curls. His fingertips brush my cheek and a surge of something I can't name spreads through my body. He's caught me off guard, but he doesn't seem to notice, twisting the tendril of hair between his fingers.

"How did you end up with this color?" he asks, bewildered.

"My mom's great-grandfather had red hair and blue eyes, actually. He has some European somewhere down his ancestral line. It's either that or I'm adopted," I say, laughing.

"I'd guess adoption because it's entirely too weird," he teases.

"Gee, thanks."

He lets go of my hair and leans back in his chair. "Either way, I like it. It's different."

I smile and have to look away, pretending he didn't just make me swoon.

When lunch is done, I find myself not wanting the encounter to end. It isn't because I'm hoping something will come out of this. I know that isn't possible. Had I met Ben first, maybe things would have gone differently, but that wasn't the case. He doesn't even look at me that way, his vision too cluttered by images of Sara.

I just like being around him.

I like the way he laughs, the way his smile stretches across his face exposing his crooked bottom teeth. How he has these amazing dimples that make his face appear kinder somehow. I like how he's easy to talk to and that the conversation flows naturally between us. How he puts all his attention on me when I speak, as if there isn't another person in the room. I love how he makes me feel important.

When he suggests we take a walk along the beach, I hear myself agree instantly. I try not to think too deeply about the giddiness I feel or the swirl in my stomach. Sara may not like it. Maybe it's wrong to prolong the afternoon with him, but the truth is, at this moment, I don't really care.

The breeze is blowing harder along the shore. The sun is still out, but a chill settles into my bones as the wind rushes across my bare arms. I left my sweater in Ben's car. There's a flock of seagulls overhead, squawking as they fly in a circle above us. I pray one of them doesn't poop on my now-wild, unruly hair. That would be *lovely*.

Ben makes his way over to a patch of smooth sand and plops down. I follow, sitting beside him, digging my feet beneath the warm grains. We stare at the horizon, neither of us saying anything. The sound of the crashing waves hums like a lullaby. I slowly start to relax, my muscles loosening as I sink further into the beach.

"Isn't it peaceful?" he asks.

"Yes, it's beautiful."

"It was one of our favorite parts of the city," he says. "It's why we agreed to take jobs out here."

"I can see how it would be a deciding factor." I wait for him to continue, silently urging him to unload his burden.

"I still can't believe it."

Something about the sadness in his voice pulls my gaze to him. He's staring out into the ocean, lost in his thoughts. I don't know what to say to help lessen this blow, to take away the pain that is so obviously written across his face. I'm angry with Sara for doing this to him. No one deserves to have his heart crushed like this. But I can't tell him that. I can't betray her, even if I don't support her actions. We've been friends since we were babies, and no matter what she's done to him, my loyalties lie with her.

So instead, I just say, "I'm sorry, Ben."

He tries his best to smile, but it doesn't reach his eyes anymore. I can see him struggling beneath the surface of his calm exterior, trying desperately to keep it under control. My heart constricts at the demons he's battling behind those beautiful eyes.

"Thanks," he says. "It sucks. You know?"

"I do," I offer, but I don't. I've never been in love.

"I really thought we were going to have this amazing life together. That Santa Barbara was just the first big leap for us. I don't understand how she could walk away so easily. I mean, we were talking about marriage," he says, facing me.

He looks at me expectantly, as if I hold the answers to why my best friend did what she did. I don't know how to fix this, or what to say to help him understand how easily she left him behind. I don't even understand it enough myself to make it clearer for him. How do I explain to him that Maziar was her one true love and he just wasn't? How do I make him see that it had nothing to do with him? Not really. No one else was ever going to be Maziar for her. He should be thankful it happened two years in and not ten. Sara and Maziar were inevitable —it was just a matter of time. I've never known people more meant for each other.

I can't tell him any of that, though, without breaking his heart further. I turn back to face the water, unable to look him in the eyes when I deliver my explanation. I'm grabbing at straws, trying to find a way to make the excuse sufficient enough for him that he can find some relief in my words. I don't want him to see that I'm improvising.

"Honestly, it wasn't easy for her to make that choice. She loved you; she did. But sometimes that isn't enough. She has a lot of history with Maziar. And I just think the accident terrified her enough to realize that she hadn't completely gotten over him. I know it doesn't seem like it, but she was trying to be fair to you." I turn back toward him when I say the only truth I'm certain of: "You deserve someone who loves only you."

He looks at me silently, running his gaze along the length of my face. My nose, my lips, sweeping across my neck, settling on a curl lying against my collarbone. He lingers there for only a moment, then returns to my eyes. I don't have the answers he seeks; no one does other than Sara, and she's not available to ask. She may never be. But he gives me his crooked smile anyway.

"Thanks," he says.

He suddenly gets up and reaches out his hand to me. I look at him, confused at the gesture.

"The water looks amazing, don't you think?" he asks. "Let's go get our feet wet."

I laugh as I put my hand in his. We run toward the receding ocean's edge and dig our toes into the wet earth beneath us. As the tide comes rushing back, the cool water splashes along our feet. He sets out in a slow jog, kicking droplets playfully toward me.

"You're going to get me all wet!" I protest, giggling.

"And?"

"And I'm Persian. This," I say, grabbing a strand of my hair, "does not mix well with sea water. It's like a science experiment gone horribly wrong." I'm failing miserably at being serious, a ridiculous smile stretched across my face.

Ben bends down toward the tide, peering up at me with a mischievous grin.

"Don't you dare do it!" I warn.

When he splashes me, I squeal, despite being ready for it. He winks, then takes two big strides further away as I kick water up at him in retaliation.

I'm so elated at the change in Ben's demeanor that I'm not paying attention, making my way into the ocean farther than I should. The cool rush of a wave hits the back of my pants, knocking me tumbling into him. He grabs me around the waist but loses his footing, sending us both into the crashing surf. I can feel his muscles pressed hard against my chest as the ocean floor meets us. I almost forget where we are until another wave comes crashing over us, pulling him away from me. I come up coughing and laughing hysterically.

The happiness is settled back in Ben's eyes as he pulls me up. I'm sure I look like a wet dog, but he's so close to me now that I can't think. There's an expression in his eyes I haven't seen before, and it stops the air from passing through my lungs. It doesn't linger, gone as quickly as it came, making me wonder if I imagined it.

"Might as well enjoy the water now," he says, pointing at his wet clothes.

He pulls me gently behind him as we play in the ocean for a few more minutes. Then we head back to his car, where he gives me a spare sweatshirt he has in his backseat. It smells of all things Ben, and I stop myself before I bury my face in it.

What is wrong with me?

Once we get to Ben's apartment, he gives me a pair of sweats and a T-shirt to change into, along with a towel to dry out my hair. He makes a fresh pot of coffee to help warm my insides and sets to the business of packing my trunk with boxes.

"This was fun," he says, as he walks me to my car.

He steps over to the driver's side door and opens it, allowing me to take my seat. As he leans against the door frame looking down at me, the sun setting behind him creates a hazy backdrop. The perfect romance novel scene. If we were characters in a story, he'd lean down and kiss me right now. For an instant, I wish there could be a different reality between us. Sadly, there isn't, and this reality is all we've got. I look up at him, confused by the misplaced sadness I feel.

"It was," I say, trying to hide it behind a smile.

"Let me know if you're ever back up this way, Leyla. Maybe we could hang out again?"

"Okay."

He gently shuts the door and takes a step away from the car. He waves one more time, a sheepish grin stretched across his lips, then steps onto the curb watching me pull away. I can see him standing on the sidewalk until I'm well down the block before heading back inside.

The entire ride home I think of Ben, despite how wrong it is.

* * *

"How did it go?" Sara asks, as she helps me unload my car.

"It went okay," I say.

"Was he really upset?"

There's worry in her eyes, and it bothers me. I know she's genuinely concerned about Ben, but there's a protectiveness I suddenly feel that makes me want to reach out and shove her. She should have thought of him before this entire mess began. I swallow my need to tell her off. *It isn't my place.* Ben's a great guy, but even great guys get their hearts broken. Shit happens.

"At first."

She stops midway to the front door and stares at me. I'm balancing a box beneath my arm a few steps below her on the porch, waiting. She doesn't say anything.

"What?" I ask.

"What is up with you?" she says, making my heart drop into my chest. "Why are you giving me these one-word, snippy answers?"

She isn't irritated, she's confused. I can hear it in her voice. After a lifetime of friendship, it's easy to read each other. Something I've obviously forgotten.

"Am I?" I reply, playing innocent. Why do I feel like I've done something terribly wrong and need to hide it? "I'm just tired. It was a long drive."

I stopped at home first to change out of Ben's clothes. I couldn't think of a viable excuse to explain why I was wearing them, other than telling the truth, and for some odd reason, I don't want to. I'm not sure why. I want to keep the details of the day to myself. It's not like Sara is going to find out anyway. Ben's in Santa Barbara and she's here. He's brokenhearted and she's with Maziar. I highly doubt they'll have a conversation any time soon. And if they do, I don't think I'll be the primary topic. Besides, she's his ex, but he's my friend. Does one cancel out the other? I'm going with no.

"Well, how was he? Give me details."

Why do you care? "He was upset, obviously. But you know Ben; he does his best to keep it positive."

"Did he say anything?"

"He was mad at what you did and he's confused about it all."

"He told you that? That he was confused?"

"Yeah."

"What did you say?"

"What could I say? I just told him I was sorry he was feeling that way."

Frustration boils inside me like hot molten lava at her inquisition. I try to swallow it down, needing to keep my head. My moment to tell her I spent the entire day with him, much of which had nothing to do with her, is gone. And I certainly don't want to explore the confusing emotions I experienced either. The more she asks me questions, the more I fear I'll get twisted up and expose myself. I just want her to stop.

She stares for a few more moments, reading me. I try my best to keep my face passive, devoid of the emotions I shouldn't be feeling. Then I nudge toward the door.

"This is getting heavy," I say, urging her up the steps.

She takes another moment, then smiles.

"Okay." She laughs. "My mom just made *nazook*. Let's go have some *chayee*." *Pastries and tea.*

I exhale as I follow her inside, relieved that I made it through the interrogation unscathed.

CHAPTER TWO

I stand back as Sara is swallowed into the crowd of family surrounding her. The women *quiil*, a high-pitched trill made when the tongue repeatedly creates a *leh* sound. It's a sign of celebration in the Iranian culture, showing happiness in a joyous occasion. It will be the trumpets that follow the bride-and-groom-to-be until their wedding day, announcing their entrance into every gathering like they're royalty.

The women in her family cluster around her, showering her with hugs and kisses as they pull her left hand every which way to get a closer look at the ring. Pride beams off of them like headlights. Sara has arrived, at least in their book.

The diamond catches the light off the foyer chandelier, and even from this distance, I can see the pattern of shimmering crystals it's throwing onto the walls behind her. They just got back from Mexico, where Maziar proposed.

She's plastered a smile on her face, but there's doubt huddled in the back of her eyes. Maziar's parents are nowhere to be found. This is a big deal for Iranians, and I can tell it's stressing her out. Maziar's sister, Bita, and his cousin, Neda, are trying to compensate, but it isn't really working. Sara's mom is trying to put on a good show too, but she's fuming.

"*Mobarak basheh, Sara jan,*" *Congratulations, dearest Sara,* her aunt squeals, pulling Sara to her chest.

She looks at me, overwhelmed. A silent conversation of understanding passes between us. I try to encourage her by smiling and nodding, all of the chaos expected. The desperation in her eyes pleads for rescue. We know each other so well that words are rarely necessary to get the point across. But before I can get there, Maziar grabs her around the waist, spinning her in a gentle circle. She giggles as he twirls her, the edges of her pastel skirt inflating like a parachute. He looks down into her eyes, and although he doesn't kiss her, I can see that he wants to. It wouldn't be acceptable to show that type of affection with the grown-ups around. Despite being in our late twenties, the parental generation makes us feel like children by comparison. But a public display of affection isn't necessary anyway. The love Maziar feels for Sara and the dedication that he so fiercely emanates toward her is undeniable.

I want that.

I haven't felt that type of love. Sure, I've been in relationships, and I've cared for men, but never like this. I've never known what it feels like to be certain that there is no other person in the world meant for me, to wake up each day wanting nothing more than to spend every moment with him. I'm jealous.

"So, Leyla *joon, key nobateh toh meesheh?*" *When will it be your turn,* Sara's grandmother asks, startling me as she comes up behind me.

I look at her and try to smile despite my irritation. I hate how single girls are always asked this question, as if the union of one person flashes a spotlight onto us less fortunate, potential old maids.

"I'm not sure, Shahla *khanoom.* Hopefully soon," I reply. The traditional Persian girl response. It's neutral, safe, because admitting that it's not top priority on my 'to-do' list would only earn me a baffled expression. Then probably a somewhat disgusted glare.

I don't understand what the elders want us to say; maybe never, outlook is grim? Or any day now; I can feel it! It's not like we have a crystal ball in our bedrooms we confer with each night on the status of our Prince Charming.

"Leave her alone, *Mamanbozorg*." Sara swoops in and saves me, wrapping her arm through mine and leading me outside to where the younger generation is seated.

I plop down on a lawn chair, its once-bright-red cushion now the color of rust from the constant sun exposure. My unruly hair is tied up in a bun, which I'm sure is an accent in color coordination with the pillows against my back. Maziar is passing out flutes of champagne. Neda grabs two and makes her way over, sitting down in the seat beside me. She hands me one, then leans hers toward mine. The thin sheets of glass chime out in a high-pitched hum as they collide.

"Cheers to the single girls," Neda says. "May we find our Prince Charming too," she adds, laughing at our predicament.

Amen to that. I longingly stare at my best friend and her fiancé.

CHAPTER THREE

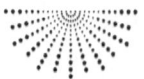

"You ready?" Maya asks.

I throw my overnight bag into her back seat. It plops down on the chair beside her blue and gold UCLA duffel. One of our many outlandish spirit day purchases to celebrate the last year of law school.

"Yup." I slide into the passenger seat.

"Okay. Let's go!" she says. "Everyone left an hour ago; we aren't too far behind." She's bouncing in her seat, bubbling with excitement as she pulls away from the curb.

"Apparently someone is looking forward to this," I tease.

"Hell yes!" she says, laughing. "A weekend in Santa Barbara! Why aren't you more excited?"

Maya's sister, Lisa, just transferred to UCSB and we're going to get her settled in, which really means we're going to party our asses off.

I spend the next two hours listening to Maya chatter on. My phone is in my lap, burning a hole through my jeans. I've picked it up numerous times and started a text to Ben, only to leave it partway done. When we saw each other a few months ago, he told me to let him know when I'd be back in town. I'm itching to do just that.

"Who are you texting?" Maya asks. She glances over at the phone in my hand trying to get a glimpse of the name on my screen. I don't say anything. "Well?"

"No one," I say, unconvincingly.

"Bullshit!"

"It's nothing."

"Don't make me pull over and wrestle that thing away from you to look for myself," she threatens, her lips upturned in a daring grin. I know she'll actually do it.

"Ben," I admit.

"Ben," she repeats, her lips stretching into a full-blown smile, a glimmer of approval in her eyes. "Excellent."

"Stop it," I say, swatting her playfully.

"What?" She feigns innocence.

"Don't humor me. I haven't decided if I should send it yet."

"Of course you should," she encourages. "He told you to let him know when you're back around. What's the hesitation?"

"You already know the answer to that question."

"Sara. She's moved on, Leyla. And you aren't doing anything wrong. You're just inviting

a friend to come hang out. It's not a big deal. Just send it!"

I look at Maya, her pearly whites urging me forward, and take a deep breath. I drop my gaze to the lit-up screen, wanting nothing more than to tell Ben I'm coming. But I can't do it. I shut the phone off again.

"Chicken," Maya says.

She squeezes my hand and smiles. She doesn't push me any further. Instead, she turns up the radio, singing at the top of her lungs to the song blaring through the speakers. I laugh at her rendition of Bruno Mars, throwing the phone into my purse and joining her.

I try to shove thoughts of Ben out of my mind.

* * *

We make it to the hotel at dusk. The sun is dropping down beyond the horizon, sending a swirl of pink and purple clouds dancing along the water's edge. The view is breathtaking from our fifth-floor hotel room.

I stand at the window ledge, absorbing the last few moments of the peaceful silence that accompanies the sunset. It seems as if the entire world stands still, watching.

"Are you ready?" Maya asks, as she fills her gray clutch with the night's necessities: lipstick, money, ID.

"Yup."

I glance out the window one last time, taking in the vibrant tone of the cotton candy sky before turning to follow her out of the door.

We arrive at the bar a few minutes later. The ten-minute walk from the hotel has my feet aching. We're trying to be responsible and drinking is definitely in our future. Sadly, I couldn't pass up the heels for a pair of flats. My short stature requires additional height to make me feel sexy. Tonight, I want to feel sexy.

I run my fingers through my hair one last time, separating the curls so they don't look like a messy nest. I'm praying the plethora of products I used are still working and the wet dampness of the ocean breeze isn't having its way with me. My wild waves settle midway down my chest, a stark burgundy against the white of my tank top. My jeans fit snug, cinching in at the waist, accentuating my hourglass figure. I'm looking to have fun tonight, far enough away that my bad choices can't follow me.

We show our IDs at the door. The bouncer stands tall and wide like a tank, his muscular frame resembling an MMA fighter. His arms are tatted from shoulders down, tribal vines wrapping around his wrists, highlighting his edgy, bad-boy vibe. A predatory smile stretches across his face while he stands aside, giving us passage.

His eyes bore into me, running the length of my body. I can feel them almost as distinctly as a touch. I tingle with his innuendo, wondering if he's the type to throw me up against a wall. My skin is on fire with the possibilities. I bat my eyes, stare a moment longer, then turn and walk away. I make sure the sultry sway in my step is noticeable enough to catch his eye. I glance at him over my shoulder one more time to find him still watching me before I'm sucked into the crowd.

The night is starting off well.

The familiar beats of Rihanna beckon me forward. I feel the

melody make its way into my hips, instinctively. There's a small dance floor to the left of the wraparound bar, with bodies jammed together like sardines, bouncing in rhythm to the music. I can't wait to make my way over.

Maya spots Lisa talking to a tall blond resembling an Abercrombie model. They're standing at the far end of the bar and she's flipping her hair side to side, giggling at something he's said. Alexis and Jen are standing beside her having a conversation of their own. They're looking out into the crowd of dancers, no doubt sizing up the potentials. The whole crew is here. Time to get the party started.

* * *

A round of tequila shots lies across the bar. The Abercrombie model, along with two of his friends, have joined in our mission for intoxication. I've lost track of how many I've thrown back, but judging from the blurred edges of my vision and the warm buzzing vibration in my limbs, I'd say the mission has been accomplished. I'm feeling good as Maya grabs my hand to lead me to the dance floor. I turn to follow, but something catches my attention out of the corner of my eye, and I come to an abrupt stop.

Standing at the entrance, chatting it up with the hot bouncer, is Ben. I have to blink a few times, unsure if the alcohol is playing tricks on me. When he doesn't disappear, my pulse begins to race. Apparently, fate has intervened.

He's dressed in a pair of dark blue jeans and a light blue button-up shirt, his sleeves rolled up to his forearms, accentuating the veins that run down to his wrists. They outline each of his muscles, tight beneath his skin. His eyes are electric, complementing his outfit like a well-placed accessory. They glow like fireflies against the dim background of the bar.

I don't recognize his friends, not that I should. I've only ever seen him with Sara and their pharmacy school crowd. Memories of her wrapped around him suddenly bubble up to the surface, tasting of bile. I try to push them away, allowing myself the simple pleasure of drooling over an incredibly hot man. There's no room for Sara here. Not tonight.

I'm frozen in a strange trance, unable to pull my gaze away from him. I'm aware of Maya saying my name, the confusion in her voice noticeable despite the loud base beating against the walls, but I don't look at her. I can't take my eyes off of Ben. *Damn, he's so handsome.*

He must feel me staring because he looks in my direction. We lock eyes and for a brief moment, nothing else exists. There's no crowd, no loud music, no Maya yanking on my arm. It's just Ben and me. The smile that breaks out across his face in recognition, the playful, subtle flirt dancing in his eyes, is thoroughly delicious. It feeds my soul in ways that it shouldn't.

I can hardly breathe as he cuts through the crowd toward us. Maya finally sees him and her arm falls away.

"Well, look at that," she says, leaning in close to my ear.

"Right?" I reply, still bewildered at the turn of events.

"Have fun." She turns and heads into the crowd with her sister before Ben has made his way over.

"Hey!" he says. His voice runs over me like warm butter.

"Hi."

"How are you?"

"I'm good." My voice is coming out in breathless spurts and I wonder how flustered I must look.

"Good," he says.

He looks over my shoulder at the small group of people behind me, no doubt seeing the guys. He raises a brow in question.

"Lisa's friends," I explain. "Maya's sister," I add.

"Hmmm," he says, not sparing them another glance. "Have you guys been here long?"

"I think."

"You think?" He laughs, his chuckle laced with an electricity that runs through me.

The alcohol has caused me to lose all ability to filter so I stare at his lips, uninhibited. The color matches my hair, the definition so distinct it's almost like he's wearing lip liner. I imagine how soft they'd feel up against mine. I'm lost in the daydream longer than I should be.

When I realize what I'm doing, I quickly return my gaze to his whole face. It's too late, I've already been caught, evident in the teasing glimmer in his eyes. I can feel heat spread up from my neck and I pray the lights of the bar don't give me away. The lack of pigments in my skin turn me a deep shade of scarlet when I blush. That, along with my hair, transforms me into a Crayola crayon.

His friends have made their way over to us and are ordering drinks at the bar.

"Want anything, man?" one of them asks.

"Yeah, a Guinness," Ben says. "Can I get you a drink?"

"Vodka tonic, please."

My request stops him dead in his tracks. His eyebrows pull together in concentration as he works the muscles in his jaw. *Shit! That's Sara's drink.* I find it thoroughly annoying that she's always present despite her absence. But in true Ben fashion, he quickly shakes it off, turning toward the bartender.

Alexis cuts through my thoughts as she pushes her way playfully in between us, leaning against the bar where Ben's standing.

"Who's your friend, Leyla?"

She's turned in toward him, barricading me out with her back. Red flashes before my eyes and I'm startled by my own reaction. *What is happening? This is Ben; I shouldn't be jealous.* But I am. Alexis has a better chance with him than I do. No Sara entanglement to get in the way.

Ben's looking down at her as she bats her eyes at him. He's caught in an expression halfway between amused and shocked. It's obvious that he doesn't understand the effect he has on woman. He never has; one of his finer qualities.

"Alexis, Ben. Ben, Alexis." I make the introductions.

The DJ spins a Beyoncé track and Alexis squeals.

"I love this song! Dance with me," she demands, pulling him toward the dance floor before he has a chance to answer her.

I exhale as Alexis drags Ben further into the crowd. With my back against the bar, I watch her expertly swoop in for the kill. She exudes sex appeal in the swells that roll through her body in time with the music. She dances in a sultry circle around him, her index finger running a slow seductive line across his bicep. He isn't having any trouble keeping up–an exceptionally good dancer. As he meets her move for move, a stab of jealously kicks me hard in the gut.

Maya appears beside me, composed out of thin air, startling me when she speaks.

"You know, if you stand here long enough, I'm going to try out my chance with him."

I turn toward her, lines of irritation furrowing across my brow, creating what I imagine is an amazing scowl.

"Ha! I knew it. You dig him," she says, laughing. "What are you doing letting Alexis take him?" She waves in the direction of the dancing couple as if I haven't been honing in on them for the past five minutes.

"What do you want me to do?" My frustration is thick, weighing heavily on the end of each word.

"Uhm, maybe go in there and take back what's yours?"

"He's not *mine*," I protest.

"Not like this he won't be." Her brows are raised in challenge.

"What am I supposed to do? Go in there and ask to cut in? I can't just push her out of the way and take her spot."

"Ugh," Maya groans. "You're intolerable sometimes, Leyla, seriously."

She pushes off of the bar and walks over to where Alexis is dancing with Ben. I can tell she's still feeling the effects of the last tequila shot as she staggers. When she leans in to whisper something into Alexis's ear, I stop breathing. I don't know what she says, but Alexis winks at me before letting Maya lead her away.

My heart starts to beat uncontrollably in my chest, ready to burst through my ribcage. Ben's watching Alexis as she gets swallowed up by the crowd, and I worry he may be disappointed by her departure. What if he was interested in her?

I don't have time to thoroughly interpret his reaction as he turns to face me. We're ten feet apart, drinkers and dancers creating a path between us. The DJ continues spinning hip-hop and the crowd is bouncing in time to the beat. Ben's standing still, watching me. There's a devilish look in his eyes that sends goosebumps along my skin. He motions me over with his head and I can barely feel my legs moving beneath me. It's as if I'm floating.

"Hey," he says, once I'm in front of him. "You feel like saving me from looking like an idiot since your friend just left me hanging?" He doesn't look upset; the tone of his voice indicates he's joking.

"You need me to save you, is that it? Are you worried all these drunk people might think you have no game?"

"Oh, I have game," he answers, reaching out and wrapping his strong arm around my waist, pulling me in closer. "Want me to show you?" he whispers in my ear.

His breath is hot against my cheek. My heart has stopped mid-beat and I'm getting dizzy from his proximity. The smell of his cologne has invaded my nostrils, intoxicating me further.

"Show me what you've got."

He just smirks and begins to move. I place my hand on his arm, feeling the muscles flex beneath my fingers. We sway to the beat of the music, my hips against his, his chest on mine. I lose sight of everyone around us, entangled in a moment I can't define. There's a playfulness in the way he's moving, but an edge in the way he touches me. I look up at him, beckoning him further with my eyes, silently telling him I want more.

Neither of us says a word, our bodies doing all the talking. I lose myself in the feel of him, in the idea of what could be, if only for the night. He leans his head down until his lips are inches away from mine. When he speaks, his hot breath caresses my skin. I'm overwhelmed by a desire I didn't realize I had. When the air catches in my throat, I fear I may pass out.

"I'm *so* happy I ran into you tonight, Leyla."

Just like that, the sound of my name on his lips pushes me into dangerous waters. I lose sight of the consequences. All I can see is Ben.

CHAPTER FOUR

"**S**o what do you think?" Ben asks, staring at me expectantly.

"It's good."

"Just good?" he replies, in playful disgust. "You have no taste at all."

"I'm sorry I'm not up to par on my burger connoisseur skills."

"Such a waste," he says. "These are the best burgers I've ever had. I was so excited when I found this place. I feel like you're not truly appreciating their artwork."

He makes a snobby expression of distaste, making me laugh so hard, my soda almost comes out of my nose. He smiles, handing me the spare napkin off his tray before I have a chance to spit my food across the table at him.

When Maya asked me to keep her company on another drive up to Santa Barbara, it didn't take much convincing. She knows I've been chomping at the bit to see Ben again, despite the fact that I won't admit it. Not even to myself.

We've been talking since the club. Nothing serious, just friendly conversation. But every time he sends me a text or calls me, butterflies make a mess of my insides. I simultaneously feel sick and giddy. I shouldn't be thinking of him this way. He's Sara's ex. It's wrong. Or maybe it just feels like it is? I'm not quite sure.

I can see Maman now, freaking out at the idea that all her friends will know that her daughter ended up with Sara's sloppy seconds. I'll make the front page of the *Iranian Mothers Gazette*, if that were actually a publication. It may not technically be wrong, but two of the most important women in my life will definitely think so.

But what if we could have something amazing? That little question torments me as I lie awake in bed at night. The dreaded *what if*? I try to let it go. It's a lost cause. Regardless of how great things could be between us, destiny put him in Sara's life first, complicating the situation.

I don't even know how he feels about me. He's fun and playful, but other than the night on the dance floor, he hasn't given me a reason to think he's into me romantically. We're definitely friends, that much is obvious. We never stop talking and we're always laughing. But beyond that, there hasn't been any indication that he wants more from me.

I was hoping today would be different. We've been talking for weeks and I desperately wanted to see a spark. Even though I know nothing can come of it, I still can't help but wish there was something there to deny myself.

"You ready?" he asks, snapping me out of my thoughts.

"Sure." I wipe my hands, standing up to grab my bag.

"Is Maya at the dorms?" he asks. "I can drop you off with her on my way."

The disappointment punches me in the stomach. Is he taking me back *now*?

"I don't think we're heading home until tonight," I say. Maybe he thinks I have to leave.

"That's cool. You guys won't hit traffic that way."

He holds the door to the restaurant open for me as we step out onto the sidewalk. His chivalry just adds to the rejection, making it worse somehow. Why couldn't he be a jerk? Or at least less perfect so I didn't feel like I've just been passed up by Mr. Right? I follow him down the sidewalk, dragging my feet, trying to come up with a way to turn it all around.

"What are you up to tonight?"

"I have dinner plans," he replies, adding nothing more.

The heavy weight of dismissal drops me into the front seat. I stay quiet most of the drive, my stomach twisted in knots. He doesn't seem to mind, making the music louder to hide the awkward silence. When he pulls up to the dorms, panic rushes through my veins like ice water. I search my mind for something clever to say, but come up empty. He doesn't turn off the ignition, indicating that he's just waiting for me to get out. There's no room for the possibility of more this evening.

"Thanks for the ride," I say, opening the car door slowly. Like a moron, I'm still hoping he stops me.

"You okay, Leyla?" he suddenly asks. Concern is etched into his features, constricting my heart further. I feel like crying.

"Yeah, I'm fine."

"Are you sure? You got all quiet on the drive. What happened? We were having fun."

A dam breaks open in my chest. For the first time, I truly feel the depth of my feelings for Ben, of the possibilities I've created in my head in the dark hours of the night when I'm alone. Despite his past with my best friend, my better judgment has taken a back seat to my heart. I've allowed myself to dream of a reality where he could be mine and I could be his. I want more, but it's clear I'm alone in my desires.

When Ben was with Sara, it was evident she turned his world upside down. Every word she uttered seemed like his bible. Devoted and worshipful till the day she left him. But he doesn't look at me that way. I won't ever have the ability to shatter his heart into a million pieces like she did. Up until now, I hadn't realized I wanted to.

"Everything is good, Ben. Really," I say. Then I turn and get out of his car.

* * *

"Why do you keep checking your phone?" Sara asks.

She's currently cleaning out her closet, which for Sara means making meaningless piles across the floor.

"No reason." I manage to answer without stumbling over my words.

"You've checked it a million times already. What aren't you telling me?"

"Nothing," I snap.

I'm not in the mood to be pushed today. It's been over a week since I saw Ben and there's been nothing, just radio silence. I know I should feel guilty that I even care, but I don't, which makes me feel even worse.

She stops what she's doing, dropping the shirts in her hand onto the floor. Doesn't make much of a difference considering her piles are meshing into one large lump anyway. She makes her way over to me on the bed, sitting down beside me.

"What's going on?" she asks.

The tenderness in her voice is a sharp knife being pushed deep into my chest. I'm desperate to talk to her, to tell her about Ben's rejection. She's my best friend. She's who I should be confiding in. But as I stare at her deep, dark eyes, seeing the concern in them, I can't. I don't want to deal with the consequences of my feelings. What would be the point? Ben's not interested.

"Are we okay?" she asks.

I don't know how long I thought I could be distant without her calling me out on it. The reality is, as I secretly obsess over Ben, I blame Sara for his disinterest in me. My frustration with her isn't fair. Maybe his feelings for her are part of why he doesn't see me as more than a friend, and maybe they're not. Either way, she's not really at fault. I've been so blinded by my jealousy of the life she's building with Maziar that I've found a way to be angry with her despite how much I love her.

"Yeah, we're always good," I say. I wrap my arms around her, trying to erase my recent neglect.

"Great. I was worried I did something to make you mad. I know I've been preoccupied with Maziar and all the shit that comes with it, but you know I'm here for you, right? You can talk to me about anything. I'm always here."

There's a pleading in her eyes as she apologizes for making me invisible within the chaos of her life. My feelings for Ben transform into a blade that slashes at my skin, leaving me torn and tattered. They sit heavily on my shoulders, trapping me between the guilt of my feelings for him and the realization that I've made Sara into the monster keeping us apart. The truth is, it just wasn't meant to be.

"I know."

* * *

"I've asked you ladies to join me for dinner tonight because I have a very special request of each of you."

Sara pulls out a turquoise blue Tiffany bag from beneath the table, placing it on her lap. She sets six small blue boxes, each with a white ribbon tied in a neat little bow, in front of her. Ellie, her cousin, sits across from me. She winks, smiling widely at what we all know is coming. Neda is to my left, Bita to my right, each of us lifting our glass of wine to toast the other as Sara makes her speeches. Then she turns toward me.

"Leyla, you're more than my best friend, you're my sister. I don't know how I would have gotten through the past few years without you. Seriously. You've always given me strength when I can't seem to find any on my own. And you've always stood by me through everything. I can never tell you how much that means to me. Would you please be my maid of honor?" she asks. She's crying, which sparks my own tears, as she wraps her arms tightly around my neck. "I love you," she says.

"I love you, too."

Later that evening on the drive home, Sara leans her head against the window. She moans incoherently, making it obvious she's queasy.

"You okay?" I ask, giggling. She never could hold her alcohol.

"Ugh," she moans. "I feel sick."

"I know, but we're almost home." I pat her leg. "Let me know if you need me to pull over." Cleaning puke out of my car in the middle of the night doesn't sound appealing.

"Oh my God!" she says suddenly, jumping up in her seat, giving me a heart attack.

"What?" I screech, almost swerving onto the curb. "What's wrong? Are you okay?"

"Sorry. Yes, I'm fine, I just forgot to tell you what happened this weekend."

"Sara!" I reprimand her. "I almost killed us!"

"I'm sorry." She's laughing.

"You're so annoying!" I swat her, but I'm smiling. "Now tell me this big news that was worth us dying over."

"Leyla, you're so dramatic." Despite not feeling well, she still has the ability to roll her eyes. "Guess who I ran into at the store?" She waits expectantly, as if I'm actually going to play this game.

"I don't know. Who?"

"Ben."

I almost choke on my own spit, the panic rushing over me like a tsunami. I try my best to keep my features calm, praying the confines of the car, and her intoxication, keep me from being discovered. She stops talking. Her head is against the window again and her face looks a little green. Her eyes are closed. *Is she asleep? No! I need to know what happened with Ben.*

"Sara!"

"Huh? What?"

"You were telling me you saw Ben," I probe.

"Oh, yeah. I saw him at the grocery store Saturday night. He was there with some girl," she mumbles before dozing off again.

No sooner have the words left her lips then my body is numbed by disappointment. It courses through my veins, making me sick to my stomach. A girl. The word tastes bitter on my tongue. *How did he not tell me? Is this the explanation for his distance at lunch? Did he have plans with her?* The thoughts reel through my mind at light speed as I try to find my bearings.

I'm grateful Sara's too drunk to stay awake, her eyes closed, head bobbing in her seat. I welcome the dark solitude of the car, giving me the privacy I need to deal with the magnitude of this information.

CHAPTER FIVE

The smell of fresh-brewed coffee and the clanging of dishes beckon me to the kitchen. I find my sister, Raha, filling her coffee mug while Baba is cooking up another one of his *healthy* concoctions on the stove. I sneak up behind him, wrapping my arms around his waist, planting a kiss on his cheek.

"Sobekher, Baba." Good morning, Dad.

"Sobekher, dokhtaram." He pats my hands. *Good morning, my daughter.*

I stand on my tiptoes and glance over his shoulder. Egg whites and tofu, no surprise there. He's gone hippy this past year, after having been told he had high cholesterol and was at risk for a heart attack. Now he's vegetarian, bordering vegan, and he's taking the rest of us down with him.

I miss bacon. Turkey bacon, of course, being that Muslims don't eat pork. Regardless, I miss the mornings I was awoken by the delicious smell of bacon filling the air, mixed in with the nutty aroma of a cup of joe. Or *sosees. Sausage.* At least our version, which means turkey hot dogs, sliced up and fried into scrambled eggs. Sadly, those good old days are long gone.

I look at Raha and a silent exchange is made between us. I know we're both thinking of a stack of pancakes and a side of turkey bacon at the local IHOP. She winks; I giggle.

"Don't even think about it, ladies," Baba says. "You will not be supplementing this meal with a cadaver. It's not good for you. You're too young to be clogging up your arteries."

"Oh, Baba, you're so dramatic. You're the one that made this house a no-meat zone. This isn't a dictatorship," my sister replies. "Besides, we're healthy."

"Today you are, but you're young. You two keep eating the way you do, and you'll regret it when you're my age!" Baba chuckles, shaking his head at us.

I sit down at the kitchen table, finding comfort in the harmony of my family. Baba at the stove joking, Raha at the coffee pot playfully arguing with him. Maman's late to the party, a fan of sleeping in. The familiarity of it fills me with a calm that only my family can provide.

I love the way Baba sounds when he laughs. His baritone voice translates into a deep rumble that starts at the bottom of his toes and erupts through his body like a volcano. As his mouth stretches across his teeth, his thin upper lip is hidden beneath his mustache. It's now peppered with grays, giving away his age. I happily tie it to every memory of my past. I can't recall a moment I've ever seen him without it, a permanent fixture in the makeup of my dad.

I pick at a mushroom on the plate of eggs he's setting down on the table, earning me a gentle whack of the wooden spoon.

"We use utensils, Leyla. *Heyvoon neesteem.*" *We aren't animals.*

"Are you sure about that?" Maman says, as she walks in. "Those beds still aren't made, Ali, and don't get me started on how long the laundry has been sitting folded on their dressers. They look like animals to me." There's a playful tone in her voice, a glimmer in her eyes as she teases us. She thinks we're lazy; I just think she's overly organized.

Maman pours two glasses of *chayee* for her and Baba. They're tea addicts like most Persians, unable to kick the habit. Baba calls it their one guilty pleasure, a common staple among Iranian households. Maman says it's a necessity. Most of my generation grew up with watered-down tea in our sippy cups.

Raha and Baba make their way over, my sister handing me a cup of coffee as she sits down beside me. Like every Saturday, we take part in our ritual of breakfast as a family. It's the one time a week all our schedules overlap and we can actually hang out together. It gives my heart a very necessary recharge.

"How was last night?" Maman asks.

"It was good," I say, my stomach rolling as I remember what Sara told me about Ben.

I earn a quizzical look from Raha, who is watching me closely. I widen my eyes giving her a slight shake of my head as I pray she doesn't ask questions. I don't want to have this conversation in front of our parents. She gives me a subtle nod, letting the subject rest for the moment.

"Sara asked me to be her maid of honor," I add.

I take a bite of my dad's tofu scramble. It's not half bad.

"I expected she would," Raha replies.

"Yeah, I know."

"That means you're in charge of the bachelorette party, right?" There's a mischievous glimmer in her eyes.

"Crap, I didn't even think about that!"

"Don't worry. I'll help you plan it." Raha winks.

"Oh, lovely," Baba says. "That's going to go well."

"What?" Raha protests. I'm too busy laughing to come to her aid.

"Try not to get these girls in trouble, Raha. You're the older one," he warns.

"I resent that, Baba. I'm very responsible."

"True, but you love to party. That's no secret." He gives her a loving grin.

My family is different from your average Muslim Iranians. My parents are as progressive as it gets, religious regulation having no place in our home. I call my parents hippies to be funny, but they really are in comparison to most. Maman and Baba eat healthy, do yoga, believe in energy and its healing powers. They are also open to the idea of their daughters dating, and although they don't like the idea of premarital sex, they aren't naive about it either. And they've never shamed us for not falling somewhere in the perfect Persian girl box.

Raha went to beauty school and is now a hairdresser at a swanky salon on the west side. In the traditional family, that would definitely not fall within the limits of acceptable careers: doctor, lawyer, pharmacist.

It took me a while to figure out what I was doing. I flapped around at UCLA, changing majors every which way, until I decided I wanted to go into law. I actually like it. Otherwise, I could have been a basket weaver if that's what made me happy. My parents are much more relaxed about futures than most.

But now that the idea of Ben has made its way into my mind, I wonder how open-minded they actually are. I'm not entirely sure where they fall when the norm of cultural expectation is questioned.

I know race wouldn't be a swaying factor. Maman would prefer we married Iranian men, as most mothers would, but she'd never stop us from being with anyone on that note alone. However, with the added details of Ben's past with Sara, and the common knowledge it is among the community, the complications get sticky. Iranians are close-knit, family among friends, bound by our race alone. And the fact that Sara was with Ben for so long, about to move in with him, equates them to a married couple. It would be like I was stealing her husband. Not only that, but that I was stealing my *sister's* husband, being that we're best friends.

Maman doesn't like to be the center of a gossip fest. Neither does Baba. They like their privacy. I'd surely be the talk of the town, and they wouldn't be happy. I guess the fact that it's unlikely Ben is interested has its benefits.

"Want to go for a run?" Raha asks as we finish up cleaning the kitchen.

"We just ate!"

"Eh, we'll just jog." She gently bumps my hip as she dries the last dish. "Come on, it's such a pretty day."

"Sure, why not," I say. "But you're holding my hair if I puke."

"Deal," she answers, winking at me.

Fifteen minutes later, we're jogging through the neighborhood.

"What happened last night?" Sometimes, it's uncanny how well Raha knows me.

"Sara saw Ben."

"What? Where? Isn't he in Santa Barbara? Did he tell her about you guys?" A sheen of sweat gleans across my sister's forehead beneath the mid-morning sun.

"No, I don't think so," I say, between pants. "She didn't mention it. But she did tell me she saw him with another girl." I pull my shoulder blades together, trying to dislodge the sweat pooling between them.

I take a couple more strides before I realize that Raha isn't beside me. I turn to find that she's stopped a few feet back, staring at me in shock.

"What?" she manages.

"Yup."

"You have got to be kidding." Her voice rises a few octaves. "What an asshole!"

"Is he, though?" I question whether he's even done anything wrong. "We're just friends. Just because I'm starting to have feelings for him doesn't mean he owes me an explanation," I rationalize.

"Yes, but friends discuss these things. And I doubt he doesn't know how you feel. Or at least he's questioned it. He should have told you."

"Maybe."

* * *

I'm sitting on my bed with bar review books sprawled out all around me. I'm knee-deep in torts while most of my friends have graduated and started their careers. The price I pay for being indecisive. My phone begins to buzz on the nightstand. I lean over and grab it without looking up, trying to avoid losing my concentration.

"Hello?" I say, half-paying attention.

"Hey."

Hearing his voice through the receiver feels like a bucket of ice water's been dumped over my head, snapping me to attention.

"Ben?"

"Yeah. Hi."

"Oh. Hey. What's up?"

"What are you doing?" he asks.

"Um, studying."

"Oh," he says, suddenly sounding disappointed.

"Why?" I add, because I can't help myself. I'm desperate to keep him on the phone, despite knowing he's with someone else. I know it's pathetic, but at least I'm finally being honest with myself.

"I'm in LA, came down for an interview. I just finished up and thought I'd take you to lunch. But I see that you're busy."

"An interview, here? You're moving back?"

"I don't know. A position opened up so just thought I'd feel it out. Anyway, I'll let you get back to it."

I should hang up the phone, go back to my studies. He's dating someone. He doesn't have feelings for me. I repeat it as if it's a mantra, trying to convince myself to walk away. But it's useless. I want to be around Ben too badly to pass up the chance. I'm a lost cause headed down a very bumpy road.

"No," I say, more assertively than I intended. In a voice that feels desperate, I add, "I was just going to take a break anyway. I've been at it for hours. I could use some food." Total lie, but I'm hoping I sound authentic. I have a few hours left in me, but I'd rather spend them with Ben.

I smack my forehead, silently reprimanding myself for sounding so easy. If Ben likes the chase, I'm doing nothing to provide him with one. I hold my breath, the fear of rejection laying heavily in the pit of my stomach. He's asked *me* to lunch, but somehow, I feel like I'm begging him to take me.

"Great! I can be there in twenty," he says.

I exhale, unaware I've been holding my breath.

"See you soon." I have to work on keeping the giddy out of my voice. I'm failing miserably at playing hard to get, something Maman says is necessary when dealing with men.

"*Khodetoh arzoon nafroosh*," she always says. *Don't sell yourself cheap*; don't give your heart over to him without making him work for it. I feel like I've already handed Ben a receipt. At a discounted price, for that matter.

I jump to my feet, running to my closet in an attempt to find something more presentable to wear. The green sweats and black tank top I have on seem inappropriate. I throw on a pair of jeans and a gray top, with just enough time to pull my hair up in a ponytail before Ben sends me a text indicating he's outside. As I grab my bag and head toward the door, I'm grateful that my parents are out with friends today. I don't feel like having to explain where I'm going, and definitely don't want to defend who I'm going with.

"Hey," Ben says, as I shut the door behind me. "Shouldn't I say hello to your family?" His well-mannered ways don't allow for such rude behavior.

"Nope," I reply. "They aren't home."

"Oh. Okay." He almost sounds disappointed. "Where should we go?" he asks, as we walk over to his car.

"I'm really craving Indian."

I can think of a restaurant a few cities over with decent food that will put us far enough away from home, where we'll be less likely to be seen. Sara also hates Indian.

"Cool."

* * *

The server puts the hot dish of tikka masala between us, along with a freshly made platter of naan, then leaves. Ben is telling me about some issues at work, shaking his head at the ridiculous arguments that unfold between some of his coworkers. As managing pharmacist, he plays internal HR as well.

I stare at his lips moving but don't hear a word, dreamily focused on the dimples that flash at me each time he uses long vowel sounds. His blue eyes sparkle like gemstones set perfectly in his sculpted face. I struggle with the irrational need to lean across the table and kiss him. Then I remember the "other woman." Suddenly, I want to throw my food at him.

"Isn't that funny?" he asks, between spoonfuls of rice. When I don't answer, he looks at me quizzically. "Did you even hear me?"

"Yeah, sorry."

"You okay?" He raises an eyebrow waiting for my reply.

This is my moment. I should ask him about the girl, demand an explanation. I could hear it from the source, have him tell me that he's into someone else. Maybe then I could walk away from the mess I've created in my mind. But as he sits across from me waiting, I know there won't be any turning back. I'll just be the fool that continues to hold on despite his confession. I change my mind. I can't hear the answer, afraid to know the truth. I want to pretend reality isn't what it actually is.

"Yes. Sorry. I'm just worried about the bar. I remembered something I forgot to look up," I say, chickening out.

"I totally get it. Those exams are the worst. Don't worry. I know you'll do just fine."

He reaches across the table and squeezes my hand. The heat from his fingers burns through my flesh, breathing fire into me. I don't want him to let go, so I hang onto to him for a second longer than I should. He doesn't say a word; I'm not even sure he notices.

When he leans back in his seat, smiling at me, I know it with certainty. I'm willing to risk it all if it means having a few moments in this life with Ben.

* * *

I hold my breath when we pull up to the front of the house, praying my parents aren't home yet. As if the luck gods can hear me, the driveway is empty. I exhale a sigh of relief; Ben doesn't notice. I expect him to leave the car running like last time, saying a quick goodbye and heading home, but he doesn't. He turns off the ignition and faces me. There's an expression on his face that I can't place, causing something to stir inside me.

"What do you have going on for the rest of the afternoon?" he asks.

I need to study. I'm scheduled to take the test in less than a month and I need to review. But the unfamiliar glitter in his eyes makes it difficult to say no. I can't think of anything I want more than extending this date with him.

What I should do is turn and leave. I need to walk back into my house and throw the idea of Ben out the window, along with the confusing emotions that go with him. This won't go anywhere. I try to remind myself that he's dating someone else. I try to remember he's been with Sara.

"Nothing," I say, against my better judgment.

"I have to go to Crate and Barrel to order something for my brother and sister-in-law to be. Want to take a drive with me?"

The store is right here in the valley, too close to home. There's a big chance we will be seen, a thought that only seems to cross my mind, not Ben's. He doesn't appear the least bit concerned with getting caught. He probably doesn't even care. Why would he? I'm the one pining over my best friend's ex. He no longer has any loyalties left to Sara, not after the way she treated him.

"Okay." I know I'm taking a risk, but I can't seem to keep my mouth from saying what it shouldn't.

"Great." He turns the ignition back on and pulls away from my house.

* * *

I'm breathing a bit easier. I've made a thorough scan of the shopping center on the way into the store and now I'm hidden behind a rack of pots and pans while I wait for Ben to place his order. I'm keeping myself busy reading labels and comparing steel as if I know what I'm doing. Anything to keep from thinking about getting caught.

I've come up with a few different excuses I could give if indeed someone spots us. Provided Ben plays along and doesn't blow my cover. I'm running my finger across the edge of a red cast-iron skillet when I feel a light touch on my side. I turn to find myself only inches away from Ben. For a second, I forget where I am.

"I'm done," he says, smiling.

"Okay."

"Ready? Or were you looking at stuff?" He glances over my shoulder at the pan I still have my hand resting on.

"Oh, no. Just keeping busy," I say, flustered.

"Cool. Want to grab some coffee?"

"Sure."

We pull into the parking lot of the coffee shop a few minutes later.

It's a quaint, family-owned establishment, with cute wicker chairs and wooden tables. I've always loved it here. I come to study when I need a change of scenery. The Starbucks down the street has taken a lot of their business, creating a quiet, calm ambiance. Good for me, but bad for them. Nevertheless, I try to stay a loyal customer.

"What do you want?" I ask Ben. He's paid every time we've gone out. It's time I returned the favor.

"I got it," he says.

"Nope, you always pay. It's my turn."

"You don't have to do that. I like paying."

"I know, but I want to. It's just coffee. I think I can handle it," I joke.

"Okay," he says reluctantly, realizing I'll put up a fight. "Can I have a cappuccino, please?"

"Got it."

I turn toward the counter and he grabs my hand. Electricity rushes up my arm at his touch. I have to fight the sigh that wants so desperately to escape my lips. I turn back in his direction to find his eyes trained on me, melting me beneath their gaze.

"Thank you."

"You're welcome."

I order the drinks, then lean against the pick-up counter, waiting.

My mind wanders to thoughts of Baba, as I absentmindedly twirl a honey stick between my fingers. He'd like Ben's chivalrous ways. He says a real man should always be a gentleman.

"This newer generation knows nothing about how to treat women. In my day, we opened doors, paid for dinners, even brought flowers. Said please and thank you when we spoke to parents. And we worked hard for what we had, not like these young kids that are so entitled." I can see him cutting through the air with his hand in irritation. It makes me smile.

Despite the dying breed, I've managed to find one of the good ones. Too bad he isn't technically mine. I'm not exactly sure how Baba would react; it might not be enough to tip the scales given Ben's history with Sara. Iranian scrutiny can easily over shadow Ben's chivalry.

The barista repeats my name and I whip my head up to find her holding two mugs in my direction. I take them, trying to bury thoughts of Baba and his opinions. There doesn't seem to be a reason to worry about him right now. There may never be.

Ben's chosen the table in the far-right corner of the shop, against the front window so we can see the passersby. I should come up with an excuse to move, put us in the back where we're harder to spot, but I'm still reeling from the high of his touch. *Let them see. I don't care.*

"Here you go." I put his drink in front of him as I sit down.

He just smiles and takes a long sip of the coffee. His eyes light up when the caffeine passes through his lips as if he's a kid in a candy store. It makes me giggle.

We spend the next hour chatting as usual, discussing his work and my test. The conversation twists and turns naturally, encompassing any topic that pops up. We never fall victim to awkward silences or uncomfortable subjects. I relax into my seat, slowly losing the worry of being discovered.

For the first time today, I'm just enjoying his company. As I loosen up, he does too, becoming more playful and witty with his responses. He makes me laugh. And it feels good. Each time he touches me with either a gentle squeeze of my hand to emphasize a point, or a nudge at something sarcastic I say, my heart flutters. I lose myself in it.

Suddenly, he reaches out and pulls a stray curl back behind my ear. His fingertips graze my cheek and I inhale sharply, trying to keep from unraveling. He's staring at me with a dreamy look in his eyes.

"You're really beautiful." He sounds like he's talking to himself, like I'm not in the room.

My heart stops and I hold my breath, waiting for something. I'm not sure what it is, but I can feel it coming. Forgotten is everyone and everything surrounding me. All I want in that moment is to hear the words I can see he's about to say. At the same time, I'm terrified of what they'll mean.

"I don't think you know just how amazing you really are, Leyla."

He runs his thumb softly down the side of my jaw, still drinking in my features.

The glimmer in his expression, the way his full lips are beckoning me, the heat of his touch. All my senses are alive, buzzing with the need to get closer to him. I wish he'd lean in, put his lips against mine, and kiss me. I don't think I've ever wanted anything more.

Suddenly the door to the coffee shop opens and the bell attached to the frame rings, snapping me out of my trance. Sara. The girl he's dating. Both of them come crashing into me with the reality of our situation. I pull back, disconnecting from Ben. His arm falls to the table and his eyebrows pinch together in confusion.

"I have to go," I say shakily. I grab my bag and head out the door. I need to put distance between us.

I step into the parking lot to find that it's dark outside. How long have we been together? The entire day has escaped me, lost in the idea of something that could never work. Even if I could talk Sara into being okay with this, he's with someone else.

I didn't drive and have no way of getting home without him. But I can't go back inside. I'm not sure how I'd face him after what I just pulled. He'd never let me get away without an explanation and I just can't do it right now. I don't want to admit that I'm a stupid girl with stupid girl dreams that won't come true. I start walking toward the street, pulling my phone from my purse so I can call Raha.

Before I have a chance to make it more than two feet, Ben grabs my arm.

"Leyla, where are you going? What just happened?"

I stop but don't face him. I'm not sure why I feel so embarrassed; I haven't done anything. He's the one with another girl and spending the entire day with me. I try to pull away, to keep walking toward the street and away from Ben, but he won't let me.

"Talk to me." His tone is soft and comforting, wrapping itself around me like a warm blanket.

I'm suddenly angry. Why does he have to be so perfect? Why is he always so kind and understanding? It just makes things worse. This isn't fair. I whip around to face him.

"What are you doing, Ben?" I ask, accusingly.

"What do you mean?"

"Why didn't you tell me about her?" I blurt out.

"Who?"

"Sara told me she saw you." In one sentence I've made reference to both of the reasons why we can't be together.

Understanding crosses his face as my words settle in.

"I don't know," he says honestly.

"What? That's not an explanation." I don't even care if he doesn't owe me one. I want it anyway.

"I know. I just...I don't know what's happening between you and me. I'm not even sure if anything is? But I didn't want to ruin it before it began. I'm just dating Liz. We aren't exclusive. There isn't anything to tell yet." The skin around his eyes crinkle when he asks, "You've told Sara about us?"

"No! She just mentioned that she ran into you at the store and you were with some girl."

Subtle disappointment settles on his features but he doesn't say anything more. I try to attribute it to my lack of bravery and not the idea that he wants Sara to know about us. I try not to think about what the intentions behind that might mean. I need to get away before I lose all my nerve. I can't do this. He can't do this. Both of us are bound to other women somehow.

"I have to go," I plead.

He just stands there for a few moments, then releases my arm. Defeat knocks the air out of my lungs. He gives in when I was hoping he'd put up a fight. The confusion of my feelings is making me dizzy. I can't even keep up with my own mood swings. How do I expect Ben to?

"Okay. But I'm taking you home. You aren't walking or whatever it is you were planning on doing." He doesn't leave room for me to protest, just heads toward his car.

I follow, trying to fight the tears threatening to expose me. I should be happy he's giving up, letting the notion of us go before it's had a chance to take shape. This is what I thought I wanted, but the idea that he doesn't care enough to try to convince me to stay breaks my heart.

He opens the door for me, then makes his way to the driver's seat. I wish he'd stop being such a damn gentleman, just adding insult to injury. He turns the car on and as the engine purrs to life, my heart aches knowing this is all about to end. But he doesn't throw the car into reverse, instead he faces me. I have to hold my breath. The slightest movement will cause me to burst, a tidal wave of emotions waiting to drown me.

"What are we doing?" he asks.

I can't look at him, too afraid I'll start to cry.

He reaches out and gently grabs my chin, forcing me to meet his gaze. "Leyla, what do you want?"

"I don't know," I manage. My voice quivers and I hate myself for being so vulnerable. But Ben doesn't judge, his eyes soften, a small, kind smile pulling at his lips.

"Yes, you do," he urges.

"Ben, please. Just leave it."

"No. I can't."

"Why not?" I ask, trying to find the anger I need to push myself down a road I so desperately don't want to go down. I come up empty. All I feel is sadness.

"Because I need to know what it is that you want from this. From us."

What good will saying the words actually do? Despite how badly I want to be with Ben, I can't figure out a way to make it real. And I really don't want to hear myself say it out loud.

"I can't," I repeat.

The radio is playing Jordan Davis's "Dancing in a Parking Lot." It competes with the sound of my heart pounding in my ears. Ben grins, then suddenly gets out. Not the reaction I was expecting. I stare at him in confusion as he walks around the car to my side. He opens the door, leans over me and turns up the volume. Then he extends his hand. I look at him as he flashes his irresistible dimples at me and can do nothing else but put my hand in his.

He pulls me up before him, our faces inches apart, and places his hands around my waist. He begins to dance, gently swaying me back and forth. My arms find his neck and I lean in until our bodies feel like one, never taking my eyes off of him.

We dance, in a parking lot, along to the music. I can hear the words swirl around us, lifting us up into the night. No one exists. No one matters. It's just Ben and me. In this moment, on the pavement, we are in a world where maybe, just maybe, I could be his and he could be mine.

"What do you want?" he asks again, his breath tickling my lips. He's so close that all I need to do is stand on my tiptoes to close the distance between us.

I can't deny my feelings any longer, can't pretend I don't want this. I can't tell myself to walk away, to turn and leave him behind. I can't do anything I should and want everything I can't have.

"You," I whisper.

"Good," he says. Then he leans in and kisses me.

CHAPTER SIX

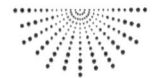

I lie on the couch, curled up beneath Ben's arm, my legs resting on his. The sun is shining through the living room window, draping us in a blanket of warmth beneath its rays. This has become my favorite pastime in the past two months. The hours move slowly here, nestled in the cushions, protecting us from the big, bold world beyond the windows. The one that houses best friends kept in the dark and disgruntled parents.

Ben's lazily twisting a red curl between his fingers as we watch a Dairy Queen commercial.

"Ice cream sounds good," he says.

"Yup."

"Should we go get some?"

"No," I answer, yawning. He's still playing with my hair and it's making me sleepy. "I just want to stay here." I pull my body in close, place my head firmly on his chest, and close my eyes. The weight of sleep weighs heavy on my lids.

I should be studying, getting ready for the bar exam, but I'm burnt out. And it's the weekend. Ben works all week long, and I don't get to see him that much. Or at least that's the excuse I'm telling myself so I don't feel guilty about not hitting the books.

I don't realize I've dozed off until I'm startled awake by a car alarm outside. I open my eyes to find Ben quietly napping beside me. I lift myself up on an elbow and drink in his details. The sharp outline of his jaw, the perfect curve at the tip of his nose, and the soft whistle sound his breathing makes. His skin, glowing from the Santa Barbara sun, shimmers with stardust.

I reach out and run my finger through a small curl at the nape of his neck. He stirs beneath my touch and opens his eyes. Neon blue shines back at me in the dim light of dusk that has now settled on the living room. He doesn't say a word, just meets my gaze, and in the silence that passes between us, the desire we feel wraps around our bodies.

Until now, I've never felt how badly he wants me. But deep in his eyes, I can see something new, a primal longing making an appearance. It causes my hair to stand on end and a chill to run up my spine.

Without saying a word, he reaches up and wraps his fingers through my curls, pulling me down to him, placing his lips against mine. Explosions go off around me. The soft flesh of his lips, the heat of his tongue as he pushes it into my mouth, the way his hand is resting on the back of my neck, amplify my senses. I become incoherent with just one kiss.

His free hand traces the length of my body, teasing the hem of my top. When his fingertips brush across my skin, it takes my breath away.

He searches my face, silently asking for permission to undress me. I respond by pulling my shirt over my head, then grabbing the edges of his own and doing the same. I watch him as I unfasten my bra, letting it fall on top of the pile we're creating on the floor. A devilish grin tugs at the corner of his lips, sending my heart into sprints.

I'm suddenly nervous, keenly aware of all my insecurities. I feel vulnerable and exposed. As if he can read my thoughts, he sits up until his back is leaning against the couch, taking me with him. I'm positioned comfortably in his lap, a porcelain doll in comparison to his godlike body. *He's so damn sexy.*

He places his hand against my cheek, the lines around his eyes softening as he speaks.

"You're beautiful," he says. "I don't think you realize it." He gently pushes my hair behind my ear. "You're amazing, Leyla."

I smile to hide the emotions lodged in my throat. He runs his thumb over my lower lip, his gaze tracing the arc it makes. Then he leans in until our mouths are almost touching.

"I want you so bad."

My stomach drops down into my toes like the fall of a roller coaster ride. When he finally presses his mouth against mine, my entire body ignites with electricity. He kisses me deeply, gently guiding me down to the couch. The heat of his body washes over me, melting me into the cushions.

I wrap my arms tightly around him, pulling him close. He places his lips on the tender skin of my neck, slowly drawing a path across my chest, until he's teasing my nipple between his teeth. The sensation is overwhelming, muddling my senses, causing a moan to escape me before I can stop it. Everything I feel for Ben seems to build with each touch, bright and furious, threatening to tear me open.

I'm desperate for him, to feel him inside me, to join our bodies into one. But there's part of me that's terrified of what's about to happen, to commit myself when I'm not entirely sure how any of this will play out.

What if he's comparing me to Liz, or worse, to Sara? What if he still isn't over her? Could this just be a ploy to get back at my best friend?

I don't realize my body has stiffened beneath him until Ben pulls back and hovers mid-air above me.

"Where did you go?"

"Nowhere." I shift on the pillows, trying to hide my discomfort. I do my best to smile up at him, hoping I look convincing.

He leans back on the couch. I feel a pang of disappointment at the cold breeze that now replaces his body on my skin. *Damn it, Leyla, you're ruining it!* This isn't the memory of our first time I want to have. Tears lodge in my throat and I rapidly blink up at the ceiling when they pool in my eyelids.

"Don't do that," he says, pulling me up until we sit face to face, again. "Don't you dare do that, Leyla."

"Do what?"

I can't look at him, darting my gaze away from his face, trying to find anything else to focus on. If he stares at me with that expression of concern another minute, I'm going to start crying. So, instead, I avert my eyes. But he doesn't buy it. He places his hand beneath my chin, gently forcing me to turn toward him.

"No one else is here other than you and me. No one," he says. *Damn him and his psychic abilities.*

A stray tear escapes and I curse my eyes for their betrayal. How pathetic I must seem to him right now. He doesn't say a word, just wipes it away with his thumb.

"There's nobody else but you, Leyla," he whispers. As my name leaves his lips, I come undone.

He kisses me, soft and slow at first, silently confirming his feelings. The heat builds from down low, coursing through my veins, covering the length of my body with its urgency. I imagine it bursting out of me, splattering along the gray walls in crimson paint. Before I know what I'm doing, I'm pulling my pants off and encouraging him to do the same. Our remaining pieces of clothing frantically rain down around us, settling where they may. He flips me onto my back until his body is hovering above mine. I can feel the desire radiating off of his skin.

"Are you sure you want to do this?" he asks.

"Yes." I've never been more sure of anything in my life.

He grins his crooked half-smile, then eases himself inside of me. The feel of him takes with it whatever small hold I still have on my emotions. We fit like the rhythm of a song, musical notes that mold together on a page.

My body arches up to meet his, each movement laced with the magnitude of our forbidden love affair. I want him. I need him. And I don't ever want this moment to end. When the world comes crashing down around us, I cry out his name.

We lie wrapped around each other on the couch when it's over. My body is heavy with exertion, the weight making my thoughts fuzzy and dreamlike. My head is on his chest and I can hear the beating of his heart underneath my ear, feel his pulse slowing beneath my fingertips.

He's playing with my curls again. It's a small gesture, but it's mine. The fact that he does it unconsciously makes it even more endearing.

In this moment, I know there is nowhere else I'd rather be. Ben has managed to surprise me, make me feel things I've never felt before. He's given me something I've always wanted. Lying here on the couch with him, I know I'm doomed. I'm stuck in a web I can't untangle; in a situation that won't be resolved easily.

I also know that I don't care, because I'm falling in love with him.

"You slept with him?" Raha sits back on my bed, her dark chocolate eyes wide with amusement. She's almost giddy with the news.

"Don't look at me like that," I say, giggling. "I feel like I've just told you I lost my virginity or something."

"Please, we both know you gave that up a long time ago," she teases.

"You're such a bitch," I laugh, throwing a pillow at her. She ducks out of the way.

"I just wasn't expecting this."

"Why not?" I ask, suddenly self-conscious about telling her.

"Don't freak out. I just meant I didn't realize it was getting serious."

"I wasn't expecting it to be either." I'm playing with a stray string on my comforter, daydreaming about my night with Ben.

"Oh my God, you're falling for him!" she says, as if she's just made a big discovery. "You're blushing." I can tell from her elated expression that she approves.

The innocence of her happiness tears my heart open, and I can no longer conceal the fears I've been holding tight against my chest. My eyes fill with tears and I fight the urge to cry.

"Leyla, what's wrong?" She scoots closer to me, reaching out and grabbing my hand. Her concern pushes through my defenses, bringing down the shield I'm hiding behind.

"Raha, I think I'm falling in love with him. I know it hasn't been that long, but I can't help it," I whisper. My voice is barely audible as I try to form the words around the lump in my throat. "What am I going to do?"

"What do you mean?"

"How am I going to do this? No one even knows we're together, other than you and Maya. I'm in a secret relationship with Ben. And I'm already falling in love with him." The tears break through my lashes, wetting my cheeks.

"So why are you keeping it a secret?"

"You know why. *Sara*."

"That's your choice, Leyla. No one is making you hide. If you really feel that strongly about Ben, you have to tell her."

"What about Maman and Baba? They'll have a fit too," I say in protest.

"Why? Because he's not Persian? They aren't like that."

"No! Because he's been with Sara. They're open-minded, but they won't like the fact that everyone knows about the two of them. You know how they are about what we look like in front of the community. They'll never approve."

"Leyla, don't get ahead of yourself. One step at a time. Do you want to be with him?" she

asks.

"Yes." A tiny sob escapes my lips.

"Then fight for him."

Raha has always fought for what she wants regardless of who she pisses off. I don't know if I can do that, if I can be as fierce as she is. I'm not sure if I can battle my parents on this and not crumble beneath their disappointment. More so, I'm not brave enough to face Sara. I have no idea how she'll react, but the fact that I haven't told her for two months only makes it worse.

My sister reaches over and pulls me into her arms, letting me cry for the first time since this all began. My vulnerability makes its way to the forefront and I embrace the confusion I've found myself in. I allow myself to accept how I feel about Ben, knowing I'm not willing to lose him.

"It's going to be okay. I promise," Raha says.

"I hope so."

I desperately want to believe her.

CHAPTER SEVEN

Another weekend in Santa Barbara under the pretense of Maya's sister. My parents don't hassle me much. At twenty-six, they've loosened the reins, realizing I'm an adult. Raha knows I'm staying at Ben's. I figure one person knowing the truth is good enough.

We're sitting at a swanky restaurant for dinner, on our second round of drinks, when my phone buzzes. I'm so busy laughing at what Ben's just said that I don't look down at my screen before picking it up. There are moments I forget I'm keeping him a secret.

"Hello?"

"Hey!" Sara's voice comes through the other end of the line and the blood instantly freezes in my veins.

"Who is it?" Ben asks, his eyes crinkled in concern.

I whip my finger up to my lips, silencing him. I earn a scowl in return. "Hey, Sara," I say, enunciating her name clearly, leaving no question who I'm on the phone with. "What's up?"

"Where are you?" she asks.

"I'm out to dinner. Why?" I'm trying to stay vague, praying she doesn't ask for more.

"With who?"

"Maya," I say, not skipping a beat.

Ben is leaning back in his chair, watching me. I wish the restaurant were louder so I could mask the conversation better. The fact that he can hear me deliberately lying to Sara makes me fidget with discomfort. I can feel his disappointment, the anger beginning to boil inside him from across the table. I try not to get flustered, ignoring the anxiety taking shape in my stomach.

"Oh, so you aren't around, then?"

"No. I'm in Santa Barbara. Why?" At least I'm giving her part of the truth, if I can't give her all of it.

"Maziar and I wanted to know if you'd join us for some drinks. Guess not." In her reality, I've been spending a lot of time with Maya. She has no clue that Maya is actually home tonight, in L.A., with a cold. "Maybe next weekend?" she asks, hopeful.

"Yeah, maybe." I don't want to commit, not knowing what my plans with Ben might be. "Can I call you tomorrow and we can figure it out?"

"Sure." She tries to sound chipper, but there's hesitation in her voice.

I've been avoiding her because I don't want her to know the truth. Not yet. Maybe not ever, despite that being impossible.

"Cool. Call you tomorrow." I quickly hang up, leaving no room for a drawn out conversation.

When I look across the table at Ben, his icy blue stare feels like the frigid cold water of the ocean when I first step in. Tension lines run across his forehead, the edges of his eyes pulled tight with dissatisfaction. His normally plump lips are bordering on a thin pink line. He doesn't say a word, just continues to pin me down with his gaze.

"What?" I finally say, unable to take his judgment any longer.

"How long do you plan on keeping us a secret, Leyla?"

"I'm not." I say it as forcefully as I can but it's still unconvincing, even to my own ears.

"Okay, then who knows about us?"

"My sister does," I say.

He raises a brow indicating he already knew that, and that she doesn't count.

"And Maya does." A pathetic attempt at redeeming myself.

"Does Sara know?" he asks. There's an accusatory tone in his voice.

"No, but it's more complicated with her."

"Okay. I can accept that. What about your parents? Do they know?" He leans forward in his chair, placing both hands around his drink, perched on the edge of his seat, ready to pounce when I give him the answer he already knows. He oozes strength, largely in contrast to the weakness I feel.

"No."

"Why not?"

"I don't know."

"Yes, you do, Leyla. So tell me. Why haven't you told your parents about us? Are they going to have a problem with the fact that I'm not Persian?"

"No!" I reply instantly. "They aren't like that."

"Then why?"

"I don't know!" My voice rises with irritation. Why does he have to be the only guy on the planet that's all about meeting the family? Any other twenty-six-year-old would think he'd won the lottery if his girlfriend wasn't trying to orchestrate a big reveal with Mom and Dad. "Can't we just enjoy this fabulous dinner? Please," I say, trying to redirect his focus.

Judging from the way he's aggressively running his hand through his hair, it's not going to work.

"No, we can't," he says, exhaling loudly. "Look, I know this is a tough situation. I'm not entirely on board with why you think it is, but I understand that for you, it's hard. That being said, we're not children, we're adults. Twenty-six to be exact. I'm too old to get into another relationship that's doomed from the start. You know I care about you, Leyla." He reaches out and grabs my hand in his. "But I won't do this again. I can't be with someone who's too afraid to tell people about us. I can't fall in love with you just to have my heart broken again."

Did he just say love? My heart melts, pooling on the floor around my feet.

"You're going to have to make a choice," he continues. "You either choose to be with me and all that comes with it or we end this now, tonight, and go our separate ways."

I can see he means it. The anger of a few moments ago has left him. Now he looks at me with a longing in his eyes, urging me to make the choice we both desperately want. I know how difficult this is going to be, but the alternative is more than I can bear.

"Why did I find the only mature twenty-six-year-old who's all about futures and long term?" I tease.

That manages to get me a smile.

"No more secrets?"

"No more secrets."

I don't want to be a coward anymore. Everyone has found their happy: my parents have each other; Sara has Maziar. I refuse to let my fear keep me from mine.

I choose happy. I choose Ben.

* * *

Raha sits to my right at the kitchen table, giving me moral support. Maman is to my left, Baba across from me, both engaged in a conversation about *Mamanbozorg, Grandmother,* and her cold. Maman has been taking care of Baba's mother for years, despite the fact that all her children are living close by. My grandmother adores Maman, but juggling her schedule along with *Mamanbozorg's* is hard.

"It's not like I don't have a job. Your sister is home all day while the kids are in school. It would be so much easier for her to take your mom to her doctor's appointments."

"I know, Simeen *joon,* but my mom really appreciates it. *Nemisheh kari kard. Zaneh peereh. Gohnah dareh." There's nothing we can do. She's an old lady, poor thing.*

"*Meedonam*, Ali." *I know.* "But it's still upsetting. Your siblings should help us."

Baba reaches out and pats her arm. She smiles, their love visible like lines of smoke from a fire.

I'm sitting eerily still as I take deep breaths trying to calm my nerves. Raha squeezes my knee under the table, nodding her encouragement. I know she has my back, but I can't help but feel like I'm standing in front of a firing squad alone.

"Leyla has something to tell you guys," Raha suddenly blurts out.

I turn toward her, wide-eyed and shocked. *What the hell!* She just smiles and nods again, as if I asked for her help. I feel the urge to punch her, but Maman reaches out and gently grabs my arm, distracting me from plotting my revenge.

"Leyla?"

My parents are staring at me, patiently waiting for the news. It's time to jump. I've made my choice; I won't leave Ben.

"Okay, don't freak out."

There's a quiver in my voice despite my attempts at a calm exterior. I don't want to sound doubtful before I've even begun. They'll be all over me in less than a second if they think there's a way to dissuade me from my decision.

"Oh boy," Baba says. "That doesn't sound good."

"I've met someone."

"She's *dating* someone," Raha clarifies. I throw my sister a sideways glance and she raises her hands in surrender.

"Okay," Maman says. "Who is he?" Her lips are curling at the edges, hopeful at the potential mate.

"Ben," I reply. No use in stalling any longer. Let the avalanche fall.

"I'm sorry; what?" Maman says, the smile suddenly turned into a frown. "Ben? Sara's Ben?"

The indication that he belongs to anyone other than me, especially my best friend, sends fury reeling through my body. It burns like fire through my limbs. I have to remind myself that losing my cool won't help the situation.

"Yes. But he's not Sara's Ben," I say, through gritted teeth.

My parents simultaneously sit back in their seats and stare at me, speechless. I don't know what to say to alleviate the situation, so I just stay quiet. Raha and I exchange nervous glances, waiting on the explosion we both know is coming.

"What are you thinking?" Baba finally says to me.

"Why him?" Maman throws in.

"He's a really great guy," I protest. "You'll think so, too, when you meet him."

"No!" my mom snaps. "We aren't going to meet him. You're not going to continue dating him." Her voice is final, leaving no room for debate.

I stare at her baffled, the words caught in my throat. My parents have never told me who to date, and they've definitely never forbidden me from seeing anyone in particular.

"That's not fair," Raha says, finding the voice I can't.

"I don't care if it isn't fair." Maman throws my sister an icy glare, causing Raha to pause.

"Okay, *Simeen*, calm down," Baba urges. "Raising our voices won't help." Living amongst three dramatic Iranian females has made my dad the rational one. "How long has this been going on?"

"Three months." I look down at my hands, avoiding the look of betrayal I know is on Maman's face.

"You've been dating him for three months and kept it from us?" she asks.

"Yes." I have no valid excuse to give for my omission so instead I don't try.

"Why?"

The pain in her voice stabs me in the gut.

"Because I knew you guys wouldn't like it. I didn't want to deal with it."

"No," she says, "I mean why *him*?"

"He's a great guy," I repeat.

"He really is," Raha adds.

"Enough, Raha." Maman holds her hand up like a crossing guard. "Enough with your commentary."

My sister sits back in her seat, reprimanded. I give her the only smile I can muster in this shit storm and turn back toward my parents.

"There are so many guys. Why pick the one who almost married your best friend?"

"They didn't almost get married!" I say, frustrated.

"They were moving in together. Same thing!" Maman yells. "What will people think, Ali?" she asks Baba, as if he has some sort of crystal ball that will answer her question.

"Is that what you're worried about? What your friends will think?" I'm appalled at my parent's close-mindedness. How could they let other people's opinions dictate our lives? My life?

"It's not just our friends, Leyla. You know how the community is. Everyone knows about Sara and this boy. They all know she was planning to move away with an *amricayee*. Don't you see? They'll not only think you aren't good enough to find your own boyfriend, but that you can't even find an Iranian," Baba says. "You're much better than that, *azizam*." *Dearest.*

"I don't care."

"You should care," Maman says.

"But I don't! I care about him. He's one of the best human beings I've ever met, and he treats me really well. Why do I have to walk away from that just because of what other people will think?"

"Leyla, why are you making life so difficult? How do you plan on being with him? Sara won't be comfortable around him, and even if she is, what about Maziar? Do you think he'll want to spend time with someone who has been in a relationship with his future wife?" Maman won't ease up. "No man would want that."

She has the familiar look of determination in her eyes I'm so accustomed to seeing. The one that indicates she's on a mission. Operation "break up Leyla and Ben" is definitely underway.

I stare at my parents in disbelief, the despair of their disapproval like a boulder in the pit of my stomach, pulling me beneath the ocean. I feel like I'm suffocating, the walls of the kitchen closing in on me. I unconsciously pull at the collar of my shirt in an attempt to get more air. I can't believe they'd let other people dictate anything that had to do with us. I thought I knew everything about my parents, but now I'm wondering if I've had them wrong all along.

Who are these people? "You've always said that we should be who we want to be and not worry about anyone else. Why is this different?" I ask.

"Because this *is* different. Picking a career or what clothes to wear to express yourself isn't the same as being someone's second choice. And he's not even Iranian, which makes it that much worse." Maman's eyebrows are knit together. She reaches up and pinches the bridge of her nose as she takes two slow breaths, her hand shaking with rage.

I knew this would be difficult, but I wasn't prepared for them to outright forbid me to see him.

"I'm sorry, Maman, but I won't stop dating Ben," I say, with finality in my voice. I won't be bullied, by anyone, including her. "I'm an adult. I can make my own decisions about who to be with. I like him. I really do. And we're good together. This could be something amazing for me, and I refuse to walk away just because people will be talking behind my back."

"Leyla, don't say that. Why would you want to give anyone a reason to say bad things about you?" Baba asks.

"It doesn't matter what any of us do! Don't you guys understand that? People gossip all the time, regardless. It's a Persian pastime, and you know it."

"And Sara?" Maman interjects. "Are you willing to lose her, too?"

"I won't leave Ben because of Sara, either." The force in my voice wavers.

The thought of losing Sara is more difficult than I would like to admit. But I can't show my weakness here. They'll swoop down on me like vultures.

"She no longer has a right to have an opinion on who Ben dates. She has Maziar now. If she doesn't want me to be happy despite what that means for her, then maybe we aren't the friends I thought we were."

Maman stares as me, the moments dragging into decades before she speaks. "I don't know who you are right now, Leyla. But you aren't who I thought you were."

I'm rendered speechless, having no idea what the rebuttal to a comment like that should be. I do know that my chest aches in response to the despondency in Maman's eyes.

I stand up and walk back to my room, wanting to put distance between us. I don't make it to my door before the tears start falling from my eyes. By the time I lie on my bed, I'm quietly sobbing. I need their support. I already know telling Sara will be a nightmare. I hadn't even thought of Maziar. But now that they've planted the seed, I can't help but worry. He's going to throw a fit. Maybe a bigger one than Sara.

I suddenly want nothing more than to see Ben. I wipe my eyes, grab my keys, and head out the front door. I don't respond when Baba asks me where I'm going or when Maman asks if it's to see Ben. I don't bother telling them if and when I'll be home. I just ignore them and keep moving forward.

I catch a glimpse of Raha smiling broadly in my direction before I make it outside. At least someone is on my team.

* * *

Ben looks puzzled when he opens the door to find me standing there. I didn't call him to tell him I was coming. I could have made the long drive only to find him gone for the night.

"Leyla?"

I don't respond, just wrap my fingers through his messy dirty-blond hair, pressing my lips against his as my tongue asks for passage. The heat of his mouth burns life into me, reminding me of why I wanted to see him in the first place.

He grabs me by the waist and I become airborne. I wrap my legs around his waist as he takes a step into the apartment, swinging the door shut behind us.

I frantically place kisses on his lips, his neck, while he carries me to the bedroom. I'm a rag doll, as he expertly maneuvers my weight, never losing stride. By the time he lays me down on the bed, he's already shirtless and pulling my top over my head. He doesn't say a word, just meets my advances with his own. Within moments, we're naked.

The smooth feel of his skin, the hard muscles bulging beneath my fingertips, has me in a frenzy of need and wanting. I can't get enough, pulling him closer, arching my body to meet his.

His lips are an erotic flutter of butterfly wings touching my skin as he works his way down the length of my body, each agonizing caress taking me closer to my demise. When he nestles his head between my legs, I'm dizzy with desire. I moan as his tongue caresses my tender flesh, aching for release, like an addict to her heroin.

Just when I think I can't take anymore, he lifts himself up, entering me. The fireworks I've grown accustomed to explode around us. I see stars, burn with electricity, feel a cosmic boom ignite in my soul. We move in unison, each wave bringing us closer to the climax. And when our bodies tighten and the world pauses around us, we find that euphoric moment we've been chasing. I collapse back onto the sheets, orgasmic tremors leaving their heavenly imprint across my limbs.

Sweat glistens my skin as sweet exhaustion claims my mind. He kisses me tenderly one more time before lowering himself beside me. We lie side by side in the silence of the room, with only the dull sound of car engines purring outside the window.

"Leyla?"

"Yeah," I whisper, behind close lids and a dreamy smile.

"You want to tell what that was all about?" he asks.

"What do you mean?" I say. I turn onto my side to face him, still riding the high of our lovemaking.

"Don't get me wrong, you can show up here and do that whenever you want to, but that didn't just feel like you missed your boyfriend."

Boyfriend. I love how that sounds. I almost sigh before I notice the worry lines etched around his forehead.

My chest tightens as reality comes crashing back into me. I know I have to tell him that my parents are against our relationship. But I'm terrified it may be a deal-breaker. After all the drama he experienced with Sara's family, he may not want to take mine on. And honestly, I wouldn't blame him.

The heat of fury flushes my skin, replacing the euphoric calm of just moments ago. I'm suddenly angry with no real person to condemn for it. Had fate brought Ben to me first rather than Sara, things would have been so different.

Damn you, destiny, for screwing me over. Apparently, the universe is at fault.

He scoots in closer, lifting himself up on his elbow. The sheet falls down, pooling around his waist, exposing the definition of his chest. I unconsciously reach out, outlining the muscles with my finger. He places his hand on top of mine, pressing my palm against the spot where his heart is. I can feel it beat beneath my fingertips. Suddenly, I can't stop the tears from filling my eyes.

"Talk to me, baby."

"I told my parents."

"Okay. I'm guessing it didn't go well?" He chuckles, trying to make light of the situation. It tears into my already-broken heart.

"No," I say, shaking my head. I swipe the back of my hand across my eyes.

"What did they say?" he asks. "Is it because I'm not Iranian?"

I can see now how traumatized he is from his experience with Sara. She really did a number on him.

I place my hand on either side of his face, look him straight in the eyes, when I say, "No. It has nothing to do with that."

"Sara, then?"

"Yeah." I have to look away, ashamed by my parents' reaction. "They're worried about what people will think if we're together now."

"I can get that."

"I don't! They've never cared what anyone has thought before."

"Yeah, but you've never done anything they've ever had to worry about. Not until now." He has a point, but I'm too upset to accept it.

I shift uncomfortably on the bed, causing the sheet to fall away, exposing my breasts. I don't move to cover myself like I would have so many times before. I hardly even notice, a newfound comfort between us. In the past few weeks Ben has made me believe that when he looks at me, I'm the only one he sees. I no longer live in Liz' or Sara's shadow. He belongs only to me.

"Can I ask you something?" My heart is crashing against my ribcage and I'm about to lose my nerve, but I need to know.

"Of course."

He smiles, his dimples deep on either side of his face. He reaches out and pulls a curl back behind my ear. I've become so fond of this gesture—my life vest in the storm. I have to pinch back the tears as they threaten to consume me again. The thought of losing Ben is crushing.

"Do you want this? What's happening between us, I mean. I know you said you do, but I need to make sure you have no doubts. I'm going to have a lot of people angry with me, and I just need to know I'm fighting for something real."

His eyes are trained on my face and I force myself to meet his gaze. This is the moment of truth, when I have to decide if this fight is worth what I stand to lose. I hold my breath as I wait for his answer.

"Leyla, I love you."

He's looking at me, his eyes clear passageways into his heart. There's no doubt muddling his irises, no ulterior motives hiding in his pupils. Every fiber in my being knows he's telling the truth.

"I love you, too."

A smile stretches across his face at my admission. I return the gesture, scooting in closer, nestling against his chest. I feel like I'm in a dream, afraid I'll wake up and find that my life really isn't as amazing as it feels right now.

He loves me. The realization lifts a heavy burden off my shoulders, making it easier to breathe. I lean in and kiss him.

In that moment, I hand every piece of my heart over to Ben for his safekeeping. I lose myself in a world of love I've never known before.

And I refuse to look back.

* * *

The television screen flickers from the den as I enter the foyer. It's two in the morning and at least one of my parents is awake. With a boulder of dread in my stomach, I force myself down the hall to meet them, bracing for their disappointment.

Maman is lying across the couch sleeping, an infomercial on a waist trainer murmuring in the background. I tiptoe to the coffee table and grab the remote, shutting it off. I think I may make it away unscathed, but she stirs on the couch behind me. I freeze as if standing still will make me invisible. I hear her sit up and realize I'm too late—I've been caught.

"You're finally home," she says. The disgruntlement is evident in her tone.

"I am." I slowly turn to face her.

"You didn't pick your phone up when I called you."

"I didn't want to talk to you."

I'm terrified to engage in a battle of wills with my mother. She's an Iranian woman. I don't stand a chance, but I force myself to meet her gaze, despite the urge to run and hide.

"When has it ever been acceptable, Leyla, to throw a tantrum and storm out of the house, not telling us where you're going? And then to ignore our calls? *Deevooneh shodee?*" *Have you gone mad?*

"No, Maman, I haven't lost my mind. I wasn't ready to talk to you," I answer.

"Oh, grow up, Leyla."

"I am grown up," I throw back at her. My frustration is building; my hands are shaking by my sides.

"Then act like it!" Maman is whispering, but she's somehow still managing to yell at me. "We have a problem here. Whether you want to admit it or not, it's there. And throwing a tantrum and storming off to be with *him* isn't making it better." She emphasizes "him" making it clear he doesn't even deserve to have his name acknowledged.

"His name is Ben," I say.

"What?"

"He has a name. Give him enough respect to use it. And as far as this problem you keep talking about, I don't see one. So if you ask me, you're the one with the problem." With that I turn and head to my room.

"Leyla." I hear Maman whisper loudly in my direction but I don't turn around.

I'm done with the Ben saga for the evening.

I pull my phone out of my purse before I climb into bed. As I set my alarm, I notice I've missed a text message.

Miss you already, baby. Come back.

I curl around my pillow, sheets pulled up beneath my chin. I let thoughts of Ben wash over me, grabbing onto the moments of the evening like a lifeline. I allow them to replace the panic and dismay that have settled permanently in my stomach. The idea that I've disappointed my parents eats away at me like a plague. I don't want to be a disappointment to them, but I can't walk away from Ben. As my mind engages in a confusing battle against my heart, I fall into a fitful sleep.

CHAPTER EIGHT

Months pass, but nothing changes with my parents. We struggle at first, each trying to get the opposing side to see our point, Raha and I against Maman and Baba. We make no headway. I push to keep my relationship and they forcefully insist I move on.

Soon, we fall into a new normal, one where we co-exist well enough while never discussing the unmanageable topic of Ben. When I'm with him, they turn a blind eye. I've given up on trying to make them see the flaw in their ways.

The circumstances surrounding our relationship only prove to propel Ben and me forward, despite the cloud of doom. Soon the word "love" passes frequently between us. I spend as much time with him as I can. The bar exam comes and goes, leaving me nothing to do but wait. And so I do. In Santa Barbara.

Despite having been with Ben for six months, I still haven't broached the topic of my new relationship with my best friend. Sara has grown suspicious of my frequent "plans;" I'm never available to hang out like I used to be. With her wedding around the corner, the distance between us is just more evidence of the shitty friend I've become. I'm surprised she hasn't revoked my maid-of-honor title.

Ben has also grown weary of my lack of bravery. He's given me time to sort through my feelings. But the novelty of standing up to my parents has worn off.

"It's just hard," I say desperately. "I told them. What else do you want me to do?"

"I know you have, but that's all you've done. It's like the entire topic has disappeared, taking me along with it. You guys are just ignoring our relationship. Your parents are fine because no one knows about us yet. You've kept it a secret from everyone but them." He shakes his head.

I open my mouth to defend myself then close it, realizing I have no idea how to. There's validity to his point. I just don't want to accept it.

"Don't get me wrong," he says, his features softening. "I love having you spend time here with me, but that's the only place we can be. Santa Barbara works because you won't run into anyone here."

He sits up in bed, scooting away from me. He's been nothing but patient with the situation, never pushing me past my limits. But I know he's right; it's time to come out about us. Telling my parents was just the beginning.

He runs his fingers through his hair. Each strand settles in an odd direction, giving him a porcupine appearance. I have the urge to reach out and pat it down but refrain, knowing it will just aggravate him further. I exhale, a long, drawn-out breath. It adds more dramatic effect than I anticipated.

"You're right," I say. "I need to start being honest about us. I'm just scared, okay?"

"I know."

He doesn't turn to face me, his voice deflated and worn down. My heart begins to race in my chest. *Has he given up? Have I waited too long?* I sit up and slide closer to him, gently placing my hand on his bicep. My fingers break up the dark lines of the phoenix's wings.

"I'm going to tell everyone," I say.

"Okay."

"I love you. You know that, right?" I can hear the edge of desperation in my voice.

When he turns to face me, there's disappointment in his eyes.

"I know you do. But how would you feel, Leyla, if I kept you a secret for six months? Even if I kept telling you I loved you? Would that be enough? There's a whole version of your life I'm not a part of."

I wrap my arms around him and settle my chin on his shoulder. Staring up at his beautiful eyes, I can feel every fiber in my body yearning to be near him. I can't risk losing him, despite who I might lose in the process.

"I'm going to tell them. I promise you."

"I've heard that before."

Panic rises as bile in my throat.

"I mean it this time, Ben. I swear. I'm going to tell Sara and then it won't matter who knows."

I don't know if he believes me, but I pray that he does. I close the distance between us, kissing him hard, trying to convey the truth through unspoken words. He doesn't pull away, and I take it as a good sign. When he pushes me back into the pillows, a sigh of relief escapes me. I wrap my body around his and wish, for just a moment, that I could melt into him. I've never loved anyone as deeply as I love Ben. The magnitude of my feelings is almost painful.

* * *

"Hey!" Sara says, as I approach the table.

"Hi."

I smile shyly at her, an awkward funk having settled over our friendship these past few months. I've been MIA and she's had no idea why. She's trying her best to seem normal, so I do the same.

"I'm so hungry," she adds. Her voice sounds squeaky, a failed attempt at enthusiasm.

"Me too," I reply.

The truth is that I can't even imagine eating. My stomach rolls with the idea of doing what I've come here to do. I'm trying desperately to hide the fact that I'm shaking as I reach out to grab the glass of water sitting before me. My throat is parched and I have to cough a few times to clear it. I pray Sara can't tell how nervous I am, even though I'm doing a horrible job of hiding it.

She appears uncomfortable too. She's leaning on the table, her hands wrapped around a vodka tonic, her index and pinky fingers rapidly tapping on the glass. Her eyes are pinched together in concentration as the waitress approaches us and asks if I'd like anything.

"I'll have a vodka tonic too, please."

"Coming right up." She turns and walks away.

"I didn't know what you were going to want so I didn't order for you."

"No worries."

We fill the silence with small talk.

"How are the wedding plans going?" I ask. The date is rapidly approaching.

"We are still trying to figure out things with Maziar's parents. His dad is cool, but you know how his mom is." She rolls her eyes in annoyance. "It's freaking me out, to be honest. My mom's losing her shit."

She continues, telling me about their latest run-in with the mother-in-law-to-be. I listen patiently, nodding every few minutes to show I'm paying attention. But, my mind wanders to the discussion I know is coming, trying to figure out a smooth transition into the topic of Ben.

The waitress returns with my drink, not a moment too soon, and I take a long sip, welcoming the sterile tang of alcohol as it burns its way down my throat. Liquid courage is highly necessary at the moment.

The waitress hangs around for our food order. I ask for a salad I'm sure I won't eat and agree to share a plate of fries with Sara. It's our customary date tradition. Things already feel so off between us that I don't have the heart to tell her the idea of greasy potatoes makes my stomach cramp with nausea. Finally, the waitress leaves.

An awkward silence swallows us up as we run out of safe topics to discuss. Sara tries to busy herself with the edge of the table cloth, scraping her nail across the hem. I watch her as she looks anywhere but at me.

"I have to tell you something," I blurt out. I can't take the weird vibe strangling us any longer.

"Sure," she says, leaning forward, placing her elbows on the table.

She has her fingers wrapped around her glass again, furiously tapping the side. I reach out and steady them.

"I know things have been really strange between us. I'm sorry. That's been my fault."

She's about to launch into a rebuttal, no doubt refuting my blame, when I raise my hand to stop her. I won't have the nerve for long and I need to get out what I came here to say. I promised Ben I was done hiding. Come what may.

"I have to tell you something that I should've told you a long time ago, but I've just been too afraid about what you'll say."

"You can tell me anything, Leyla."

She reaches across the table and intertwines her fingers with mine. I give her hand a gentle squeeze as my heart constricts in unison. The potential of losing her stabs me in the chest.

"I know." I smile at her. "But this is a big deal, and you're going to have a tough time with it."

"What is it?" She's hesitant, her features scrunching with worry.

"I've been seeing somebody."

The muscles in her face relax almost instantly at the news. But before she has a chance to start an inquisition, I continue.

"It's been six months and it's pretty serious. I've really fallen for him and I'm truly happy, Sara."

"Okay?" The intonation of her voice beckons a question rather than a statement. I'm presenting this information in a way that sounds like I'm delivering grave news. "I don't understand. You've been dating someone for six months and you're just telling me this now?" The hurt is evident in her eyes.

"Yes." I take a deep breath as I deliver the blow. "Because it's Ben. I've been dating Ben."

She just stares at me at first, and I wonder for a second if she's heard me. Then the lines on her forehead furrow deeper as her skin runs pale, and her eyes widen with understanding.

"You're dating Ben? My Ben?"

Her clarification angers me, and I suddenly feel a rush of heat invade my cheeks. I'm so tired of everyone identifying him as *Sara's* Ben. Even her. I wonder if there will ever be a time that people tie my boyfriend to me, rather than to the ex that broke his heart. I have to remember to stay calm, dissuading myself from storming out of the restaurant.

"Yes. Ben."

She leans back in her seat. She looks ill, an almost green hue to her now-pale skin.

"How?"

"I'm not entirely sure how it happened. After I picked up your stuff from his apartment, I ran into him again and we started talking. We were just friends at first, but then things evolved into something more."

"Why didn't you tell me?" Her lips are pursed together, a sad look settled in her eyes.

I'm not sure whether she's more hurt that I've started something with her ex, complicating our relationship in ways that may be irreparable, or that I've been in a relationship for months and I've kept it from her.

"I couldn't," I say, by way of explanation.

She cringes at my response as if I've leaned across the table and slapped her. I might as well have, judging from the betrayal I can see in her eyes.

"I'm sorry." My lame attempt at amends.

"How could you?" she accuses. "Why would you start something with *him*? What am I supposed to tell Maziar?" Her cheeks are flushed with anger. "How could you do this to me?"

She's glaring at me like I've just told her I killed her cat. It sparks my own rush of fury and I lean forward in my chair. My red hair falls around my shoulders, the tips resting on the pink tablecloth, creating a Valentine's Day color scheme. Ironic, since currently love is nowhere to be found.

"I didn't do anything to you," I reply, enunciating each word slowly, leaving no room for the misinterpretation of my rage. "I didn't go to Ben's apartment looking to be with him. I went because you were too scared to do it yourself. Life happened and we hit it off. My relationship with him has nothing to do with *you*." My voice is low, barely audible as I try to fight the anger threatening to burst through me. I grip the edge of the table, steadying myself.

"How can you say that? It has everything to do with me. It's going to directly affect my life. And our friendship, for that matter."

I remind myself that I never thought Sara would accept the idea of Ben and me immediately. But no amount of preparation could dull the sting of her reaction. Despite how small, there was a part of me that held onto the hope that she may see past herself and be happy for me. I've wanted so badly to share this part of my life with her. There's no hope for the pajama *chayee* sessions I've prayed for when we discuss and dissect all the wonderful things I've experienced these past few months, like the best friends we used to be.

"I'm happy, Sara," I say, trying to desperately find a way out of this mess. I don't see a light at the end of the tunnel, but I can't help but try to get there anyway.

She leans back again in her chair, downing the rest of her drink as her eyes bore into me. She doesn't say anything at first, but her features soften when she asks, "Do you love him?"

"So much."

"Leyla, I just..." she says, then stops and purses her lips together. It's what she does when she's trying not to cry, prompting tears to well up in my own eyes. "I just don't know what to do with all of this," she manages to shakily say.

"I know."

I can't afford her any comfort other than the acceptance that our new reality is difficult for us both. We're standing at the edge of an abyss, both staring down into the black hole that awaits us. Neither of us has any idea if our foundation is strong enough to withstand this push.

"You're in love," she finally says, mustering up a small smile.

"Yeah, I am."

"Well isn't that something? Love looks good on you."

I lose my hold then, unable to withstand the wall of tears that have been pushing against my eyelids. I'm losing her, and the mere idea of it feels like a blade through my heart. I don't do life without Sara, and now somehow, I may have to figure out how to. She begins to cry along with me, startling the waitress as she sets our food down before us.

"Is everything okay?" she asks hesitantly.

"Yes," I say, wiping the tears off my cheeks. "Can we get this to go?"

"All of it?"

There's a silent exchange between Sara and me. No words are necessary, but there's an understanding that despite how much we love each other, neither of us knows whether we can get past this. The dinner is over and we both know it's pointless to sit here under false pretenses.

"Yes," Sara says. "All of it."

* * *

"What do I do?" I ask.

"Give her some time, Leyla. You barely told her. It's going to take a minute for the dust to settle. Sara will come around," Raha says.

I don't know if I believe her, but I grab hold of her words because it's necessary. I need to stay afloat despite the loss I'm experiencing.

"What if she doesn't?"

Raha has always been the big sister, taking on her role with mastery. She finds ways to guide me when I'm lost and never lets me go at it alone. Now, as I lie across my bed, crying over the destruction of my closest friendship, it's she who will pull me from the storm.

"Do you love Ben?" she asks. My head's on her lap and she's gently stroking my hair. It's transporting me to my childhood.

"Of course I do."

"Is he worth it?"

"Yes."

"Then you can't worry about Sara. Or anyone else. You have to be true to yourself and follow your heart."

"But what if it's a mistake?" I ask.

"What do you mean?"

"What if I think it's worth it and it's not? I mean, I love him and I know he loves me. But what if this doesn't end up working out and I've lost Sara, and maybe even Maman and Baba, along the way? What do I do then?"

I look up at Raha, waiting for an answer she can't possibly have. She isn't psychic, she doesn't know how this story will end. But I'm terrified and broken. I just need a confirmation that I'm doing the right thing.

"Well, I suppose that's a risk you take when you love someone. No one knows how things are going to go, Leyla. But you can't always make the safe decision. Sure, you could break up with Ben and make everyone else happy. It's the easiest option. But would you be happy?" she asks.

"No."

"For the first time, you're letting yourself feel things you've never felt before. You deserve that. You're aren't doing anything wrong by choosing you."

Suddenly my door opens and Maman walks inside, her arms piled high with laundry. One of the perks of still living at home.

"What's wrong?" The edges of her lips pull down in a frown in response to my tear-stained face.

Raha looks at me and I nod, giving her permission to tell Maman.

"Leyla just got back from lunch with Sara."

"I see," Maman says.

She has the ability to sound condescending using just two words. I roll my eyes at her.

"Don't tell me you're surprised?"

"No, Maman, I'm not surprised," I say, straightening myself on the bed and wiping my cheeks. Time to find strength again as I go back into the next battle of the day.

"Is he worth this?" She sweeps her hand in front of her as if my relationship with Sara is encompassed in this room.

"Yes." I don't break eye contact, asserting my position.

"Ugh, Leyla! Nothing is worth losing your best friend and fighting with your family over. He's just a boy."

"That's not fair, Maman. She loves him," Raha throws in.

I flinch as the words fly out of her mouth. Maman's about to lose her shit. No one's said anything about love yet.

"Love! What is this nonsense about love? No, Leyla, no! I won't allow it."

"What?" I say, because I must have misheard her. She did not just forbid me from loving who I want to.

Raha is stunned silent, looking back and forth between Maman and me. Now would be a good time for some of that strength she so easily exudes.

"*Sheneedee manoh*," Maman yells. *You heard me.*

"No, I don't think I did, actually. What I thought you said was that you're not giving me permission to love Ben."

"Like I said, you heard me."

She stands her ground, laundry now placed on the edge of the bed, her hands balled in fists, resting on her hips. Spiderwebs fan out from the corners of her eyes as she scrunches them together in a fabulous Iranian mother scowl. Her dark eyebrows are almost touching, creating two perfect parallel lines between them. If this were a cartoon, steam would be rushing out of her ears.

I begin to laugh. A sarcastic chuckle at first that soon increases in stride and vigor to a full-out crazy cackle. Maman and Raha stare at me, wide-eyed, bordering on terrified. I feel like I may be having a nervous breakdown. *This is not happening.*

"You've done it, Maman. *Deevoohen shodeh!*" *She's gone crazy.* Raha's hands are out in front of her like she's getting ready to approach a rabid animal. "Leyla, you okay?"

"Oh, Leyla, that's enough. You're so dramatic," Maman says. There isn't an ounce of remorse in her voice, causing the anger lying dormant in my chest to explode in a storm of flames, threatening to bring the house down around us.

"Dramatic? I'm being dramatic because I find it funny that you actually think you can tell me what to do?" The fury has taken over, making its way into each cell of my body. I'm buzzing with it, cheeks hot, hands shaking uncontrollably.

"I'm your mother."

"I don't care!" I start screaming.

Maman takes a step back. She's fuming at my outburst, but there's concern in her eyes as well. This isn't like me. This is what Raha does, making a big scene. I've always been the quiet, rational one. I'm suddenly unpredictable and I can see it worries her.

"I'm a grown woman. I'm not a child you can control. I'll love whoever it is that I want to, regardless of how difficult it is for you." My voice is eerily calm, despite how upset I am.

Maman continues to stare at me in disbelief.

"You haven't even given him a chance. He's a really good person and if you would take a minute to just see that, you'd be happy that I'm with someone like him."

The crinkles of dismay soften around Maman's eyes.

"I know you think you love him, Leyla *joon*. I remember those feelings too. But this isn't going to work, *dokhtaram*. It's already more complicated than it needs to be. You're blinded now by your feelings, but if you go down this road, all the talk you'll have to endure and all the people you'll lose will ruin how you feel about him. At some point you'll look back and resent what he's done to your life. By then, it'll be too late." With that, Maman turns and walks out of the room.

"Shit," Raha says, after she's gone. "This isn't going to be easy."

As if I didn't understand what challenges I'd be facing.

"You think?"

CHAPTER NINE

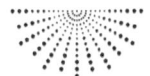

W ord spreads quickly, once I decide to step out into the open with Ben. Not only do my parents' friends hear about me, but it burns through the entire community like wildfire. I'm not surprised; Middle-Easterners are always up for a good gossipfest. I try to take it in stride.

Maman's fury continues to grow like an ugly tumor eating away at my insides. Her scowls deepen each day and she rarely speaks to me. She feels as though I've put her in an impossible situation with her friends.

Baba's disappointment remains evident in the way he looks at me too, but he doesn't cut me out like she does. He resorts to cornering me and *talking* about my relationship, which translates into his list of reasons why I shouldn't be with Ben. I listen quietly, nodding every so often so he feels like he's being heard, because there's a part of me that's terrified of losing both my parents.

But Sara's silence hurts the worst. It's a constant reminder of what I've already lost.

I missed Sara's dress shopping. She didn't even call me to let me know she was going. I saw it in a picture Bita posted on Facebook, of their lunch afterward. A stabbing pain shot through my chest at the smiles stretched across their faces. I should've been there.

It appears as though Sara no longer needs me.

Losing her is more than just losing a friend. Someone has reached into my soul and pulled out a piece of my core, leaving me empty. I don't know if there's a way to fill the immeasurable void I harbor in her absence.

Maman and Sara's mother are still okay despite the crumbling relationship of their daughters. Yet my mother makes it a habit to constantly tell me how uncomfortable she now feels around her old friend.

"I can't even look Shireen in the eyes," Maman says.

"But she isn't giving you a hard time about it," I reply.

Sara's mother has proven to be very supportive in the situation. Shireen has just voiced concern over my relationship with her daughter. Plus, I took Ben out of the equation; she never wanted him for Sara, so there's that too.

"It doesn't matter. She's being polite. *Khejalat bekesh, Leyla. Aberoomoonoh bordi!*" *Be ashamed of yourself; you're embarrassing me!*

Maman makes it a habit to remind me daily of what my actions have done to her.

"I know. I'm sorry." My standard response. Anything more prompts an argument I'm not interested in.

Despite disagreeing with my decision though, my parents defend me against the negativity. They're fiercely loyal to their children, a commonality among most Iranian parents. Raha and I mean the world to Baba and Maman, and they won't allow anyone to drag us through the mud. But behind closed doors, they continue to try to sever my ties with Ben.

Raha and I lie lazily across the couch, channel surfing, when the final confirmation that I've officially made headline news happens. Maman and Baba come storming in from their brunch date with their friends.

"Can you believe her?" Maman is shaking her head as she drops her bag on the loveseat. "Acting like someone has died!"

"Well we knew this could happen," Baba says. His tone is somber and thoughtful.

"What's going on?" Raha asks.

"Nothing. Just a few people have heard about your sister and her new boyfriend," Baba explains.

"A few? More like *everyone*." Maman is staring daggers in my direction. I nestle down further in the pillows trying to escape her wrath.

"Oh," Raha replies. Of all the times I need her to come up with some witty, confident response, she's got nothing. *Brilliant.*

"Maryam had the nerve to give me her condolences over the situation. As if Leyla has up and died somehow!" Maman's voice is shrill with agitation.

"She gave you condolences? Seriously?" I ask. The conversation is just baffling.

"No, not literally, but you know what I mean. Don't annoy me further, Leyla. I told you this would happen. Everyone knows you settled for second best and now Baba and I are doomed to defend you each time it comes up."

"Well don't defend me, if that's easier. I don't care what they say about me." I'm trying to be helpful, but the crimson in her cheeks just deepens, spreading across her forehead.

"*We* care! You're our daughter. Regardless of how we feel about this boy, no one is going to disrespect my children." With that, Maman's expression saddens. "I wish you'd stop this nonsense already, Leyla. I don't know how much more of this I can take." She turns and heads to her room.

"It will all settle down, *dokhtaram*," Baba says, running his hand across my head and cupping Raha's cheek as he follows Maman down the hallway.

The disconnect with Maman makes me feel horrible, but I refuse to compromise. I can't keep defending my choices. It's exhausting. But although I'm stubborn and unyielding, I secretly wish there was a way to come to an agreement. I need my family.

* * *

With the recent avalanche of my life, Ben has been trying desperately to cheer me up. He's taken me to fancy dinners, lazy picnics on the beach, funny movies, and fed me more chocolate than I care to remember. Aside from enhancing my Persian girl weight insecurities, this had no effect on the hole still sitting prominently in the center of my chest.

His newest attempt is a trip to the observatory. I just want to crawl into my pajamas and sleep the day away after seeing Bita's picture, but I know how desperately Ben is trying, so I go along obediently. I plaster on a smile for good measure, but it isn't fooling either of us.

It's a clear night and the stars are vivid against the black sky, even without a telescope. We make the windy trip up to the top of the hill, slowing as traffic builds near the parking lot. I'm more quiet than usual, my mind racing with thoughts of my lost relationships. My friends have divided, the mutual ones silently stating their allegiances. I don't know why I'm so surprised. I should have expected even they'd have their opinions.

Ben weaves his car through the rows of parking spaces until he finds one in the far-left corner, closest to the observatory. The walk up the hill is torturous from down further, so the location brightens my mood. He helps me out of the car, always chivalrous. I'm convinced he was born in the wrong time, a reincarnation from a different era.

His lashes brush against the side of my cheek when he presses his lips against mine, small fluttering butterfly kisses. I giggle against his mouth. He smiles, his dimples deep and beckoning, making him appear stellar against the dark sky. He's so handsome. Sometimes it hurts to look at him.

I still can't wrap my head around the fact that he's mine. I'd never have guessed a year ago that this would even be possible, that I'd fall in love with my best friend's ex, and that he'd love me back. I guess destiny can be confusing sometimes.

The observatory sits on the southern slope of Mount Hollywood in Griffith park. Its large white building is decorated with three copper-clad domes. Mounted in the two domes on either side of the building are the large telescopes used for viewing. Their hatches are open now and I can see the tips of their cylinders peeking out from where I stand.

There's a crowd forming at the entrance, trying to push their way in. A family is walking in front of us, a baby on Mom's hip, a toddler holding Dad's hand. A third child, around eleven, stands beside him, her blond hair tucked behind her ears as she stares curiously at the massive building before her. Dad reaches out and guides her closer to him, running his hand lovingly down the back of her head. It makes me smile. Ben pulls me closer to him, kissing my forehead. I wonder if he's thinking the same thing: our potential family someday.

Once we're inside, we make our way over to the planetarium to look at the times, then purchase tickets. We have forty minutes to kill. I grab Ben's hand and drag him upstairs to the balcony. There's a panoramic view of the city we can see from up there.

I lean against the wall, staring out at the backdrop of shimmering street lamps. They throw a zigzag pattern into the darkness, mimicking little bulbs on a Christmas tree. Ben wraps his arms around my waist and I lean into him, feeling the warmth of his chest against my back. There's a comfort in the feel of him, his strong arms and broad shoulders caging me protectively between his embrace. For a moment, I forget the real world and all the problems that come with it. I'm frozen, in the present, here with Ben.

"I love you," he says. His breath is hot against my scalp, causing goosebumps to rise across my flesh.

"I love you, too."

I spin around in his grasp until I'm facing him. He leans in and kisses me, his lips warm and inviting. I wrap my arms around his neck, running my fingers through his hair as I stand on my tip toes to reach him. He pulls me in closer, holding me tight. I get lost in his strength, making me believe I could do anything as long as he's beside me. We're too tangled in the moment and in each other to notice the couple that has just come up the staircase.

"Leyla?"

I freeze. I don't need to turn to know who's calling me. Her voice is as familiar as my own, and currently laced with surprise and a little disgust. Recognition flashes across Ben's features, so when I pull away, he lets me. My cheeks are warm and flushed with embarrassment as I slowly turn. I'm a child caught making out by her mother.

"Sara."

Ben steps in behind me, his frame positioned in a protective stance.

"What are you doing here?" she asks, as if she currently owns all of Los Angeles after our breakup.

"It's obvious what they're doing here," Maziar says.

I hadn't noticed he was standing behind her, too preoccupied with the expression on Sara's face. Shocked, hurt, and slightly annoyed? It's hard to tell. But Maziar is an open book. There's no question as to how he feels about this encounter with Ben and me. He's staring at my boyfriend, his gaze shooting shards of glass in our direction. Ben's returning the sentiment. The four of us are locked in some sort of battle that hasn't yet begun.

"We came to see the show," I say.

I steady my voice, trying to stay calm. The situation can get ugly quickly, with both men fluffing their feathers, trying to prove their dominance. Sara looks between Maziar and Ben, then at me. A silent acknowledgment of a truce passes between us, if only for the moment. Neither of us wants the evening to get out of hand.

"We just saw the last showing. It was great."

Her voice has lightened as she modifies her posture. The tension has disappeared from her shoulders and her expression looks light and airy. Just a normal night among friends. If only that were true.

"Cool," I say. "We should actually head down. It's going to start again soon." I smile, hoping I'm convincing. Not that it seems to matter, Ben and Maziar haven't broken eye contact, both trying to win the staring contest.

I place my hand on Ben's arm, pulling his gaze down to me. He startles, as if he's just remembered I'm there. He must see the worry in my eyes, because his features soften. He sheds the tough exterior he's wearing, reaching out and grabbing my hand.

"Sorry. We aren't making this very easy for you guys, are we?" he says.

I shake my head. I'm so overwhelmed by the situation that I don't trust myself to speak without betraying my emotions. He pulls me closer to him and faces Sara and Maziar.

"You guys really need to talk, Sara," he says, addressing her for the first time since they walked up. "I think there's a lot you both have to say." Before she can respond, he focuses on Maziar. "We're going to have to figure out a way to be civil around each other. For the girls' sakes."

Sara and I exchange glances, both shocked speechless by Ben's candor. I know I should say something, if the hollowness in my chest is any indication. I want to reach out to her, find a way to make things right. I'm angry, and I know she is too, but I can't help the fact that I still don't want to lose her. I need my friend. She can't hear the thoughts running through my mind, but when she gives me a small halfhearted smile, I pray she's telepathic.

Maziar has been backed into a corner. If he continues his macho bravado, he'll look like an ass, only proving to Sara that he's more concerned with his ego than making an already tough situation easier. Regardless of what he feels, he has no choice but to back down.

"You're right," Maziar says, looking at Sara for approval.

She smiles broadly at him, reaching over and hugging his waist, finding a spot beneath his outstretched arm. He pulls her in close, two puzzle pieces in perfect unison. They kiss, and I'm consumed with an unexpected pang of jealousy. As I watch their uninhibited expression of love, I get the urge to physically pull them apart, upset by the unfairness of the situation. Why can Sara parade her happy life around for all to see, but when I do, it's met with opposition and disdain? She's Muslim and he's Jewish, yet somehow, it seems as though Ben's past with Sara is a larger hurdle for us to climb.

"Well, enjoy your show," Sara says.

"Thanks."

Sadness washes over me. The awkwardness of our friendship has me on an unpredictable roller coaster ride, my emotions fluctuating so rapidly it's exhausting. As I turn to head down the stairs, I feel her hand on my wrist. Disappointment becomes a lump in my throat, wanting nothing more than to get away from the two of them. I don't think I can deal much longer but I turn to face her anyway.

"We need to talk. I'll call you?"

She's asking, making me believe she's as hesitant about my reactions as I am of hers. We're on uncharted territory and the normal rules no longer apply. Apparently, neither of us has any clue on how to proceed in these harsh waters.

"Yeah, I'd like that."

She gives my wrist a tiny squeeze just as Ben leads me down the stairs. It's a small indication, but I wrap myself around it, pulling it in close. I can feel their eyes on my back, but I don't look over my shoulder. I already know I'll find pain in Sara's expression, and only anger in Maziar's. Instead, I focus on the way Sara's fingertips felt on my skin, the subtle gesture as they pressed into my flesh, and the tiny seed of hope that has begun to bloom in the center of my chest, despite my better judgment.

CHAPTER TEN

My foot taps in nervous succession on the tile floor beneath me. It sounds like gunfire, a millisecond between each beat. I try to breathe, to calm my nerves, to no avail. My heart stammers in my chest and I feel lightheaded. I pull the mug up to my lips, wrapping both hands firmly around it, allowing the warmth of the coffee to seep into my fingertips. They are frigid and stiff, despite the comfortable temperature of the coffee shop, my anxiety mimicking colder weather.

I try to focus on the parking lot, staring at the spot where Ben and I had our first kiss. I imagine the hazy glow of the streetlights creating a halo on the asphalt. I think of the way his hand felt resting on my waist, the heat from his fingers burning into my skin. I remember the soft touch of his lips on mine, the way something so gentle could still invoke such vigorous desire inside me.

I take a sip, feeling it warm the tender flesh of my mouth, followed by a hot path down my throat. The steam rising off the mug blurs my vision, creating a dreamlike scene. Suddenly, the bell on the door frame jingles and apprehension drops into the pit of my stomach. I look up just as Sara scans the room. Our eyes lock and she makes her way over to the empty seat in front of me, in silence. A tight, apprehensive smile is stretched across her face.

"Hi," she says.

She sits down, hanging her bag across the back of the chair. Her hands quiver as she fiddles with the purse strap. I find comfort in knowing I'm not the only one with frazzled nerves.

Her deep brown eyes are a complicated sea of emotions. Sadness mixes with her anger, darkened by betrayal, until they appear like onyxes set in her face. I have to look away.

"Is this for me?" There's a steaming cup of coffee resting on the table.

"Yes."

"Latte?"

"Yup," I answer. It's a small peace offering. Something to take the edge off. *I should have suggested we meet at a bar.*

"Thanks."

I lean back in my chair, hands still folded around my own mug, giving me something to do other than tap them furiously on the table. I sit patiently, waiting on Sara to begin. Although I know there is much to say, I feel as if she holds the power, the deciding vote on whether this relationship lives or dies.

I've tried to convince myself that what I've done isn't the worst kind of betrayal, but I can't shut up the voice in my head that relentlessly reminds me I should never have gone for my best friend's ex. I didn't do it intentionally, but I'm not entirely sure that I'm absolved from the guilt because of it. I spend nights losing sleep. I've asked myself numerous times what I would have said if Sara had told me that another one of our friends had done the same. Would I be furious for her? Would I agree that she'd been horribly wronged? I think I would.

For that reason, I can't help but feel as if I'm the one asking for forgiveness. If Sara chooses not to give it, I would understand. Matter of fact, there's a part of me that expects it.

She's eyeing me from across the table and I try not to squirm. Despite the confusion of thoughts flying through my head, I still want to hold up the image that I'm confident in my position. She's my best friend. Going for her ex wasn't the right choice, but now that I've made it, I refuse to apologize for how I feel. I love Ben; she needs to see that.

"I'm not exactly sure how we're supposed to start this thing," Sara says, sweeping her hand across the table to indicate she's talking about our current situation. "I mean, I don't even know where to really begin. What you've done has put us in a very awkward position. Don't you agree?"

She's passed the ball in our tennis match. Perched on the edge of her seat, she's ready to retaliate no matter my defense. I'm annoyed that she's already placed the blame on me and we've only just begun. But I can't react. It would be counterproductive.

"I agree it's become awkward for sure. I'm hoping we could talk about it, maybe see if we can figure this out? Find a solution to our current situation," I say.

I'm trying to keep my voice even, to remain neutral and rational. Losing my cool and turning this into a screaming match won't solve anything.

"What kind of solution can we come to? You ended up with my ex, Leyla. I'm not sure how to handle that."

The anger is blazing in her gaze now, and I can't help but wonder if there are any unresolved feelings I failed to notice.

"Do you still have feelings for him?" I blurt out.

Her eyes widen in shock at my question. Her mouth twists into a grimace. It opens, but then shuts without a word as she continues to stare. Maybe there's a hint of insecurity she can recognize behind my accusation. Maybe she knows that her answer could be detrimental to my current status. Either way, her features soften and she inhales slowly before she speaks.

"No, Leyla, I don't have feelings for Ben."

I exhale, not realizing I was holding my breath.

"Then what is it? I know I let things get too far with Ben before talking to you about it. I never intended for this to happen. I fucked up. I apologize for that. But I can't take that back. And honestly, I wouldn't change anything other than coming to you sooner. The time I've spent with him has been like nothing I've ever experienced before.

It's been amazing. I really love him, Sara. And I can't apologize for that. I won't."

I can see the internal struggle, the silent battle she's in, written within the lines of her forehead. Neither of us want this friendship to end; we wouldn't be here if we did. Both of us are too intricately woven in the fibers of each other's lives.

How we move forward from this moment will define who we become. Whether we grow old together like we used to talk about when we were children, raising families side by side, rests in this conversation. I wait for her move.

"That's not fair," she says.

"What do you mean?"

"You don't get to do that. You don't get to tell me you're in love with him and take away my right to be angry."

"You have the right to be angry," I say.

"Yeah, but what kind of asshole would I be to tell you that you shouldn't be with a guy you love?"

"Is that what you want? For me to leave Ben?"

"No. Yes. I don't know," she answers. "This is all so twisted and complicated."

"I know."

She looks at me, her big brown eyes like warm pools of chocolate. The dark and light tones of her irises match the various shades of her hair. She's tight-lipped when she speaks, trying not to cry.

"It's more complicated than you think, Leyla. You just don't understand."

"Then explain it to me."

I want to reach out and grab her hand, comfort her in a moment that feels monumentally difficult for her. I forget for a second that she isn't sure whether she's wishing my relationship will implode. I've always been protective of Sara. It's in my nature to see past myself to take care of her. The one time I don't do that, I get us wrapped up in a colossal mess.

"Even if I was fine with the idea of you and Ben, it still wouldn't work," she says. "Maziar is furious with you for bringing him back into our lives."

At the mention of Maziar's name, anger flashes before my eyes. How dare he dictate my life? Who does he think he is? I'm about to say something to the effect of he can go to hell when Sara raises her hand to stop me.

"Don't get pissy, Leyla. I get it. He shouldn't have a say. But he's my fiancé, so he does by association. Think about it. How are we supposed to hang out together when you're with my ex? And not just some random guy I dated. I was with him for a long time and we were about to move in together!"

The reminder of Ben and Sara's past makes my stomach lurch. I hate thinking of the two of them together. It's understandable that Maziar does too.

"Honestly, I didn't think about how he would react. I was more worried about you. But I can totally understand where he's coming from. I don't like to think about you and Ben together much, either," I confess.

Sara leans back in her seat, raising her coffee mug to her lips. Her eyelids squint, scrunching up her face as she loses herself in thought.

"What a mess we've made," she says. For the first time in the past few weeks she refers to our predicament as a result of the two of us rather than just me.

"Yup." I smile halfheartedly. "What do we do now?"

"I'm not sure what there is we can do."

Her fingers are tapping furiously on the edge of her mug, her eyes glossed over in concentration. A few moments of unbearable silence pass before she exhales slowly. Her shoulders fall forward and she drops her head, a definite sign of defeat. Panic settles in my gut, and a boulder lodges in my intestines, nailing me to the seat.

I shake my head, responding to a conversation in my own mind. Sara crinkles her nose and raises a brow, for clarification.

"Nope, I won't accept that," I say.

"Accept what?"

"That there isn't any hope. So stop that giving up business I can see you are doing right now. There's a way to fix this where we can both be happy and still be friends. We just need to figure out how."

"I don't know." There's hesitation in her voice.

Maybe she can't see the light at the end of the tunnel, but I can.

I lean forward in my seat, reach out, and grab her hand, intertwining my fingers with hers. I look her in the eyes when I speak, making sure she can't misinterpret how I feel.

"I don't want to lose us, Sara. We've been friends for too long to just walk away. I love you."

"I love you, too," she says. "But I don't know how to fix this." She can't hold back her emotions any longer. Tears pool in her eyes, and despite her best efforts to blink them away, they fall toward the table. "Great, now I'm crying," she says with a sad giggle.

"The question really is, Sara, are you the one who can't get over it, or do you think Maziar can't?" I address the elephant in the room because there's no way out until I do.

"I can get over it, I think." She doesn't seem sure of her answer, but it's not a flat-out no. It's a start. "But I'm not sure Maziar ever will. I don't think he can be in the same room with Ben."

Anger momentarily surges through me again. I refuse to let Maziar be the deciding vote in our predicament. It's a group effort here, all of us equally involved and thoroughly uncomfortable. But if three out of four of us can see past ourselves, then he will have to as well.

"Well, let's find out," I say.

"Find out what?" The confused expression on her face has been a constant companion the entire afternoon.

"How long your future husband can stand to be in the same room with my boyfriend."

Her eyes widen and she starts to gnaw on her lower lip. I can feel her apprehension from across the table. I squeeze her hand.

"It's going to be okay," I encourage. "We have to at least try, right? The alternative is we just walk away. Can you do that?"

"No, Leyla. You know I can't. Give me a second. I'm not as brave as you." She exhales a few times, rolling her neck as if she can rid her body of the tension visible in her stiff posture. "Okay," she finally agrees.

"Good. Then let's set this date up."

* * *

I intermittently bounce back and forth on my toes then pace around my living room, waiting for Ben to pick me up. Maman is trying to appear busy in the kitchen. She shoots me sidelong glances every few minutes as she shakes her head before going back to the dishes. Raha is sitting on the recliner reading a book.

"Would you sit down?" she demands. "You're driving me crazy."

"I can't help it. I'm so nervous."

"Dear God, you need a shot of something," she mumbles, scooting off the couch. She walks over to the hutch in the dining room and opens the bottom cabinet. She returns with a bottle of vodka and two shot glasses. "Here," she says, pushing one into my hand.

She opens the bottle and the medicinal scent hits the back of my throat as I breathe in the fumes.

"I don't want a shot," I protest, but she fills my glass to the rim, anyway.

"It's not about what you want. It's about what you need." She winks, then taps her overflowing shot against mine. "Bottoms up."

Baba walks in just as we throw them back.

"*Cheshmam roshan*," Baba says sarcastically. *The light of my eyes.* He shakes his head in disappointment as he makes his way over to the couch.

"What?" Raha asks. "She's nervous. I'm just trying to help her calm down."

"You don't need to make her drink for that. You guys drink too much," Baba replies.

I don't say anything. My palms are sweating and I rub them against the side of my black skinny jeans. I hope the dark tone of the fabric doesn't create any visible damp marks. I pull on my gray top, feeling as if the collar has suddenly tightened around my neck. I just want to get this whole night over with.

I don't know whether I'm more nervous about our dinner date with Sara and Maziar, or the potential of Ben meeting my family at the door. I begged him to text me when he got here, but my gut tells me he won't listen. Right on cue, the doorbell rings, causing me to choke on the next breath. I look at my sister, wide-eyed and terrified, and she jumps to her feet to open it before Baba has a chance to make it to the door.

I'm frozen in the center of the living room, the walls closing in on me. I notice Maman out of the corner of my eye as she exits the kitchen. She takes a few steps closer, a bewildered look on her face as she dries her hand on a dishtowel. I don't think she expected Ben to have the courage to face them.

He's standing in the doorway, towering over my sister's petite figure. His navy blue button up causes his eyes to pop. I sigh, relieved that his tattoo is covered up by his sleeve. I know that wasn't by accident. Despite how much I love it, I'm not entirely sure how my parents would react. If they only knew that it was a tribute to his grandfather after his passing.

"*Salom*, Ali *aghah*," Ben says, with his thick American accent. *Hello, sir.*

My family stands motionless, shocked at his gallant attempt at speaking Farsi. I try to hide my cringe as he looks over at me, his dimples pressed into the sides of his cheeks, flashing me his crooked smile. He's so proud of himself for trying, but a memory crosses my mind. There was a time he tried to learn Farsi for Sara. Now it's just one more reminder for me of their past.

"Hi, Ben!" Raha says. Her voice is high-pitched and singsong, more enthusiastic than a greeting should be. She's trying to compensate for the discomfort we're all feeling.

Baba steps forward, returning to his well-mannered ways.

"*Salom*, Ben." *Hello.* He reaches out and shakes Ben's hand, acknowledging Ben's effort to connect with my family through language.

Ben's eyes light up with joy as if he's actually winning them over. He has no clue; this is one step on the mountain he has to climb to get there. He turns toward Maman, moving in her direction, despite the condescending expression on her face. He acts as if he doesn't notice.

"Hello, Mrs. Amini."

Maman eyes him cautiously, her thick, dark eyebrows wrinkled in scrutiny. But he doesn't let her demeanor deter him, taking three big strides until he's peering down at her small body through long, thick lashes. She doesn't smile, but I notice a subtle twitch pull at the corner of her lip in amusement. He hasn't won her over yet, but for the first time, I feel the glimmer of hope prodding at the edges of our reality. Maybe all isn't lost.

"Hello, Ben," Maman offers. "It's nice to finally meet you." She doesn't mean it, but her proper Iranian ways don't allow for unnecessary rude behavior.

Before she has a chance to protest, he leans down and gently wraps his arms around her. "I'm very happy to finally have the pleasure of meeting you."

Maman's eyes widen and her cheeks become rosy. Another point in Ben's favor.

Before there's time to ruin the moment, I quickly say, "Ben, we have to go."

"Okay," he replies, reluctantly allowing Maman out of his embrace.

She pulls on the hem of her shirt, straightening out the creases caused by Ben's sudden show of affection. She looks at Baba, flushed and flustered. He smiles at her, and she gives us the first grin of the evening.

I exhale.

* * *

We pull into the parking lot of the restaurant and my heart crashes into my ribcage. I don't know what is awaiting me inside that building, but I know I'm dreading having to face it. I'm trying to calm myself down when I notice the car is off and Ben is staring at the entrance, deep in thought.

It dawns on me that this entire time I've been so focused on how difficult this situation with Sara has been for me that I never thought to ask how Ben felt. He's been a true partner in all of it, pushing his own feelings aside as he finds a way to see past himself in an attempt to help me save my oldest relationship. He's been so convincing that he's okay with it all that I've believed him. Now I'm not so sure.

"Hey," I say, reaching out and gently touching his arm. "Are you okay?"

"Yeah," he answers. He turns toward me and smiles. "I'm good." Despite his words, there's worry etched in his features.

"I'm sorry for not realizing this is hard for you." Sara was a pretty big bitch in the way she left Ben hanging. It makes sense that he'd be apprehensive to have her back in his life in any capacity.

"It's fine, really," he assures me.

"Ben," I say, squeezing his arm.

"Okay. I'm not thrilled about trying to find common ground with Sara and Maziar. But, I know she's your best friend and that's more important than my bruised ego. She did me wrong and made me feel stupid, that's all." He leans in and kisses me softly. "Now let's go get this over with, shall we?"

Despite the chaotic flutter of nerves wreaking havoc my stomach, I follow his lead. We're already here. It's too late to turn back.

"The rest of your party has been seated," the hostess says, when we give Sara's name. She leads us toward the back of the restaurant.

We follow her through the double doors, onto a secluded patio area. Most of the tables are empty, except for one in the far corner. A couple sits facing each other, their fingers intertwined on the blue table cloth, while the server places a plate of lava cake in between them. A deep wanting nestles inside me, wishing I was walking into an evening like theirs rather than the war I know I'm getting myself into.

The sky is changing colors, the sunset pulling an orange-and-red tail behind it as it descends beneath the mountain's edge. The stars begin to twinkle one by one, reminding me of the fireflies from my trip to the east coast when I was little. It's Tuesday, so the city streets are relatively quiet, the melodic sound of crickets chirping in unison, filling the night air.

Sara and Maziar are sitting in the two adjacent seats facing the patio entrance. She's in a blush pink blouse, highlighting her already dark hair, her waves fanning out across her chest. Their deep chocolate hue clashes against the pale background. Her equally dark eyes are wide and enamored as she gushes over her fiancé.

Maziar is laughing at something she's said while leaning down to kiss her knuckles, which are protectively clutched in his hand. Our movement catches his attention and we're greeted by his icy glare. It causes the uneasiness settled in my stomach to amplify. The green in his eyes bounces off the color of his shirt, a fiery fierceness blazing within them. Ben squeezes my hand tighter, silently pledging his loyalty to me. I try to pull from his strength, plugging up the voids in my armor. *It's going to be a long night.*

"Hi," Sara says, when we make it to the table. She's keeping her gaze trained on me, glancing in Ben's direction for only a moment to give him a quick smile before returning her focus back to me.

"Hi." We reply in unison, our voices bouncing off the emptiness of the patio. It's loud and cringeworthy.

Ben pulls my seat out before taking his own. He rests his arm protectively on my chair, his hand fanned out across the exposed skin on my back. His fingertips press lightly into the base of my neck and goosebumps rise along my flesh. Even at the slightest touch, my body responds. I try desperately to grab hold of the feeling in an attempt to find light in this unbearable tension pinning me down.

"How are you guys?" I say. I'm looking between Sara and Maziar, acting as

as if this is a normal evening among friends. Far from it.

The twisted roots of the past have securely embedded themselves between us, drawing lines in the sand. Two best friends, a fiancé, and an ex. I know there's joke in there somewhere, but I'm too busy fidgeting under Maziar's unwieldy gaze and distracted by Sara's obvious discomfort to think of one.

"We're fine," Maziar responds, in a clipped tone.

"Sara, how's work going?" Ben asks, jumping to my rescue. Not before glaring at Maziar. "How's Setie?" Their mentor from the internship is a safe neutral topic.

Ben's directly speaking to her now, and she has no choice but to acknowledge him. I can see hesitation in the creases around her eyes as she glances at Maziar, an odd expression passing between them, almost like she's asking for permission. He responds with a disapproving glare, his lips turned down in a frown.

"She's good," Sara says. She falters, at first, stumbling over her words.

Ben pays no attention to her demeanor as he continues.

"How's the baby? I've been meaning to go visit her, but with the move and the new pharmacy, it's just been crazy."

"She's good. Super cute. She's trying to crawl already. And she started saying da-da."

Sara's voice loosens as she dreamily describes Setie's child, forgetting this *isn't* just a regular evening. It's clear Maziar disapproves because he squeezes her hand. She drops her gaze to the table, reprimanded.

My protective nature rushes to the forefront, witnessing this strange new development between Sara and her fiancé. I start to forget my discomfort, becoming offended at his old traditional behavior. Disgust slowly burns its way into the crevices where only nervous energy lived a few moments ago.

When did Maziar become an old Iranian man?

I sit up straight, squaring my shoulders, leaning slightly forward in my chair. My senses are heightened, perched on the edge of my seat, ready to pounce on the predator. My sudden transformation has caught his attention and he appears flustered. He quickly shakes it off, rising to meet my position, just as I'd expected.

His Middle-Eastern male ego doesn't allow for him to shy away from a challenge, especially one proposed by a woman. My lip creeps up in a smile, welcoming the threat. I'm game. He laughs, a low, menacing chuckle that only I can hear.

Ben pushes forward, reeling Sara back in.

"Do you see Seti at work often?" he asks.

"Yeah. We usually work back-to-back shifts, so she hangs out for a while and chats with me while I set up."

"That's awesome. I miss her. I'm going to have to call and see if we can do lunch soon. Maybe go see that little girl of hers finally."

The tension in Sara's shoulders begins to dissipate again, and the lines furrowing on her forehead smooth out across her skin. Her and Ben fall into a familiar ease as they continue reminiscing about their old friend. Maziar attempts to send her another silent warning, but she expertly pulls her hand away, never skipping a beat in the conversation. Ben doesn't even notice, too engaged in their discussion. But I do. So does Maziar.

Our battle of wills is momentarily forgotten, both drawn to the pair sitting beside us, curiously watching their interaction.

"Why don't we get down to the reason we're all here," Maziar says, interrupting them. He's not even bothering to keep his voice calm, the aggression embedded in his words.

"I think that's a great idea," I reply. I'm suddenly uneasy with the level of comfort I'm witnessing between my boyfriend and his ex.

There's venom in Maziar's gaze as he turns back toward me, as if I've offended him by speaking. His muscles are tense, making his figure appear v-shaped and cobra like. I feel like prey waiting to be consumed. I'm gearing up for a fight when Ben places his hand on my shoulder. He gently pulls me back into my seat, having scooted to the edge.

Sara looks between Maziar and I, fear slowly paling her face. It's abundantly clear that half of the table is not as happy as the other.

My adrenaline is pumping, my heart ramming furiously into my ribcage. Maziar may have a hold on Sara, but he has no influence on me. And I want to make sure he knows that.

"Why don't we all take a minute to breathe? Let's bring it down a notch, shall we?" Ben, the ever level-headed one, says.

How does he keep his cool in an obviously outrageous situation? I try to obey, taking a few deep breaths. Anger is counterproductive. Maziar, though, outright ignores Ben, transforming fury into words.

"I don't need a minute," he says, through gritted teeth. "This dinner is pointless. I'm not exactly sure what we thought would be resolved tonight. I think what the two of you are doing is disgusting. I don't want to be a part of it." Then he throws in, "I can't even look at you, Leyla," for good measure. I have an uncontrollable desire to punch him in the face.

It takes every ounce of self-control not to hurl myself across the table. It's only a few feet wide and I'm pretty confident I could scratch his eyes out before anyone could pull me off of him. Ben's hand shoots out in front of me, reading my mind before I have a chance to make a move. I lean into his restraint, my body coiled and ready to attack.

"Screw you, Maziar." Poison drapes my words. "You can't look at *me*, because I found happiness? Are you kidding me?"

"No, Leyla. I can't look at you because you decided to be with *him*." He's leaning forward in his chair too, his disgust heavy and recognizable. "How can you even call yourself her best friend when you went after her ex? They've been together. Where's your self-respect?" I cringe at his reference to their sexual history. "I can't help but wonder if you planned this all along. Sara told me what you said at her karaoke birthday a few years ago."

"Maziar!" Sara's hand flies to her mouth, eyes wide with shock.

What? I can't recall what it is he's referring to as I dig for the memories of that night. It was years ago when Sara was in dental school so the moments are hazing and blurred at the edged, but I sift through them one by one trying to find an explanation. Then, as if a can of red paint has been thrown across my brain, it emerges.

I slowly turn my head toward Sara, who's still watching me, petrified. Understanding crosses the space between us, weaving its way through a silent exchange, two hands wrapped around our throats, suffocating our friendship.

"I was joking, Sara. You know that."

"What did you say?" Ben's voice is barely audible behind the pounding in my ears.

"It was before you and Sara were official," I say, my eyes locked on my now-mortified best friend. She can't meet my gaze. "I told her I'd go after you if she didn't." I turn toward Ben. "I didn't mean it. I was just messing around. I was trying to encourage her to make a move." The idea that anyone would think my relationship with Ben was somehow premeditated enrages me.

"I know." He pulls me in closer to him. "What is your problem, man?"

A predatory grin stretches across Maziar's face. It's obvious he's waited all night to push Ben's buttons. Now that he has my boyfriend amped up, he's going to go in for the kill.

"You're my problem. What makes you think you can just come back into our lives again? Sara got rid of you a long time ago. You should have just stayed gone!"

"Are you fucking kidding me? What a hypocrite! The one that should have stayed gone was you. But you couldn't leave it alone, constantly rearing your ugly head at every turn. Don't tell me about weaseling my way back into anyone's life."

Their voices are getting louder, stacking on each other like building blocks. The couple at the end of the patio has already left and I'm thankful for the emptiness of the restaurant. This scene would be worse if we were surrounded by spectators. Comments fly between the men, each jab thrown at each other like darts on a board, hitting the bullseye dead on.

"She loves me. She never loved you!" Maziar yells.

"How could she with you hanging around? She couldn't move on. You wouldn't let her!"

Ben's face is rapidly approaching the color of my hair. His nostrils are flaring with anger; his eyes harden with vengeance. Maziar looks like a mirror image of him. Both men seem to elevate with each stab they make.

Suddenly, a realization crashes into me; a freight train knocking the air out of my lungs. I'm invisible. Each man is out for blood, and my best friend sits on the edge of her seat, hand to her mouth, eyes wide with regret, trying not to cry. This isn't about me, yet it's my boyfriend fighting her fiancé about the past. A past that has nothing to do with me and everything to do with Sara.

A pain inserts itself in my chest like the point of a knife, fanning out in layers of heat as the blood trickles down my side with the shattering of my heart. Disappointment, deep rooted in my throat, manifests itself as a large knot blocking my air way. I clutch my throat, trying to physically subdue the scream I can feel pushing its way to the surface. I stand up, my chair crashing to the floor. *I have to get the hell out of here.*

All eyes turn toward me, frozen, as if they've just realized I was here. My gaze bounces between the three of them, each beat of my heart tearing through me.

"Leyla," Sara whispers.

No explanation is needed for her to know what's going through my head. She understands what I'm thinking without me having to say a word. Ben's still in love with her. Why else would he be fighting over her?

She slowly starts to stand.

"No!" One hand is clutching my chest, trying to keep the surge of pain from killing me on the restaurant floor. The other is stretched out in front of me stopping my best friend in her tracks.

Ben reaches out and grabs my outstretched fingers. I push him away. I don't say a word, not trusting that I could speak without breaking down in tears. He doesn't need me to explain either. It doesn't take a genius to see how I'm interpreting the scene unfolding before me.

"Leyla," he says.

In a move that feels desperate, I snatch my bag and head for door before he has a chance to stop me. I run, straight through the restaurant entrance, making my way down the sidewalk as fast as my wobbly legs will take me. I cut into a side street and keep running, finding cover beneath a dark tree. I nestle myself close to its trunk, swallowed by its shadow. My head drops into my hands, finally allowing myself the luxury of breaking down.

I sob uncontrollably, each intake of breath causing another shard of my heart to pierce the grass around me. I can hear Ben yelling my name. Sara's voice is lower but comes in a few seconds later. Even Maziar is looking for me, but I stay hidden, safe in the alcove of branches and leaves, wishing they'd disappear along with their ridiculous story. I don't want to be found.

How could I have been so stupid? How could I have believed he was over her? How did this night end up a battle of testosterone over Sara?

What am I doing?

Questions race through my mind, in time with the constant buzzing of my phone as Ben and Sara call me nonstop. I finally grab it, send my sister a text pinning my location so she can pick me up, then shut it off.

I wrap my arms around my chest, nestling my chin on the mantle they create, staring at the ground. There are no tears left to shed. Pain replaces the space left behind by my broken heart.

I can no longer hear my name being called from the street below. The search has apparently ceased. I can see Ben standing on the corner, intently tapping away on his phone. Sara and Maziar are out of view, but I imagine they are standing just farther down on the sidewalk, waiting for my next move.

I don't know how long I sit there, numb and cold, on someone else's lawn, but the bright headlights of Raha's vehicle snap me to attention. I stand and drag my limbs, now heavy with lead, to her car, dropping into the leather seat. She takes one look at me and reaches out, gently running her hand down the side of my face.

"It's going to be okay, Leyla."

I don't believe her.

She makes a U-turn and heads back from where she came. Just as she turns right at the corner, I catch a glimpse of Ben standing beneath the streetlamp, his blues eyes alight with worry. Sara and Maziar are a few feet in front of him. He sees me and his eyebrows knit together. He raises his hand trying to get us to stop but I turn my head and urge Raha to keep going.

"Nothing's going to be all right," I mumble, to no one in particular.

CHAPTER ELEVEN

I t's been three days. I've avoided Ben's consistent calls and text
messages, hiding beneath the darkness of my comforter. The
world feels too bright and blissful to live in at the moment.

My door opens, and I can sense Raha's presence looming in the
doorway. I don't need to look at her to know concern is oozing off of
her in waves. Her nervous energy crosses the room and settles on my
sheets. I roll over, turning my back toward her, snuggling deeper into
the pillows.

"I'm fine."

"Why don't you come out and eat something? Or we could go for a
run? May help to clear your mind." The hopeful tone in her voice is
obvious, but sadly misplaced.

"I don't feel like it. I just want to sleep."

"Leyla," she says, but I cut her off.

"Can you just close the door on your way out?" I command. My
clipped tone is sharp and unyielding. It leaves no room for debate. The
door shuts quietly a few seconds later.

I let the darkness consume me again, dragging me down into a
fitful sleep.

* * *

I'm awakened with a frantic knocking, followed by the world shaking around me. At first, I think it may be an earthquake. I try desperately to peel my eyes open, fighting against the heavy weights woven into my eyelids.

"Leyla, Leyla, get up!"

Raha's voice cuts through the fog of my dreams, pulling me back into reality.

"What is it?" I mumble, half-incoherently, as I yawn. "What's your problem?" I turn to face her, still wrapped tightly around my pillow, glaring at her interruption.

"Ben's here!" Her voice is shrill to my ears. There's an excited undertone that doesn't quite make sense as I'm trying to piece together the scene.

"What?" I must not have heard her correctly.

"Ben. He's here," she repeats. She pauses between each syllable as if she's teaching a kindergartner how to read.

A rush of nausea rolls through me and I abruptly sit up in bed. The comforter falls to my waist as the world spins on its axis. I've been lying down for too long. I try to get my bearings, reaching out and grabbing my sister's arm.

"What?" It feels like someone has dropped a bucket of cold water on my head, snapping me back to the land of the living.

"He's *here*," she says.

"How?"

"I don't know. He drove?" She giggles.

"Don't be a smartass, Raha," I say, rolling my eyes.

"Sorry. What do you want me to say? You've been ignoring him, so he showed up. You need to talk to him. You can't avoid him forever."

"Yes, I can."

I step off the bed, pushing past my sister and into the bathroom. I turn on the sink, let the cold water run, watching it swirl down the drain in a calming dance with the porcelain. I catch a glimpse of my face in the mirror and don't even recognize myself. There are dark circles invading the skin beneath my eyes. My cheeks are pulled in, giving me a gaunt, malnourished appearance. My hair is wild and frizzy, uneasiness settled in each strand, much like I feel beneath my numb exterior. I splash water onto my face, allowing its coolness to wash away my worries. It fails, but I welcome the feel of it anyway.

I pull my hair into a less-than-perfect bun on the top of my head. Wispy strands fall every which way in a non-flattering combination, but I don't care. I throw on a white T-shirt over my tank top and pull on a pair of UCLA sweats.

"Is that how you're going out there?" Raha asks, mortified.

"Yup."

"What's your deal?" she demands. Her confusion at my reaction morphs into irritation.

"You don't know anything, Raha. Just leave it alone. Let me get this over with."

I'm thankful that my parents are gone for the evening. I don't feel like witnessing Maman's I-told-you-so eyes and Baba's pity. Raha is annoying me enough as it is. I'm trying to ignore my own feelings; it's taking all my energy. I can't worry about theirs.

Raha reaches out and grabs my wrist as I walk past her toward the door. I exhale, my patience running thin.

"What's wrong?" Her tone has changed, her voice quieted.

Her concern is laced in the deep brown eyes staring at me. She reminds me of Sara for a moment and another swell of nausea hits me like a brick wall. I sway on my feet.

"Ben's not over Sara," I whisper.

"Did he tell you that?"

"No, he didn't need to."

"So how do you know?" she asks.

"Because he spent the entire night fighting Maziar over how he ruined their relationship. Why else would he care if he didn't still have feelings for her?"

I've rendered Raha speechless. I'm not sure if it's because she agrees with me or thinks I'm crazy, but either way, she doesn't offer any words of wisdom, no sisterly advice to make this horrendous situation, better. Instead, she just looks at me, pity nestled in her expression. A web of lines fan out from the edges of her scrunched eyelids and her eyebrows are knit tightly together. I try to muster up the best smile I can, suddenly feeling like I need to comfort her instead of the other way around.

"I'm fine." I pull my wrist away from her. "Like I said, let me go get this over with." With that, I head into the living room, leaving my sister behind.

Ben is sitting on the couch when I enter. He stands up and takes a step forward, then hesitates. I glance at him and keep walking to the front door. The walls of the room are claustrophobic and I need some air. I step out onto the porch, making my way over the steps and sit down. He follows, easing down beside me. He reaches out and grabs my palm, intertwining his fingers with mine. The connection is acid on my skin forcing bile up my throat. I pull away, protectively placing my hands in my lap. I don't want him to touch me.

"Leyla, let me explain," he begs.

"Go ahead."

I face him so he's forced to see the pain I feel when he's unable to convince me he's over Sara. I don't know what he can say to erase what I saw: Ben defending his relationship with her. Even now, the memory wraps its fingers around my throat, adding pressure to the lump lodged there.

"I'm sorry. The conversation just got away from me. I don't even know what happened. Maziar was being such a dick and I just lost my cool."

He thinks I'm angry over the fight itself, not its content. Anger rushes through my veins, turning to gasoline ready to ignite. I've spent seventy-two hours mourning the loss of our great love, and here he is thinking I'm pissed over some stupid show of immature testosterone.

"I'm not upset that you fought with Maziar." My voice comes out hoarse as it pushes against the restraints of my sanity.

"Then what is it?" he asks. A shadow of concern crosses his face.

He reaches out and grabs my hand again. I let him take it, knowing it may be the last time I feel the warmth of his fingers on mine. Touching Ben has become second nature. Two magnets pulling toward one another. But then I remember why we're in our current predicament and I pull away. I stand, making my way off the steps to the brick walkway, trying to put distance between us. I begin to pace, needing to expel the nervous energy that's consuming me.

He watches cautiously. Two sapphires, blue like the ocean. I can see waves crashing against their shore, despite his best efforts to hide them. I wonder what secrets lie deep beneath their surface. He tries to smile at me, his dimples an anchor against the night sky. I drop my gaze to the bricks lining the steps as I speak, trying not to lose my conviction. I could so easily fall back into his arms if I'm not careful.

"It's not the fight. It's who you were fighting about. You aren't over Sara, Ben." My voice comes out too quiet. I barely recognize myself. How did I become this timid?

"No, Leyla," he replies. "That's not true."

I slowing look up at him, searching his face for answers. He seems sincere, but no matter how hard I try, I can't convince myself there isn't more. Even if he doesn't realize it himself.

"Really? It's not true? Then tell me why you'd spend the entire night fighting over your relationship with Sara. That doesn't sound like 'over her' to me, Ben."

"No, it wasn't like that. He's just a hypocrite. That was my whole point." He exhales. "Leyla, please."

"Please what, Ben? I don't know what it is you want from me right now."

"Can't we get past this? Nothing has happened. It's still you and me." When I don't respond, he adds, "I love you."

Pain punches me in the gut and threatens to knock me to my knees. Those three little words are the reason my world has fallen apart, brick by brick. Until a few days ago, the struggle and loss seemed worth it. Now, I'm not so sure.

Desperation paints his face, but it doesn't make me sympathetic. Instead, it propels my anger forward, a tornado of fury still pacing the concrete walkway before him. This is all his fault. Or it's mine, for being dumb enough to believe him when he said he was over her. His lies have broken my heart, leaving a mess where my hopes once lived. Because of him, my relationship with my best friend has been altered in irreparable ways. How could I be so stupid?

"No, Ben. We can't get past this." I make an arc with my arm as if our problems lay scattered across Maman's pristine lawn. "There's nothing to get past. You still have feelings for Sara. Just admit it." The defiance is evident in my tone. The challenge obvious. I'm daring him to lie again, pinning him down with my gaze. He doesn't falter, despite the rage emanating off of me.

"No, I don't," he says.

"I don't believe you."

He's still, watching me, as he peels back the layers of my façade. I'm trying my best to stand with certainty, but judging from the softening of his expression, I don't think I'm convincing either of us. He stands up. My chest expands in and out, each breath deepening as he gets closer. I'm no longer pacing, glued to the bricks beneath my feet. I can't even blink.

When he reaches up and gently runs his hand against my cheek, I fall apart. The familiar tenderness ruins me. I know what's coming, and despite it being necessary, the panic rises to my throat, choking me. I almost shut my eyes, wishing I'd disappear so I didn't have to witness the final blow. My already-shattered heart rattles around in my ribcage, in a last attempt at survival. But it's pointless; I'm already doomed.

"There's no way I can prove it to you." His voice is smooth silk, running its thread count gently across my skin, reminding me of everything I stand to lose. "You'd just have to trust me, but it's obvious that you don't. I've tried my best to prove to you that I don't want anyone else but you. Including Sara."

As her name leaves his lips, a knife is pushed deeper into my chest. I've never wished she'd disappear more than in this moment.

"I don't know if you'll ever be secure enough in our relationship where she won't always be looming everywhere. I love you. More than you know. But I can't be with you if I need to prove it to you all the time."

Just like that, the walls I'd constructed these past few days to protect myself in this very situation come crumbling down around me. They don't stop the pain that's squeezing my heart so tightly I feel like it may stop altogether, or the panic that's clawing at my insides. They don't protect me from the hopes I've kept at bay, consuming me like cannibals. How could they? Ben has reached into my chest and pulled out my most vital organ. He's taken from me the happiness I so desperately wanted to hold onto. For that, I hate him.

"Well, I'm glad we both agree. We're better off just cutting our losses before this gets any messier than it already is."

My words slap him across the face and he flinches. I don't say anything more, just stand up and walk toward the front door, leaving Ben with nothing but shadows to keep him company. I reach out and grab the door handle, but then pause.

"Bye, Ben." It comes out in a whisper, the agony I feel strangling me.

He doesn't make a move to stop me from leaving. I hadn't realized I'd hoped he would until the disappointment crashes into me, adding another layer to the ever-growing pile of pain I'm dragging along behind me.

"Bye, Leyla," he says.

The tapping of his feet on the pavement signal he's walking to the car. I allow myself one more glance over my shoulder, taking in the contours of his perfect silhouette for the last time. I don't linger long. I can't watch him drive away from me.

Instead, I turn the doorknob and let myself inside, closing the thick panel of oak behind me, shutting out the cold.

Shutting out Ben.

CHAPTER TWELVE

The light. It's so bright. Where is it coming from?

I could swear I closed my curtains, but the sun is suddenly blinding me through the back of my eyelids. I'm too tired to open them and find the source of the rude interruption. My body feels like it's been laced with steel, an ache so deep it's woven into the fibers of my bones. I can hardly move. I let myself melt further into the mattress, grumbling as I hide my head deeper beneath the comforter.

I've been in this very position now for four days. I only get up long enough to use the bathroom and then crawl right back into my cave of broken dreams. I haven't showered or changed. I can barely even remember the last meal I ate. But I don't care. All I want to do is get lost in the darkness. I'm surrounded by nothingness here. The only place my mind can be still. If I leave the protection of the silence, I'll have to remember.

I don't want to remember. I'm not ready. I don't think my body could take it if I had to recall how Ben walked away from me. My mind would burst with all the details.

The way the muscles of his back stretch tight beneath his shirt. The phoenix tattoo teasing me from the edge of his sleeve, almost as if it's waving goodbye. I can't be haunted by his crystal eyes, with their kaleidoscope of blues, or the dimples in his cheeks, and the crooked imperfection of his smile. I don't want to think about him at all.

I want to forget. So I've been holed up in my room indefinitely, hiding from the world, but mostly from my broken heart. If I let it, all the tiny pieces will explode like pellets of a shotgun, tearing through me until I've been consumed by the pain. I can't do it.

I feel the bed shift and know someone's in my room. I still refuse to open my eyes, hoping Raha or Maman will get the hint. I send a silent prayer that I won't have to get into a screaming match with my mom as she tries to drag me out of bed, or snap at my sister while she tries to entice me with bribes I couldn't care less about. I don't move, wishing the intruder would leave me the hell alone.

"Leyla," Sara says.

My mind is fuzzy with drowsiness. *Sara?* That doesn't make any sense, her voice oddly out of place in the scenario I have playing in my head.

"Leyla, are you awake?" she asks again, this time, gently tapping me through the comforter.

My head aches. I just want to go back to sleep.

"Come on, Leyla. Talk to me."

She rubs my back, and after a few moments, I know I'm not dreaming. I'm forced to open my eyes, obvious she isn't going anywhere. I don't turn toward her right away, just stare at the cashmere paint on my walls.

"Tell me what happened," she says.

Her voice is low and soothing, causing something to tear open inside me. The emotions come forward in one stretched-out musical note played in the wrong key, loud and rumbling against the walls. I clutch my chest, shielding myself from the pounding in my ribcage. Too many feelings. I can't contain them all at once. Hot tears run down my cheeks, startling me.

"Ben and I broke up," I say, in between sobs.

"Oh, honey, I'm so sorry," she offers, rubbing my back again.

I lean into her hand, desperate for a connection I hadn't realized I'd missed so much. I can't think about Maziar and what a royal dick he was the other night, or that Sara was uncompromising when I told her about Ben. I can't be angry at her for disappointing me in our friendship, because the only thing I can feel right now is devastation. It's ripping through me, shredding all the good parts, leaving behind hollowness and voids. If I don't find an anchor soon, I'll lose myself in the darkness. So I reach for Sara, letting her guide me back to safety, pulling me through the storm.

She leans over and wraps her arms around the jumbled mess of bedding that's swallowed me, trying to squeeze me tight, despite the obstacles in between us. I reach out and intertwine my fingers with hers, sobbing into the pillows as I ride the waves of despair.

I'm not sure how long we stay in this position, but when my reservoir of tears is depleted, I scoot up against the headboard to face her.

"Why are you here?" I ask. There's no way Sara had such impeccable timing.

"Raha called me," she answers, chewing her bottom lip, waiting to see if I lose my shit at my sister's betrayal.

"Oh."

I could get mad, but I don't. There was a time Sara's mom asked me to rescue her daughter from the clutches of the same kind of heartache, when Maziar had broken her. I had found Sara in much the same way, buried beneath the blankets, hiding from a love that had betrayed her. Back then, I had been her anchor. Now she's become mine.

She doesn't speak at first, but the concern in her eyes blows her cover. I can tell she wants to say something. I can't take any kind of awkward silences at the moment.

"What?" I ask.

"Is it because of what happened the other night?"

My throat tightens, drying out my vocal cords, making it difficult to speak. Instead, I just nod my head, confirming what she already knows.

"Leyla, I'm so sorry." I'm not sure if she's apologizing for the breakup or for her indirect part in it all. It doesn't really matter anyway. What's done is done. "Maziar was being such a jerk. He pushed Ben too far. It wasn't his fault."

How is it that nobody realizes the problem is much deeper than the fight? Why can't anyone see that Ben shouldn't have reacted that way because he shouldn't have cared? Maziar wouldn't have been able to push his buttons if he didn't still have feelings for Sara.

"I don't care about the fight," I say, on a long, drawn-out exhale.

The strength seeps out of me, leaving behind nothing but a tired, battered mess. Sara reaches out and gently grabs my hand. I look at her through tear filled eyes.

"Then what is it?" she asks.

"He still has feelings for you."

As I hear myself saying the words, I feel sick to my stomach with Ben's betrayal. I can hardly breathe; the pain of the truth too much for me to bear.

Sara is staring at me, puzzled, eyebrows knit together in thought. It reminds me of the expression she'd get when we'd study for geometry tests in high school. Such an odd memory to find in the current moment.

"No, he doesn't," she says. There's a confidence in her words, causing me pause.

"Yes, he does." I don't sound nearly as sure as she does.

"Did he tell you that?" She raises a brow, challenging my reality like she's done so many times in the past.

"No," I mumble.

"Well, then, why would you say that?"

"Why else would he feel the need to defend the relationship you guys had?" My voice is rising with my frustration.

"Because, Leyla, Maziar is insecure about the past we shared and was being an ass. And despite how level-headed he is, Ben's still a guy." Hearing her refer to the time she spent with Ben makes me want to cringe, but I do my best not to react as she continues. "He doesn't have feelings for me."

"How do you know that?" My head hurts and I just want to crawl back under the covers. This is all too much.

"Because when he looks at you, it's obvious he's in love," she says.

"He didn't see anyone else that night but you. Don't let one stupid moment, in an argument that got out of hand, ruin everything."

I want to believe her, to convince myself that Ben loves me and only me. But even if that's true, I'm already too insecure to consider it. Our relationship is over.

Maybe it was doomed before it even began.

* * *

I've let Sara convince me that four weeks of moping is a sufficient mourning period. As I run the brush across my cheekbones, I'm rapidly regretting my decision. I want to trade the mascara and heels for my ratted UCLA sweats and a bun. I don't feel like putting on a happy face and smiling through a meal I can hardly eat.

The plus side to all of this? I've lost ten pounds without even trying. That's an Iranian girl's dream. Minimal input, maximum output. The quest to be skinnier, regardless of what weight we actually are, is embedded into our DNA. We couldn't even stop caring if we tried. I've already been asked multiple times by my cousins what my secret is. Having my heart pulled out of my chest and dragged all the way to Santa Barbara without me is the secret. Remedy to the stubborn weight you can't lose? A massive broken heart.

I'm just slipping on my shoes when I hear Sara ring the doorbell. With a sigh, I grab my bag and head out the door, sparing my bed one last glance, feeling the longing to climb back in with a hot cup of *chayee* and a good book. I quickly shut the door behind me so I can't change my mind.

"Hey!" Sara chirps as she sees me head toward her.

Maman turns around and flashes me a smile, happy I'm finally "over that boy," or whatever phrase runs through her head when she sees me Ben-less. I'm past trying to make her see the error of her ways. Pointless now. Peace is what I'm after these days. If everyone thinks I'm good, then I have the luxury of being a mess without their intrusions.

"Have fun, girls," Maman says.

She leans in and wraps her arms around me. She holds on a minute longer than necessary, and I have to consciously fight the urge to squirm. She kisses Sara on the cheeks and holds the door open for us as we head outside.

The sun is dropping behind the mountains, leaving a streak of oranges and reds behind it. They swirl around each other like flames, blending together until one color is no longer discernable from the other. A fiery dragon's tail. I'm reminded of the numerous sunsets that Ben and I watched together, his arm draped over my shoulders, our feet buried in the sand.

I no longer feel the pang of desperation that coursed through me before, just a cold, deep hollowness that seems to be my constant companion these days. I exhale, giving myself a moment to collect the memory of him and put it back into my memory jar. I screw the lid on tight and lock it away. Then I follow Sara to her car.

We arrive at the sushi restaurant a few minutes later. I don't feel like eating much, making raw fish sound even less appealing, but I don't argue. Sara seems excited about the outing, buzzing with all kinds of energy. I have a smile plastered on my face, going with the flow. I'll do my best to have a good time. Or at least that's what I'm repeating like a mantra in my head.

I follow her through the double doors, but she doesn't stop at the hostess station, heading straight toward the far-right corner. Her back's suddenly rigid, and she's rubbing her palms across the bottom of her jacket. She looks nervous and on a mission all at the same time.

I'm distracted by her demeanor, so I'm not paying attention to where we're heading until I'm standing in front of the table. Sitting across from me is Maziar.

He stands, pulling my attention away from his fiancée. Instantly, a rush of rage plows through me. My eyes narrow, causing him to unconsciously take a small step back. He raises his hands up in front of him like I have a gun pointed at his chest. It's understandable because I could tear him limb from limb if given the chance right now.

"Hang on, Leyla," he says.

I turn toward Sara, burning with her betrayal. First night I agreed to go out, and now I have to deal with this? *Are you serious?* My words are lost in the fury I'm trying desperately to contain in my now one-hundred-and-ten-pound frame. Sara doesn't say a word, just cowers back at the force of my gaze.

"Please, Leyla," Maziar says, reaching out and gently grabbing my arm.

I automatically yank it away from him, unsure if he sincerely wants me to hear him out or if he's just trying to protect his soon-to-be-wife from my wrath. Either way, I'm pissed.

Sara finds her voice. "Leyla, please don't be mad. I knew you wouldn't agree if I told you he would be here, but Maziar just wants to apologize. Please hear him out. Give him a chance."

The anger makes its way to my ears, ringing like a blaring car horn. I can't see my face, but I'd guess it was as red as my unruly hair. I want to turn around and stomp back out of the restaurant, leave Maziar and his stupid apology behind.

Even though it's not entirely his fault, I want to blame him for the fact that I'm now single. If he hadn't let his macho Persian ego get in the way, our conversation could have gone so differently that night. Then maybe I wouldn't have doubted Ben, and he wouldn't have been so disappointed in those doubts that he walked away. Maybe, just maybe, I'd never have let the thought of his feelings for Sara cross my mind, rendering me currently incapable of getting them out of my head. I know it's a long shot, but right now, I really need someone to condemn.

I'm clutching my purse, my knuckles so white they look like they're glowing. I'm ready to head toward the door but am stopped short as Sara's hand grabs my wrist. I want to yank it away from her, tell her to fuck off and leave me the hell alone. I want to scream at her that she's always supposed to have my back even where he's concerned. But I don't. Instead, I stop mid-step and wait to hear what she has to say. Because the truth is, I already feel so utterly alone in all of this. The idea of losing Sara again, after all we've been through, is paralyzing.

I don't trust myself to speak, so instead, I just look at her and wait.

"I know this is hard. It's all kinds of fucked up right now. None of us behaved like grown-ups, and you got screwed in the process. But we're trying to make amends for what we caused." She looks at Maziar. "The both of us."

I glance across the table at him. He's watching me with his hypnotic eyes. Dark greens wrapped in honey browns nestled in his sockets. They're clear as glass, no shadows of animosity or remnants of hatred from the other night. But his expression reminds me of a child waiting nervously to find out if he's in trouble or forgiven by his parent.

I exhale. A long, slow breath passes through my lips as I pull out the chair in front of me, sitting down in an unfeminine plop.

"Fine, I'll listen."

The fight has left me and I feel more fragile than I care to admit. Loneliness has become a dark, gloomy cave made of meat and bones that I once referred to as my body. I don't want to lose everyone. Letting go of Ben has been bad enough. Do I need to write off Maziar and Sara too?

Sara's lip twitches in triumph as she takes the seat next to her future husband. The waitress suddenly approaches, three vodka tonics in hand. She gracefully places them down in front of us, turning in a way that makes me think she's actually a ballerina and this is only her day job. I stare at her long, lean back, suddenly too aware of my own inadequacies.

I return my attention to the conundrum before me. Maziar lifts his glass and tips in my direction before taking a sip. *So you knew I needed a drink, big whoop. I'm not giving you brownie points for that.*

I sit waiting. I'm not going to start this conversation. I refuse to make it easy on them. As if Sara is reading my mind, she elbows Maziar in the ribs. He grunts, rubbing his side, but doesn't protest.

"Leyla, I'm sorry," he blurts out.

"Okay," I reply, after realizing he thinks that was the equivalent to an actual apology. "Is that all you have to say?"

"Uh, well," he stutters, looking over at Sara for guidance. She doesn't say anything, just nods her head encouragingly. "I acted like an ass the other night."

Okay, so at least he recognizes that much.

I have to stop myself from rolling my eyes at his pathetic attempt at making amends.

"I'm not going to disagree with you, if that's what you're waiting for," I say.

"I'm not. I know I was being a jerk. I'm really sorry, Leyla. It's just tough for me, that's all." His brows decorate the edge of a magnificent scowl as he's fidgets in his seat. It's obvious he's uncomfortable getting into the nitty gritty of his feelings.

"And you don't think it's hard for me?"

"It's not the same," he says.

"Why? Because you're a guy? Because you Persian men can't see past your pride?"

I emphasize the word Persian as if Maziar represents the whole of Iranian men. I'm so over this Middle Eastern crap. It never bothered me before, but now it feels like all it does is follow me around making life more difficult than it needs to be.

"No," he says. His cheeks flush in response to my unyielding attitude. "It's not like that, Leyla."

Now I do roll my eyes.

"Please, Maziar, enlighten me on how it is then." I've stopped controlling my facial expressions, displaying a road map to my frustration.

Sara reaches out and grabs hold of his hand, squeezing it. A flood of jealousy rushes through me, rocking me in my seat. I try to push it away, hiding behind the shield I've erected to keep me numb. I want to forget Ben, not miss him. This isn't helping.

"I know it looks like it was an ego thing. And in some ways, it was, I won't deny that." He pauses, clearing his throat. "I know it's hard for both of us to think about Ben and Sara. But the difference is that you got to choose. You decided to be with Ben despite knowing they were together before. I wasn't given any choice in the matter at all. I was just told I had to be around him and be nice. I wasn't ready for that. Maybe it's immature or childish, but I can't help it.

"It's really hard for me to see him and not think of them together. I can't keep the images of them out of my head. And yeah, I fucked with him so I could get a reaction. I wanted a fight. I'm sorry. It was wrong of me not to think about how that would make you feel."

Sara beams in his direction, pride exuding from her pores. Maziar's face relaxes as he takes in her approval like candy. I wonder how many times he practiced that apology with her so he could get it just right. All he wants is to please her, and by the look on both their faces, he's done just that.

They wait expectantly for me to reply. Part of me wants to give them a rebuttal, to grab hold of the anger-filled boulder in the pit of my stomach and throw it at them in a blazing ball of fire. The other part just wants to let it all go. I'm too tired, worn down, and weakened by the crash-and-burn of my relationship with Ben. I don't want to fight anymore.

I bring the glass to my lips and gulp down its remaining contents. They just stare at me, patiently. There's so much waiting in this game of hearts. Back and forth, emotions flashing every which way; it's dizzying. Sara implores me with her eyes to forgive the man she's spending her life with. A struggle between the two us would only result in dire effects on my relationship with her.

I'd love to think I could hold this grudge as long as I wanted, but the truth is that all it would result in is the loss of my best friend. I've already experienced my dose of loss. My heart still hasn't mended, fragments of pieces I've crazy-glued together this past month. Plus, grudges really aren't my style. The only person who loses from it is me. It eats away at my insides like a cancer. I have enough going on in my insides right now, no need to add to the jumbled mess.

"I'm not sure what to say," I finally offer. "I want to tell you both off, to be honest. I'm pissed at you, Sara, for the ambush, and I'm livid at you, Maziar, for your immaturity." I sigh, the air rushes out of me in a puff of defeat. "But what would be the point? The damage is already done, and I just want it to be over. What you did, Maziar, was unnecessary and detrimental in ways you don't understand. But we all make mistakes, I guess. And this is just one of them. You can't do that again. It doesn't matter how you feel about the guy I'm with or what the past looks like. I won't put up with that shit."

"I know. I'm sorry. I'll apologize to Ben if you want me to." He's sincere when he makes the offer, but his eyelids are scrunched together and his mouth is in a pout, forcing the words through the tiny opening between his lips. He's gritting his teeth; I can hear it in the muffled way of his words. He really doesn't want to swallow his pride and grovel to Ben.

"You don't have to. We broke up."

"But maybe that will help," Sara says. The hopeful look in her eyes stabs me with regret.

"No. It won't change anything. Maziar isn't why we broke up anyway." There, I've finally said it out loud. No one to blame but yours truly.

"Then why'd you guys break up if it wasn't the fight?" Maziar asks, confused. He's looking back and forth between Sara and me, trying to find the inside joke he's so clearly missed.

"Honestly, I don't want to talk about this anymore. It's over. That's all that matters." I grab the menu off the table and enthusiastically look at it when I say, "Let's eat. I'm starving."

Sara gives me a half-smile and pats Maziar's arm. He's still looking between the two of us, trying to answer the riddle. Before he has a chance to ask any more questions, Sara picks up a menu too, saving me from having to admit I've lost Ben over my own insecurities.

"Good idea. I'm famished," she says, ending his inquisition before it's had a chance to get started.

CHAPTER THIRTEEN

His deep amber eyes are chocolate coins with rings of subtle reds. His lashes sweep his top lid each time he blinks like the rapid flapping of butterfly wings. There's a smile stretched across his chiseled face as he speaks, lifting his whiskey to his lips every conversation break.

I should find Arash attractive. Any female would. And I do, in the way a woman admires the beauty of a man, dressed in designer clothes, striking a confident pose. Very model-esque, he could be found on the cover of *GQ* magazine.

He's sweet, his eyes lighting up each time he sees me. There's a boyish charm beneath his stoic exterior. He's perfect on paper, if finding a mate was transcribed into a series of guidelines. I wouldn't be surprised if Maman and her friends have already created a questionnaire, titling it, "Bullet Points for the Perfect Iranian Man to Marry My Daughter."

"This woman is ridiculous, trying to claim over one hundred thousand dollars in damages on a case that didn't even cause much more than a bumper caving in on her car!" He leans back in his chair and chuckles. It's deep and masculine, rumbling in the pit of his stomach and erupting out like the sounds of a hurricane. It reminds me of Baba's laugh. "I'm sorry. I'm boring you," he says, snapping me back to reality.

"No, you're not."

I lift an apple martini to my lips. I'm trying something new. Time for changes. The tingle makes its way down to my fingertips and I stifle a giggle.

"It's okay. I know; I talk too much." He smiles, crinkling the edges of his eyelids. His mask is down, allowing me to see all the parts of him. "Sorry, I just get carried away sometimes. I guess that's what happens when you love your job. Speaking of which, how have your interviews gone? Anything looking good?"

He takes another sip of his whiskey, waiting expectantly. Even his drink exudes masculinity. All his attention is settled on me, yet I don't feel like I'm the center of his world. It makes me think of Ben. That keeps happening.

It's been three months since we broke up. Since then, we've had no contact. I spent the first week hovering over my phone, expecting him to call. Every time I stepped outside, I prayed he would be parked beside the house getting ready to come storming through my door, determined to make me see the error of my ways. When nothing happened, I slowly started to realize he believed me when I acted like I was over us.

I reluctantly agreed to this matchmaking extravaganza for Maman's sake. I've gotten sick of watching her look at me with that ridiculous worry in her eyes. As if taking more than two weeks to get over someone is the equivalent of losing all my chances. I'm almost twenty-seven and my mother acts like I'm standing on the stoop of where old maids are sent to die.

A few weeks ago, my *zandayee* had a party for my *dayee's* birthday. Arash's family was invited. Once the two of us started talking, I glimpsed my aunt and Maman spying on us from the corner, mischievous grins on their faces. That's when I knew Maman was in on the entire setup.

It annoyed me, but I should have expected it. Iranian women are notorious for playing matchmakers, especially where their daughters are concerned. Arash ended up being a pretty decent guy, and I'm tired of nursing a broken heart.

"I'm not so sure," I say. "The last one was pretty promising. I liked the firm. Everyone seemed cool."

Bar results came in the same week of the breakup. I desperately wanted to call Ben and share with him that I'd passed, but each time I picked up the phone, I chickened out. I knew I'd screwed up. And truthfully, I wasn't sure how to convince him that I understood I was wrong in doubting him. So instead, I didn't do anything at all. Now he's gone.

"When are they supposed to get back to you?" Arash says, pulling me back into the conversation.

"They said to expect a call in a week or so," I answer.

"Well, that sounds promising." His eyes light up each time we talk law. I hope I love my job as much as he does.

"Yeah, I guess they could have given me a generic goodbye and left it at that. We'll see," I say.

The waitress walks up with the check. This is date number three. He hasn't tried to make a move yet, but in the world of dating, this would be the pivotal outing. Who knows, though, since Arash is such a gentleman. One of the many characteristics that makes him appealing. Also, one that always reminds me of Ben. You'd think dating an olive-toned, dark haired, Iranian man would be as far away from my ex as possible. But sadly, no. I can find Ben creeping in almost any crevice. Maybe it's because I still look for him.

Sara told me he's moved into the city. Setie let the information slip before a shift change at work. One of the interviews he went to must have finally panned out. A second too late, I suppose. Destiny can be such a bitch sometimes.

Now, everywhere I go, I do an initial scan of the room looking for him. And when I come up empty, there's always a small flutter of disappointment beating its annoying wings in my chest. I've gotten good at brushing it off, but still, I can't help but miss him.

Only Raha and Sara know I'm not actually over Ben. They're the keepers of my dirty little secret. People hide things like abortions and drug habits. My secret is that I'm still in love with the boy who once loved my best friend. Doesn't sound that bad, yet I still feel the need to stow it away. It's easier than dealing with my parents. Or the community, some new higher power that seems to have their fingers in the pot labeled "my life."

"Are you okay?" Arash asks.

I hadn't realized I was staring off into space, completely ignoring what he'd just said.

"Oh. Yeah. Sorry, I'm fine."

His eyebrows pull in with concern, perfect arches framing his equally perfect eyes. Not fair for a boy, if you ask me. My finger whips up to my brow bone, tracing its length unconsciously.

"I'm just tired," I throw in, hoping he believes me.

"Okay." His expression loosens but he's still watching me. I try desperately to keep my face upbeat. "You ready to go?" he asks.

"Yup."

I stand up, miscalculating the distance between us. He's suddenly inches away from my face. I can feel his breath tickling my cheek. He's looking down at me, almost six feet tall, through his long, sexy lashes. I get the sudden urge to put mascara on them.

His lids flutter ever so slightly, transforming his teddy bear eyes to predatory cat slits. I can feel his hunger build in waves, washing over my skin. My body responds, tightening momentarily, but then the feeling is lost to memories of Ben. The dark hair and amber eyes looking down at me seem out of place and unfamiliar. I look away, breaking the connection before I have a chance to stop myself.

Shit!

I busy my hands with my jacket and bag, rambling on about nothing in particular, attempting to fill the awkward silence. Arash gives himself only moments to recover, falling back into character beside me as we head out the door. He holds it open, allowing me to pass through first.

A rush of cold air hits us unexpectedly. It was warm when we went in. The sudden temperature change has us speed walking to his car, neither of us prepared. He reaches out and grabs my hand, intertwining his fingers with mine. Goosebumps run across my flesh.

Arash opens the passenger door for me before making his way over to the other side. He turns the car on and blasts the heater. I'm furiously rubbing my hands together, trying to push the cold out of my fingertips. He reaches over and envelopes them in his own, pulling my fingers to his lips and warming them with his breath.

His eyes are locked on mine, the amber flecks glowing hypnotically. There's a dangerous edge hidden in his pupils that makes my heart skip a beat. My body tightens again. I grab hold of the feeling this time, desperate to keep it running through my limbs. He leans in, kissing my fingertips, one by one, never taking his eyes off of me. They're trained on my face, missiles locking in on their target. It's sexy as hell.

He moves on to the thin skin at the base of my wrist, gently placing his mouth against it. My breath catches in my throat and a flutter stirs inside me. My body is reacting entirely on need when I lean across the center console toward him. I smirk as I move in close enough to catch his bottom lip between my teeth. He exhales in a shudder when my tongue traces its edge.

I'm halfway over the console now, balancing in an awkward position. He reaches up and wraps one hand through my hair, pushing his lips harder onto mine. With the other arm, he pulls me to him. I'm straddling him now, my back digging into the steering wheel, but I don't care. I haven't felt this burning urge for months, and now that I have, I want nothing more than to feed on it. It makes me feel human.

It makes me feel alive.

I don't let my mind wander to the fact that this is purely physical for me. Despite Arash being a "good catch" by my Iranian mother's standards, I'm not sure I feel the warm, fuzzy, butterfly wings that I should when I'm with him. But he's hot. And I want him. That much I'm certain of.

His muscles flex beneath my fingertips as I run them along the edges of his body. The hard length of his arousal is pressed tightly against my thigh and I can feel it pulsing with desire. It sets my body alight, pent-up fire exploding through my cells like a meteor shower. I ride up against him, my tender flesh yearning to be naked. I want to feel him.

I reach down between his legs and unzip his pants. He moans against my ear as my fingers find him, sliding up and down his length.

"Tighter," he commands. His tone is harsher than expected and leaves little room for protest.

I pause momentarily, a wave of discomfort consuming me. But before it has time to register, he softly pushes the hair back from my face in a gesture so gentle I forget.

His hands expertly unbutton my shirt, pulling them open in one quick swoop, exposing the lace bra beneath. There's hunger burning in his eyes as he exposes my breast and nestles his mouth around my nipple. I try to stifle the scream that wants desperately to escape. Every inch of my body he grazes with his fingers, feels like tiny explosions of heat across my skin. The desire builds inside me, pushing me forward.

There's a mischievous smile pulled across his face, barely visible beneath the convenient shadow the tree above us creates. We're nestled in our own little alcove at the end of the parking lot, hiding our indecent exposure from the public.

He keeps his gaze on me as he pulls my blouse off in one fluid motion. He slowly reaches up and unlatches my bra, seduction filling his eyes. I'm holding my breath as his fingertips sashay along the skin of my bare chest, causing a trail of goosebumps to rise across my skin.

His eyes travel along my exposed body like an artist painting his muse. It sweeps over my shoulders, onto my breast, and down to my waist like brush strokes. My breath is coming out in short spurts now and the flutter inside my ribcage quickens in pace.

When he looks back into my eyes, there's a new longing there, one I can't name. It's animalistic and hungrier than I was expecting. A cold chill runs the length of my spine, making me hesitate.

I'm not quite sure why I feel reluctant, but I'm keenly aware that I do. I was hoping for hot, casual sex, but there's something else here, something that makes me uneasy. He takes my silence to mean insecurity and lifts his hand to run it across my cheek, sliding it behind my neck. His grip is firm as he pulls my face to his. He kisses me softly, a contradiction to the feel of his fingers pressing into the back of my head. It's confusing and unnerving, causing tension to settle into my stomach.

Suddenly, I pull away. I drop into the passenger seat, hands across my chest. I frantically search the floorboard, grabbing my shirt. I quickly put it on, my fingers shaking as I button it up.

Arash's eyes narrow in on me so briefly, I barely catch the anger they possess. Then his expression transforms into a mask of kindness, so convincing I suddenly feel ashamed, as if I created something out of nothing but pixie dust. He gently runs his thumb across my cheek and smiles.

"I'm sorry," I say, as way of an apology, my voice coming out in a whisper.

He reaches out and grabs my hand. "It's okay. Are you all right?" he asks.

There's an unexpected courtesy in his tone. After leaving him hot and bothered, I figured he'd be angry, but he actually seems concerned.

"Yeah, I'm okay." I don't say anything else, silently praying he doesn't push me for an explanation of my inconsistent steam level.

He lifts his hand up and pulls a stray curl behind my ear. I'm knocked over by the familiarity of the gesture. Pain burns tears into the back of my eyelids and I have to look away so Arash doesn't see them. A deep gashing wound opens in the center of my chest, bleeding out onto the floor. I want nothing more than to make my way to Ben's apartment. I don't have any idea where he lives, but I'm sure I could find him, even if that means I drive up and down every street in the city calling out his name.

What was I thinking? What made me think I could be with someone else when there isn't an ounce of me that's found a way to be over Ben? I know Maman and Baba love the idea of Arash, but is that enough to get me through this? Is the need to please them, to help them save face in front of their friends, good enough to leave behind the only thing I want? Do I sacrifice Ben for them?

Ben. Why am I even thinking about him?

We're over. He hasn't attempted to reach out to me, leaving little hope for a future. He's moved on. And as I look at Arash, staring at me, I realize I've moved on as well. I wonder if he can see the battle unfolding behind my eyes. If he does, he doesn't say anything, allowing me to wage war on my heart, alone. I should want to end up with him. But I don't know if I do. *What is wrong with me?*

Arash rests his hand on the side of my face and I still beneath his fingers. Part of me wants to pull away but the other part is so confused, I just freeze. I can't nail down any of my emotions. I feel like I'm lost at sea without a life raft, floating among the ice-cold waves until hypothermia kicks in. I'm waiting, always waiting. For what? I'm not sure. For my life to move forward somehow? To figure out how to take the next step? Whatever that is.

"Do you want this, Leyla?" he asks me. His voice is low, gravely with his desire. But there's a hint of vulnerability too.

I know I should tell him I'm not ready, that there's a ghost in my past still haunting me. But as I stare into his eyes, feeling the warmth radiating off of him, I hear myself say, "Yes."

I don't know why I don't tell him the truth. Maybe it's because Ben seems like a distant memory in a world of hope that's just holding me down. Maybe it's because I ultimately do want Maman to be happy. Or maybe it's just because I don't want to be alone. Either way, I lie.

"Good," he says. "I like you, Leyla. I want this to work out. I can see a future with us. If you aren't ready for all of this, I can wait." He thinks I've just been spooked by the pace we're moving at. I let him believe his own explanation.

"Thanks. I like you too," I say. I smile, hoping it provides the confirmation he needs.

He winks at me, then fixes his clothes as I straighten out myself as well. He drives us back to my house, holding my hand the entire way. As he hums carelessly to the song on the radio, I stare out the window, wondering which street Ben lives on.

* * *

Maman and Baba are sitting on the edge of the couch, eyes fixed on the television when I walk in.

"Hi," I say.

"Shh!" Maman demands, raising a hand in my direction.

Baba is running his fingers thoughtfully through his beard, a perplexed look on his face as if he's trying to solve some sort of riddle. My attention is drawn to the newscaster. She's a thin, blonde, blue-eyed goddess in her designer suit. The powder blue blazer accents the ocean-like tone of her eyes. The epitome of what I wished I looked like as a little foreign girl in my dominantly Caucasian elementary school.

She's sitting forward in her chair, eyes slightly crinkled, showing concern for the material she's reading off of the teleprompter. I catch the tail end of her report, not quite sure what the hoopla is all about.

"Leyla, you need to be careful when you go out at night," Maman suddenly says.

"Why?" I ask. "What's going on?"

"There's some crazy man after young women," Baba explains.

"There's always some lunatic on the loose," I reply, making light of the situation.

"I know. But you can never be too careful. You're a young woman, which makes you a target. This guy," he says pointing to the mugshot on the screen, "is believed to have kidnapped two girls who are still missing. God knows what he's done to them." He shakes his head in despair. "This country isn't like Iran. We never worried about these sorts of things while we grew up."

"You mean to say there were no crazy people in Iran?" I laugh.

He smiles. "There may have been, but we never heard about it. Fathers and brothers would bring their own justice to anyone who tried to harm their women. It was like a code of conduct of sorts. A different breed of men. Not like these boys here."

"Just make sure you're not alone and you aren't going into any dark alleys, okay?" Maman says.

"I never go into dark alleys. Who does that?" I tease.

"You know what I mean," Maman answers, laughing. "I feel much better knowing Arash is there to protect you now. I'm glad you guys are getting serious." She always appears as giddy as a schoolgirl when she talks about him.

Serious? It's been three dates. She acts like I'm wearing an engagement ring already!

Before I have a chance to correct Maman on her misguided interpretation of my relationship, Raha bursts through the front door.

Her energy is high and dramatic, as usual. Always a grand entrance and exit for that one.

"Leyla, what did you do? I hope it's good," she says, winking at me.

I shake my head at her in disbelief. Why does she always assume I've done something? I'm about to shove her when Baba speaks up.

"We're just telling your sister that you guys should always be careful when you're out at night. You never know what kind of *ashghal, trash,* is around. We want you to always be safe."

"Actually, Maman was telling me that she's so happy that I have Arash now to protect me since we are serious." I make air quotes.

"Um, okay," Raha says.

"She didn't say that," Baba says in Maman's defense.

"She might as well have," I reply. "You realize it's only been a few dates, right?" I ask Maman, trying desperately to cut off her excitement before it gets out of hand.

"Well, I just meant that I'm happy you're dating him. Is that wrong? I can't help it I'm excited you've finally found a good Iranian man to spend your time with." She emphasizes good and Iranian.

I flush with anger at her implication. Ben was not an Iranian man, nor was he a good one, apparently. One shouldn't matter; the other isn't true. But before I have a chance to explode, Raha nudges me playfully.

"Let it go," she says softly. Then she heads toward the hallway, dragging me behind her. "Goodnight. We're going to bed!"

"Goodnight, girls," Baba says.

"Goodnight, *azizams,*" Maman throws in. *My darlings.*

I can still hear the smile in her voice. That woman won't quit. The hopefulness she harbors makes me cringe. She wants this thing with Arash to work out so badly. I'm afraid if it doesn't, her heart will be broken worse than his.

"At least I know she'll be safe with Arash. That's a relief. Thank goodness she found him," she says to Baba, not realizing we're still in earshot.

Raha squeezes my arm tighter. "Let it go," she says again, stopping in front of my bedroom door.

"But she's annoying!"

"I know. Just let her be. So she's happy about this guy. Who cares? You do what you want with it all."

"She's going to be so upset if it doesn't work out," I say, in protest.

"That's her problem."

Raha has always danced to the beat of her own drum. You either enjoy the melody or get the hell out of the room.

"Easy for you to say," I mumble.

"It's easy for you too. You just have to say it. Trust me." She smiles and hugs me tightly. "Go to bed."

"I love you."

"Love you too, sissy."

I head into my room, the weight of dread an anchor Maman has tied to my feet despite my sister's pep talk.

CHAPTER FOURTEEN

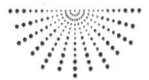

A rash pulls my chair out before taking the seat beside me. As maid of honor, I'm sitting to the left of the bride at the rehearsal dinner. Sara looks stunning. She's wearing a forest green satin dress. The material caresses her body on the way down, then fans out slightly at the floor, giving her a mermaid appearance. The hem brushes gently across the tiles when she walks, her gold peep-toed heels peeking out beneath the fabric with each step. Her bare chest leaves the perfect canvas for the round emerald pendant nestled in the hollow at the base of her neck. The diamond border catches the overhead lights, painting stars across the walls around her. It's magical.

I fidget in my mint green counterpart. Sara wanted us to match.

"I want everyone to know you're the maid of honor," she said. The equivalent to holding court in wedding politics.

It fits me snugly, accentuating my curves, tracing the peaks and valleys of my breasts and hips. It stops mid-calf, hugging my legs. My red hair stands out bold against the pastel fabric. I spent three hours at the hair salon, under the heat of a constant blow dryer, with the stylist yanking each strand of hair so many times I thought I'd end up bald. But instead, she left me with a straight and sleek do running the entire length of my back in the absence of its curl.

Arash looks handsome as usual. His black suit is fitted to his frame, the white dress shirt crisp and flattering. He decided to match my dress with his tie choice, making me feel like his prom date. All I'm missing is the corsage.

He leans in, whispering in my ear, smile stretched across his face. My parents sit a few seats down. Maman is staring longingly in our direction, stars in her eyes at the potential of a son-in-law. I get the distinct feeling he knows she's watching, thus putting on a great show. I try to ignore her, but the weight of her gaze is suffocating. Baba winks at me, always my mind reader.

Raha is across from me. She's turned toward Sara's brother, laughing at something he's said. The tight red dress she's wearing leaves little to the imagination, seductively cupping her body like hands. Dark brown waves cascade down her back, swaying as she giggles. Her plump red lips are a stark contrast to her olive colored skin, making her look even more exotic than usual. She's beautiful. At moments like this, I feel as if I pale in comparison.

Maziar clinks his fork gently against his wine glass and a hush falls over the table.

"If I could get your attention, please," he says. His eyes are lit up like green glow bugs. I don't think I've ever seen him this happy before. "Sara and I would like to thank you all for being here tonight. Tomorrow is a big day and we're very excited that all of you will be there to share in the festivities with us. We'd also like to take a moment to say thank to both of our parents for making this wedding possible." He raises his glass toward the end of the table where his parents and Sara's are sitting in a toast-like gesture. They raise their glasses to meet his. Then he turns toward his soon-to-be wife.

"Sara, I can't begin to tell you how much I love you. It's been a long road, but I've known from the first moment I met you that you were special. I'm so excited to spend the rest of my life with you. Thank you for making me the happiest man on earth."

She stands to meet him, placing a kiss on his lips and wrapping her arms around his neck. She's blinking rapidly, tears desperately filling her eyes. Maziar holds her tight, then takes her palm in his as they both sit back down.

Arash reaches out and squeezes my hand, interlacing his fingers with mine. I can feel the warmth of his skin on my fingertips, but my heart doesn't respond with the familiar acceleration. I wish it would. Maman is still staring at us, beaming at his sudden show of affection. I have to look away.

It's my turn to speak. Maid-of-honor duties require a few words at the rehearsal dinner. I try not to fidget as all eyes turn toward me at the clinking of my wine glass.

"Hi, everyone," I say nervously. "I'm Leyla, the maid of honor, for anyone that doesn't know me." Maziar's work friends, whom I've never met, are sitting at the other end of the table. "Sara and I have been best friends since we were little. We used to spend nights lying in bed, daydreaming about our weddings. I can't believe we're all grown up now and that you're going to be walking down the aisle tomorrow," I say, looking down at her. "I won't give away my entire speech tonight because I'll have to get up and say a few words tomorrow." I smile, looking around the table, making eye contact with all the guests like a good public speaker.

My phone is sitting next to my plate. The screen lights up, catching my attention. Maya's name flashes across it with an attachment. It must be a picture but it's not coming up. Arash glances down at the buzzing contraption and I quickly reach out and flip it over. His eyebrows pull together in a scowl. It lasts only a few seconds, coming and going so quickly I'm questioning its existence as usual. He looks up at me and smiles as if I didn't just hide a text message from him.

The abrupt change of emotions that Arash possesses makes me uneasy. He's difficult to gauge. For the most part, he's an incredible guy, kind and patient. But when he doesn't think I'm watching, something dark flashes across his face. It's unpredictable and makes me uncomfortable.

Suddenly, I feel a hand wrap around my forearm, pulling me back into the moment. I look down to see Sara's big brown eyes urging me to keep going.

"From the moment you met Maziar, it was abundantly clear to me, and I'm sure everyone else, that you two were meant for each other. I'm so happy for you guys." I raise my glass toward everyone at the table. "Please, join me in toasting the happy couple," I say. Then I take my seat.

I'm about to grab my phone when Arash reaches out and takes my hand. His eyes stare holes into me despite the smile stretched across his face. Dread pulls at my shoulders like a friend with a warning. Before I have a chance to call him out on it, I notice Maman still watching us. I flash him a smile for her sake. His expression softens in return, but his touch burns through me, the flame so hot it singes my skin. I have to fight the urge to recoil away from him.

"Are you okay?" he asks. Consideration emanates off his demeanor again, making me dizzy. I can't keep up.

"I have to go to the bathroom," I blurt out, hurriedly disconnecting myself from Arash and shuffling in the direction of the ladies' room. I yank my phone off the table, not waiting for his response.

Once inside, I hide in the largest stall, leaning against the cool white tiles of the wall. I pull my phone out. Maya has sent me a text message. It reads simply, "Look." An attachment is below it, but it's having a tough time downloading. I bounce back and forth on my toes as I tap the display repeatedly. She knows I'm at the rehearsal dinner, so whatever she's sent me is important.

Suddenly, a picture of Ben fills the screen. But, to my dismay, he's not alone. He's leaning in toward a magnificent blonde, whispering something in her ear, as her head is tilted back in laughter. She's tall and lanky, with perfect porcelain skin and crystal blue eyes. They almost look like they could be related. Anger punches a hole in my gut.

Just then, someone taps on my stall door.

"Leyla," Raha says.

I reach out and turn the latch, letting it swing open. I hold out my phone to face her before she has a chance to ask me anything.

"Oh," she blurts out as the image flashes across her pupils.

"Oh? Really? That's all you've got?"

"That sucks?" It comes out more as a question than an answer.

"Yeah. That sucks," I confirm. "It really sucks." I try to pinch back the tears that are flooding my eyes.

"I'm sorry," Raha says, pulling me into her. "You don't know the story, Leyla. Don't jump to conclusions." She tries to comfort me.

"What do you mean? He's with another girl."

"Yeah, but it could be a friend or a first date. You don't know the story. That's all I'm saying."

I know she's right, but does it really matter? The point is, he's moved on. Whether it be a first date, or tenth, he's out and doing his thing. He's forgotten about me. Despite the anger I feel right now, I have no one to blame but myself. I told him I didn't believe him; I let him get away.

"What difference does it make?" I ask.

"What do you mean?"

"He's over me. He's out. He's with another girl. He's done."

"You don't know that, Leyla. *You're* out with another guy. You've been dating him for months, to be exact. But are you over Ben? No, you're not. So this doesn't mean anything. He's not going to sit around and wait for you. That's not how guys are. You don't know what could happen if you told him how you feel right now."

She sounds so confident, I feel a flame begin to spark in my lungs, fanning smoke through my chest with the possibilities. Before I have a chance to give it strength, the bathroom door swings open and two women come trampling in, too intoxicated to walk a straight line. They stumble toward the stalls in a zigzag formation, leaning on each other, giggling. Raha looks at me, raising one brow in amusement. Then she grabs my hand, dragging me out of the bathroom.

I follow my sister back to the table, my thoughts permanently preoccupied with the picture of Ben. I have no idea how the night progresses from there. All I know is that I force myself to smile and engage in polite conversation. I laugh at jokes and let Arash take my hand as he leads me to the car. I lean in and lightly peck his lips as he pulls up to my house. He reaches out and places his hand against my cheek, deepening the kiss. I let him, wanting desperately to feel a spark. But none flickers and so I pull away, disheartened.

* * *

I help Sara's brother, Nima, load the gifts into his car after most of the wedding guest have gone home. The wedding has come and gone, an entire day of festivities completed in a whirlwind, feeling like just a few minutes rather than hours. He's struggling with his keys, his right hand officially swelling. Purple and red patches are stretched across his knuckles as a result of laying into his cousin's jaw.

I haven't gotten the full fight story yet, too much for Sara to fill me in on before she left. Something about Maziar's cousin, Neda, and an unwelcome suitor. I'm sure we'll be hashing out the details tomorrow. A fight at her wedding; this should be interesting.

"Thanks, guys," Nima says, appreciatively. "I know it's late."

Arash steps up behind him, putting the last box into the trunk.

"No problem," he says, fist-bumping Nima.

He reaches out and grabs my hand. It's as if he can't let me walk without leading me to our destination. Always in control. I'm about to protest when I'm distracted by the last few wedding stragglers heading to their cars.

Seti comes up behind me. She's how Sara knew Ben had moved back to Los Angeles. I can't help but wonder what other details she knows.

"Bye, Leyla," she says.

"Bye, Seti. See you tomorrow. You'll be at Sara's mom's, right?"

"Sadly, no. We don't have a sitter. But you guys have fun," she answers. "I'll see you later. Bye, Arash," she says, leaning around me. "Nice to meet you." She smiles, then heads to her car with her husband's arm wrapped around her waist.

As Arash pulls me toward our parking spot, it hits me like a cinder block wall: *Seti knows where Ben lives.* I need to talk to her.

"Hold on," I hear myself say to Arash, who responds with a quizzical look.

I don't pay him any attention, making a straight line to Seti's car. I reach her just as she's closing the door. My hand shoots out, grabbing its edge, stopping her mid-swing. She lets out a little yelp.

"Leyla?"

"Sorry, I didn't mean to scare you," I say. "I need to ask you something." I drop my voice so her husband doesn't hear me. He's trying his best to busy himself with the radio, pretending he can't. "I need Ben's address," I blurt out.

"What?" Her eyebrows scrunch together. "Why?" she asks, hesitantly. There's no mistaking the protective tone in her voice.

"Please, Seti," I plead, hoping I don't seem pathetic, but not caring if I really do. All I can think about is seeing Ben. "I need it. Please."

She's eyeing me carefully, no doubt trying to make a decision on my credibility. I wouldn't blame her if she wanted to save him from the hurricane that is me. They're good friends. That's what good friends do.

Finally, after what feels like forever, she says, "Give me your number. I'll text it to you."

I rattle off the digits quickly, before she has time to change her mind.

"Thank you, Seti." I turn to leave but she grabs my wrist.

"He's a really good guy, Leyla," she cautions. What she doesn't say, but I know she means is that he doesn't deserve to be hurt. I couldn't agree with her more.

"Thank you," I say again, squeezing her hand.

* * *

"Goodnight," I mumble quickly, turning to get out of Arash's car.

I'm hoping to get away before he has a chance to kiss me. No such luck. I almost yelp when I feel his hand on my shoulder.

"You okay, Leyla?"

Doesn't he get tired of constantly asking me that? You'd think he would realize that yes indeed, there is something wrong. Yet he continues to question me and come off all understanding. It should be endearing, but I'm starting to see the edge beneath his façade. I find it unnerving.

"I can't do this anymore," I blurt out.

His eyes widen, apparently not expecting that.

"What do you mean?" he asks. His face is calm, but his eyes pool with anger.

"I just can't be with you anymore." I say bluntly. Better to tear off the band-aid quickly instead of letting it linger.

"Okay." Still no reaction other than the sickening twitch happening at the edge of his lips likes he's trying to hold back a smile.

"Look, Arash, you're a great guy, you really are. And any girl would be lucky to have you. I just have baggage, and I've realized I'm not ready to start anything new with anyone." I'm rambling, my nerves suddenly frazzled. I feel compelled to explain myself but have no idea why.

"What baggage?" He isn't going to make this easy.

The anger moves from his eyes and flashes across his expression. It doesn't last long, but I'm sure I've seen it this time. It isn't all in my head. But as quickly as it comes, it's gone, as he falls back into the placid look of a few moments ago. His stealth ability to mask his emotions makes my blood run cold. Like Dr. Jekyll and Mr. Hyde.

I brace myself. I can't blame him for being furious, I'm breaking up with him. But I don't want to deal with it. I just want to get out of his car. But The red that invades his skin tells me it isn't happening any time soon.

"It's your ex," he says. It isn't a question, rather a statement.

"Yes."

"So these past three months have just been—what? Nothing? Wasting time until you realized you weren't over him?" His voice is thick with disapproval now.

"No. I thought I *was* over him." Total lie. "I really wanted this to work, Arash." Another lie. More like Maman really wanted this to work. "But it just isn't. I don't know what to say other than I'm sorry."

My voice is coming out in a whisper and I mentally reprimand myself for not being braver. But something about the crazed look in his eyes gives me pause. I feel like I'm dealing with a rabid animal.

"Get out," he demands. His voice is strained, pushing against his self-imposed restraints. I'm so shocked by what he's said, I don't move for a few seconds. He turns toward me, drilling me to the seat with his glare. "Go home, Leyla," he says, then throws in, "Please," for good measure.

"Arash."

I don't even know what I want to say. What will Maman think in the morning? I need to end this on somewhat good terms to save face for my family. All I can see is Maman and her concerns regarding her friends. Or worse yet, the whole of the Iranian population in Los Angeles, since that's how far Maman thinks our news travels. She's thoroughly dramatic and I have no desire to deal with it.

He puts his hand up to silence me.

"Look, Leyla, you said what you had to." His eyes burn with contempt, the only clue he's angry in his otherwise expressionless face. "You'll soon realize what a big mistake you've made. They all do."

A smile slowly stretches across his lips, exposing his teeth like a predator. My stomach turns with nausea. Something just isn't right. Then his features transform back into a passive mask of indifference, jarring me into motion. I quickly open the door, wanting nothing more than to get out. He barely waits until I've shut it behind me before speeding down the street. I stand stunned, watching his tail lights disappear into the night fog.

Mistake? What a pretentious asshole!

I shake it off. He's gone and I don't have to deal with him anymore. When I tell Maman how he acted, she'll see he wasn't good for me. I try to convince myself she won't be upset, but I know she will. Disappointed, anyway.

It's freezing outside, and my muscles are stiffening. I pull my shawl in tighter around my shoulders and contemplate going inside to change. But it's late, close to two thirty in the morning and I'm about to lose my nerve. I shuffle over to my car and get inside. I send a prayer that my parents are sound asleep and the noise of the ignition doesn't wake them. I have no viable excuse to give if they see me driving away.

I put the car in reverse and ease out of the driveway slowly. Once I make it down the street, I pull my phone out and scan Seti's text for Ben's address. To my surprise, he isn't terribly far. At this time of night, I could be in Studio City in fifteen minutes.

A giddiness wraps its tendrils around me, making me feel high. I bounce in my seat with its energy, wanting desperately to be at his place. Despite his proximity, it feels like a lifetime before I pull up to his apartment.

I almost fly out of the car and make my way to his door. I reach up to knock but realize it's early morning and I may look like a crazy person. I contemplate getting back in my car and throwing this insane idea behind me. But I can't move. The need to see Ben, to feel his arms wrapped around me, to push my body against his, is so fierce that I'm frozen to the concrete beneath my feet.

It's now or never.

I reach up and knock, lightly at first, still hesitant on my spontaneous plan. When no one answers, I bang a little more forcefully. A minute passes before I hear the shuffle of feet behind the door.

"What the hell?" he mumbles.

I gulp down a wave of anxious regret. Maybe this was a bad idea. But before I have a chance to run back in the direction I came from, the door swings open. A bleary-eyed Ben greets me. His lids droop with the weight of sleep and his hair is a disheveled mess.

"Leyla?" he says in disbelief. "Are you okay?" He's scanning me with his eyes, possibly searching for an injury. Why else would I be at his house in the middle of the night?

"I'm fine," I reply. "I just needed to see you."

"At three in the morning?"

His brows pinch together, suddenly making me feel like a stalker. My stomach rolls again, this time with the dismay of my decision. I can clearly see this was a terrible idea. I'm just about to apologize when he moves aside, pushing the door wider.

"Come in," he says, on a drawn-out sigh.

I hastily step past him. I'm afraid I'll lose my nerve if I stop to think this through. I may be sick. Puking on his carpet is a real possibility. I hear the door swing shut behind me and I jump.

Before my better judgment takes over, I pivot on my feet to face him. I'm reminded of the waitress at the restaurant and wonder if I look as graceful on my toes as she did. Ben is staring at the carpet, running his hand through his hair, avoiding my gaze. He doesn't notice me approaching him until I've successfully flung my body against his. He catches me, seconds before we both go toppling to the floor.

This isn't as romantic as I had planned in my head, my movements choppy and clumsy, but I don't stop. I'm scrambling to find a thread of bravery, feeling like water draining out of a tub. I'm spinning in circles, eaten by the pull of the momentum. If I don't keep moving, I'll be lost forever.

Before Ben has a chance to shake the shocked look off his face, I press my lips against his. My fingers wrap between the strands of his hair, pulling him closer to me. I push my body in tighter, until I can feel the taut muscles stretched beneath his t-shirt.

I get so lost in the moment that I don't realize he's stiff against me. His lips aren't moving along with mine, frozen in a disbelieving grimace. *He's not kissing me back!* The thought rams into me like a wall, causing me to stall in an awkward make-out pose. Any courage I have left shrivels up into a tiny raisin and falls to the floor. My hands drop out of his hair and fall limp to my sides. I step away.

He's just eyeing me, no doubt calculating his next move. I wish the floor would open up and eat me whole; this entire plan was a horrific miscalculation on my part. The silence stretches between us until it becomes a one-eyed green monster hovering in the shadows.

I turn and silently search for my keys. I've managed to somehow lose them after letting them fall to the floor in the heat of my one-sided passion. A flash of silver catches my eye beneath the side table. I grab them and head toward the door.

I can't manage any words, mortified by Ben's reaction. My cheeks are flushed, the heat in my skin indicating that I'm as bright as a cherry tomato. I try not to think about how pathetic I must appear as I attempt to make my getaway. Just as I reach out for the doorknob, Ben's hand wraps around my wrist and stops me. I stifle a yelp that's begging to transform into a sob. *I will not cry here where he can see me. I will not let him see he's hurt me.*

"Leyla, wait," he says. "It's late. You can't drive home. Just stay here."

My eyes shoot up at him, hopeful for a split second before I see the concern in his eyes. There's no romance, no passion. He must read my expression because he lets go of my wrist, breaking the physical connection.

Suddenly, the truth unfolds before me. Through no fault other than my own, our path has veered off course. We were supposed to be together and in love. Due to my own insecurities, I've thrown us into an entirely different direction. I should have figured. Despite being the same age, Ben is more mature than most. He knows what he wants, and he knows what he won't put up with. Now I can clearly see that I've pushed him over the edge.

"You can take the bed," he says.

"No!" I blurt out. I can't imagine being alone in his room with all our memories to haunt me until the sun rises. I'd rather gouge my eyes out.

"Leyla," he begins, but then pauses.

He stares at me for a moment, deciding what he should do. It's late and he's too much of a gentleman to let me leave. Usually, I find it heartwarming, but tonight it's infuriating. I just want to get in my car and nurse my wounds in the darkness alone. I have no intention of waiting until morning to have the inevitable conversation I refuse to engage in.

"Okay," he finally says, dropping his head.

He opens the door for me and moves aside. I walk through, each step I take heavy and forced, but I push myself forward. I don't look at him, despite the fact that I can feel him waiting, sensing the words sitting on the tip of his tongue. I don't have anything left in the way of bravery. I just want to hide in the confines of my car and pretend I didn't just make the biggest fool out of myself.

"Drive safely, Leyla," he says. I afford myself a single glimpse, trying to drink in the details of his image. "Let's talk tomorrow," he adds.

I get into my car. My hand hovers over the ignition, too afraid to turn it on. What I had come here hoping for is no longer a possibility. The realization crushes me.

Ben is gone.

CHAPTER FIFTEEN

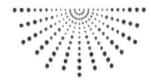

"Leyla, get up. We have to get ready to go to Shireen's house." Raha's voice is nails dragging across a chalkboard.

"Shit." I groan into my pillow. I totally forgot about the after-wedding brunch.

I sit up in bed, rubbing my eyes, hoping it will rid me of the overbearing need to sleep. I've only slept for two hours. I'm so tired I feel nauseous. My fingers come away black, the mascara from last night's make-up smeared across them. I was too exhausted to take it off. Judging from the way Raha is staring at me, I must look like a raccoon.

"You look like crap!" she says.

"Thanks," I reply dryly.

"What time did you get home?"

"Um...four-ish?" It comes out more like a question, prompting Raha to raise an eyebrow, a tiny smirk tugging at the corner of her lip. *Oh, brother, here we go.* I roll my eyes at her.

"What were you and Arash doing until four in the morning?" she asks. She playfully squeezes my leg.

"Nothing." I'm bored with her constant sex-fueled fantasies revolving around my life. I'm not that interesting.

"Bullshit." She calls my bluff. I know I should keep my mouth shut, neither having time nor the energy required for her inquisition, but I have the desperate urge to smack the smug look off of her face.

"I wasn't with Arash." Her eyes widen. "Matter of fact, I broke up with him last night. And just so you know, he's a pompous prick. He's much more full of himself than he lets on."

Raha's mouth falls open at the new morsel of information I've given her to gnaw on. It takes her a moment to recompose herself, thoroughly entertaining me with her confusion. It's so much fun to throw the know-it-all for a loop.

"Then who were you with? Don't lie," she demands, "because I know you weren't with Sara, obviously, and if you were with Maya, you'd have stayed the night. So spill the beans, sister. And by beans, I mean the truth," she adds, for clarification. As if I'm a moron.

"You're so annoying!" I say.

"Yes, but you love me. So spill." She giggles.

"I was with Ben." I sigh, counting down in my head for her dramatic reaction. *Three...two...one...*

"What?" she squeals. She bounces up and down on the bed. Team Ben to the end. I almost feel bad telling her there's no hope.

"Shhh! I don't want Maman to hear you. That's all I need. And don't get your panties in a bunch because nothing happened. It's a lost cause."

"Elaborate," she demands.

I'm so not in the mood for a recap. I spent the entire night analyzing every detail already. My head hurts with the effort. And now, as if destiny wants to screw me over further, I have to make myself presentable in the next forty-five minutes to witness how Sara's found her happily ever after.

I don't have the time or energy to indulge Raha with a play-by-play. But I know my sister and she's a force to be reckoned with. If she wants something, she's going to get it. I might as well give it to her instead of prolonging the inevitable.

"Follow me to the bathroom."

When we were little, Raha would sit with me while I showered, closing the toilet lid and using it as a chair. At first, it started out because I was too old for Maman to go in with me but too scared to be alone. Somehow, over time, it morphed into our sisterly ritual.

Our most important discussions happened there: crushes, friends, upcoming events, teenage gossip. It became a sacred time, laying the foundation for our friendship. Despite the copious amounts of water we wasted, Maman and Baba never complained. In fact, they seemed to love the sisterly bonding that happened in the magic of the steamed-up bathroom.

She takes her seat and tries to give me a false sense of privacy by staring at the floor. I strip off my clothes quickly and jump behind the curtain. Raha pulls open the vanity drawer where she keeps her makeup, grabs a hand mirror, and starts to make herself presentable since we have to be at Sara's soon.

"Okay, tell me what happened," she says, her voice distorted behind the rush of water hitting the shower floor.

"What do you want me to say? I ended up going to his house in the middle of the night like some lunatic. Then I threw myself at him in an attempted romantic grand gesture. He was supposed to realize I had seen the error of my ways and confess his love for me, but instead he froze like a statue, then didn't really say anything at all."

"He didn't say anything? Like, nothing?" she asks.

"Well, I mean, he didn't address the fact that I tried to rip his clothes off in the middle of his living room. He did say it was late and I should stay the night."

Suddenly, the shower curtain is yanked aside, startling me. I drop the container of shampoo, narrowly missing my toes.

"Jeez, Raha!"

A hopeful smile is creeping across my sister's face. "He told you to stay the night?" She raises one brow and smirks. I stop her before she has a chance to voice her opinion on the matter.

"On the couch," I clarify. "Actually, he offered his bed, but I couldn't take it. I can't sleep there without him."

"Oh. Bummer," Raha offers. She's trying to make light, but I can see her face crumble at the potential loss of Ben. Even though he was mine, I know she was rooting for him. Suddenly she asks, "What happened with Arash?" An obvious afterthought.

"Oh, don't get me started on him," I say, rinsing the shampoo out of my hair. "He's a jackass! I told him I had baggage, and he figured out it was Ben. Then he proceeded to tell me I'd be sorry I walked away from him right before he kicked me out of his car!"

"What the fuck?" she says.

"Leave it alone, Raha," I reply.

I can see the fury in the clenching of her jaw. She's protective; no one messes with her little sister. I wouldn't be surprised if she ran Arash over the next time she saw him. Or better yet, if she stalked his house until he came out so she could run him over.

"But—" she protests.

"But nothing," I cut her off. "It's done. He's gone. He was just pissed. It's fine."

Raha mumbles something under her breath that I can't hear due to the water rushing over my ears. But she lets it go, returning to her seat and picking up her makeup. I pull the curtain closed as she throws me a sidelong glance. It makes me laugh. Pretty soon, I can hear her giggling too. I change the subject, done with talk of boys and broken relationships.

* * *

Baba already has the car running as I hurriedly try to slip on my shoes while dashing down the driveway. It's evident from his glare through the windshield that he's annoyed with our tardiness. He hates being late. He's prompt to a flaw, always snapping at us and getting grumpy if we're a few minutes behind. It doesn't help that he's surrounded by women. Iranian women, for that matter. We're notorious for being late.

We all wordlessly slide into our seats, not wanting to poke the bear. He just huffs, mumbles about how rude we are, then eases the car into the street. Raha and I try not to laugh as Maman winks at us through her visor mirror.

She's checking her makeup when she nonchalantly asks, "Is Arash meeting us there?"

Dread clutches my insides, leaving its metallic taste in my mouth. I was hoping she wouldn't notice his absence. Long shot, I know, but a girl can dream.

"No, he's not coming," I reply as confidently as I can.

"Oh?" she says, turning toward me. "Why not?"

I know there's no way to avoid the truth. She'd find out eventually. Might as well get it over with. A recurrent theme in my life, it seems.

"We broke up last night."

"What?" Maman's voice rises two octaves, filling the confines of the car with its shrill. Baba reaches out with his right hand and squeezes her knee, his silent way of telling her to calm down.

"Maman, he's not as good a guy as you think. Trust me," I say in my defense.

"Are you sure about that? Or is it because you just can't leave that damn boy behind?"

Her anger has her bursting, about to tear her dress wide open, and her voice is a sharp dagger she's thrashing about in the car. I flush with my own rage. *She never gives up!*

"Seriously? You know what, Maman?" I say, ready to lay into her, but Raha reaches out and grabs my hand.

"Easy," she cautions me. "Maman, that isn't fair. And it isn't your business. Leyla is a grown woman. When she says someone isn't for her, just believe her."

My sister comes to my rescue, like she has so many times before. I smile at her for loving me enough to throw herself in the line of fire, taking the attention away from me. Maman just stares at us both, her facial expression jumping between anger and sadness. I can't tell if she's planning on yelling or crying. Baba just sits silently in the driver's seat, minding his own business, shaking his head at us every few seconds.

"He's an ass, Maman," I say.

"What did he do? I saw him with you. He seemed to be a gentleman. Maybe there was a misunderstanding? Sometimes, you come off a little harsh, *azizam*."

"It's not my fault, if that's what you're asking. Even if I did make him mad, he shouldn't have told me off."

To that, she pauses, knowing she doesn't have much of an argument if Arash was verbally abusive. The rage drains from her face, taking her expression with it. Her features crumble and my heart aches for the heartbreak that she's so visibly experiencing. I almost regret breaking it off with him, just because she looks so damn sad.

"Okay, Leyla. If he's rude, then he's no good. I just hope you made the right choice, *dokhtaram*. You girls won't be young forever. I just don't want you to pass up all your chances and then regret it. Both of you," she says, giving Raha and me a smile. But it doesn't cause the familiar laugh lines to fan out from the corners of her eyes. It only makes me feel worse.

Baba pulls into Sara's parents' driveway, pulling us out of our current conversation. They always park their cars with just enough room to leave us a spot as well. I'm relieved no one has taken it; otherwise, Baba would have been pissed. He was already grumpy because we were late and now even more irritated with our most recent feud.

We silently exit the car, trying to regain our composure before we head into the party. As I lean in to grab my bag, a car creeping down the block, catches my attention through the window. I bang my head on the door frame as I pull back to get a better look.

I watch Arash roll down the street, slow enough to let me know it's him. He stoically watches the road ahead of him, probably trying to make me seem unimportant.

"Is that...?" Raha asks, staring in the same direction I am.

"Yes," I say, baffled. The familiar dread is back, sending off warning flares that make my heart pick up pace. "What the hell?"

Maman sees him too. "Maybe he regrets your fight last night?" she says, by way of an excuse.

"Maybe," I reply, not convinced. Something doesn't feel right.

Just then my phone buzzes in my purse. I pull it out, thinking Arash has sent me a message. Surely, he's explaining why he's in front of my best friend's house the day after we clearly ended things. But when I look down at the screen, I see Ben's name across it. My stomach drops rapidly down to my toes, the dread transforming into a bundle of nerves. I forget Arash and his sudden appearance momentarily.

*11:00 Hey. Wanted to make sure you got home okay. It was
pretty late.*

11:01 I'm good. Got home safe.

11:02 Good. I think we need to talk, Leyla.

"Weird," Raha say, as Arash's taillights turn into two red dots in the sunlight.

"Yeah," I mumble, sliding my phone back into my purse without replying to Ben's last text. "Definitely strange," I say, referring to both men.

CHAPTER SIXTEEN

I've managed to avoid "the talk" with Ben for over two weeks. To my delight, a job offer came in three days after my run-in with him at his house. It not only meant some much-needed finances, but it also gave me a viable excuse to push off our coffee date. Now, I sit on the hard, wooden chair of the coffee shop, staring into the parking lot, remembering when we danced beside his car.

My heart clenches at the vivid images swaying in my mind. But I push them aside, knowing that I can't linger on them too long. I've discovered a lot about myself these past few months without Ben. The first being that my mourning period is over, and the second, that I need to move on. I just started a new job and a different chapter in my life. I need to focus on myself for a while.

Ben pulls up, unfolding his tall frame from the front seat. He doesn't know I'm staring as he takes his aviator sunglasses off and meticulously returns them to their case. The muscles of his back stretch tight as he leans down to drop them on the seat. I could trace their definition, even from this distance.

I busy myself, picking at the skin surrounding my nail bed, waiting for the familiar ring to jingle from the door. When the bells come, my insides knot up like the drop in a roller coaster ride. Seems fitting, being that I've been on this up-and-down momentum nonstop for entirely way too long.

"Hey," he says, as he steps up to the table. His voice feels like hot water from a shower the second you step beneath it on a cold day. It begins at my head, warming me up as it flows down my body.

Two piercing eyes are peering at me. Their blue glows against the bronze of his skin, reflecting off the white t-shirt he's wearing. The sleeves wrap snuggly around his biceps, hugging the phoenix tightly with each move he makes. Damn him for always looking so irresistible. As if battling the desire in my heart wasn't bad enough, now I have to stand up to the need coursing through my veins. Despite the struggle, I find a smile involuntarily stretching across my face to meet his. I stand up to greet him.

He pulls me into his chest, wrapping his arms around my waist. I'm all too aware of his hands resting on the small of my back, the heat rising off his body, the smell of his cologne and soap invading my nostrils. I want to melt into him, to throw the idea of moving on out the window, along with the past few months. Instead, I pull away gently, needing to put distance between us. I remind myself that things are different now.

He grabs the back of his seat but then notices the empty table. I silently reprimand myself for being so nervous I've forgotten to order. I hope he doesn't think I'm one of *those* Persian girls, the ones that wait for him to show up so he can front the bill.

"What can I get you?" he asks.

"I can get it. I was just waiting until you got here," I answer, trying to mask my embarrassing oversight. I move to stand but he rests his hand on top of mine, stopping me.

"It's okay," he says. "I've got you."

I pause, thinking about protesting, but decide otherwise. "Just a coffee, please."

"You sure? You don't want any of those *fancy* drinks?" The edge of his lip twitches as he makes fun of my usual caffeine choices.

"No thanks," I say. "I'm changing my coffee ways."

"Okay," he laughs, then heads for the counter.

I watch him lean against the wood panel as he turns on his charm with the barista. I wonder if he notices her batting her eyes at him and the pink flush in her cheeks? She's maybe eighteen, and it's obvious she's smitten. Pretty common when he's around.

I pull my gaze away. Gawking at him isn't going to help either of us.

When he returns a few moments later with our drinks, he's eyeing me carefully, causing the breath to catch in my throat. The playfulness is gone, his expression serious. The dreaded conversation I so desperately want to avoid is coming. I scramble to find a distraction.

"How's the new job?" I ask, hoping to guide the subject elsewhere.

"Good," he says.

"Do you like it better than Santa Barbara?"

"It's different. Busier. But everyone's cool." He leans back in his seat, lifting his mug to his lips. A billow of steam lightens his complexion as I stare at him through its fog. "How's your job," he asks, in return. He flashes his dimples at me. My heart flutters.

"It's good. I'm still getting used to it, and it's super-busy. But I'm liking it."

"What type of law is it? I don't think you told me."

No, I haven't, because we haven't really been talking. "It's civil law," I answer, smiling so he doesn't notice the wave of sadness I'm wrestling to suppress.

"What is that, exactly?"

"A lot of things. It deals with non-criminal acts, like contracts, property, family stuff."

"Oh, that's cool."

"It's okay. I like the busy pace," I say.

Ben smiles and nods. Then goes back to drinking his coffee, busying himself as the conversation stalls.

The awkwardness between us chips away at my resolve. I break eye contact and turn toward the window, holding my breath. I know he's about to ask me what I was thinking showing up at his house that night, about to stretch my stupidity across the walls of the coffee shop, forcing me to relive the embarrassment of his rejection. But just as I hear him say my name, inhaling whatever courage I have left to face him, a car in the parking lot catches my eye.

A silver Mercedes shines beneath the sunlight. Something about the talisman hanging off the rearview mirror is oddly familiar. It's hard to see the details from this distance, so I squint to get a better look. It's swaying despite the unopened windows.

The glint of the sun off the windshield makes it difficult to see the driver, but he leans forward, almost as if he wants me to get a better look. The cobra shape of his shoulders and the dark wavy hair on his head come into view. A sharp intake of breath passes through my lips. He's not looking at me, but I don't need to see those amber-crested eyes to know who I'm staring at.

Arash.

I get the distinct feeling he knows I'm watching as he meticulously gets out of the car. His movements are sharp and determined, even the smallest tasks some sort of calculated mission. Why didn't I ever notice how eerily he carries himself or the dominating look always lingering in his eyes? How did I miss all the signs? I'm not exactly sure where those signs point, but judging from the panic rapidly filling my insides, it's not good.

He looks straight at me, holding me hostage with his gaze. My heart stops mid-beat. A creepy smirk slowly pulls up at the edges of his lips, paralyzing me. Just then Ben reaches out and gently touches my wrist in attempt to get my attention.

Arash is cutting through the parking lot now, close enough to leave little room to pretend I don't notice him. He sees Ben. He falters momentarily, anger contorting his features, then quickly transforms his expression to the flaccid and unaffected one I've become uncomfortably accustomed to. His emotional swings make my stomach roll. I turn toward Ben, who's also watching Arash barreling toward us. I feel the need to explain, but given too little time to get the words out.

"Who is that?" Ben asks.

Before I have a chance to even say Arash's name, the bell on the door jingles and he's standing beside us.

"Hey, Leyla," he says.

His voice is smooth and hypnotic, his eyes intently set on mine, rendering me speechless. Then they drop to the table where Ben still has his fingers resting on my wrist. Ben must sense the tension, feel me squirm beneath Arash intense gaze, because his hand slides to my fingers, intertwining them protectively in his. I pull courage from his grasp, finding my voice.

"Hey, Arash." It's isn't clever or forceful, but at least I'm not sitting mute as he dissects me with his glare. He's still staring at our hands, prompting me to introduce my protector. "Ben, this is Arash."

"Hey, man."

Arash turns to Ben, the familiar predatory smile stretched across his teeth. "Hey," he says. The malicious expression he wears only deepens as he brings his attention back to me. "How have you been, Leyla?"

"I'm good," I say, forcing the words from my mouth. I don't provide any further explanation, hoping he gets the hint and leaves. I feel sick to my stomach and have the urge to run.

"I'm glad." There's a condescending edge to his tone.

He smirks and raises one brow in Ben's direction as if he's sharing some joke about me. It makes me want to flinch and slap him at the same time. When I provide little else in the way of a conversation, he continues.

"Since you don't seem too talkative, I'll let you enjoy your little *date*." Then he turns toward Ben. "Nice meeting you, man. I'd be careful with this one," he adds, chuckling maniacally. He winks, sending chills up my spine, then heads toward the counter.

Ben and I sit quietly as he orders his drink and then meticulously adds sugar and creamer to his coffee, pretending he doesn't know we're watching. He smiles at us as one more time before he heads out the door. Goosebumps rise across my flesh.

Why does he have me so rattled? It seems impossible that just a few weeks ago I was ready to have sex with him. Where was all this uneasiness then?

I begin to wonder if I'm making something out of nothing when Ben squeezes my hand, bringing my attention back to him. My eyes fall to the interlaced fingers lying on the table between us, pushing thoughts of Arash to the far edges of my mind.

"I'm sure there is an interesting story with that guy," he says. I'm ready to launch into an explanation, but he raises his free hand and stops me. "No need to explain. Four months is a long time. Things happen."

I exhale in relief. I'm already too shaken up by the unexpected run-in with Arash that I don't feel like reliving my past mistakes.

"Yeah, it is a long time," I say.

I force myself to pull my hand away from his. He doesn't protest when I do, causing a cloud of gloom to settle on my shoulders. I push it away. *No time for that.*

"About the other night," I say.

"How did you know I was in Los Angeles? And where did you get my address?" he interrupts, before I've had a chance to launch into the conversation I don't want to have, but know that I need to.

"Seti. She told Sara you'd moved down here. And I forced her to give me your address. Or rather pleaded, anyway." When his lids wrinkle in confusion, I add, "At Sara's wedding."

"Oh."

"I'm sorry about that. I shouldn't have made her give it to me and I definitely shouldn't have showed up at your house in the middle of the night, unannounced. I'm not entirely sure what I was thinking. Or maybe I wasn't thinking. It was Sara's wedding and it was dramatic and I was emotional."

"You can't just pop up like that though, Leyla. We aren't together anymore. I'm not your go-to when you feel sad or lonely," he explains.

"I know that." My voice quiets with shame. I feel like a reprimanded teenager.

"I need you to understand why."

"I do."

"Do you? Because I'm not so sure. You made a choice a while ago, Leyla, not to trust me or my feelings for you. You decided that believing your truth was more important than listening to mine. I loved you, and it was hard walking away. But I'm finally moving on. I can't keep jumping back in and out with you just because the feelings move you at that moment. I don't trust *you* anymore."

His words feel like daggers through my heart. I didn't come to this coffee date thinking we would rekindle our relationship. Matter of fact, I didn't want that. I'm trying to focus on me, figuring out who I am and what I want. But hearing him use the word "love" in the past tense, and then following it up with not trusting me, hurts more than I anticipated. My chest burns in response.

He watches me, expectantly. But I don't have a rebuttal. He's right. I ruined this with my lack of confidence in us; he didn't do anything wrong.

"I never meant for things to happen like they did, Ben. But you're right; we can't jump in and out of our relationship. I made a mistake, letting my own insecurities blind me to what was real. I'm sorry that I hurt you and that I didn't believe in you. In us. It kills me that you don't trust me anymore, but I can see why. I didn't come here thinking we were going to magically work things out. I'm not that naïve. But you're important to me, Ben. And I want to see if we can try to be friends again. I miss talking to you," I say, laying my feelings on display across the table.

He's staring at me, his gaze so deep it feels like he's reaching into my soul. I don't know what he's searching for, but I meet his silent advances, never breaking eye contact. After a few moments, he seems reassured, because he smiles at me, his dimples deep on either side of his face.

"I'd like that, too," he says.

CHAPTER SEVENTEEN

"What do you think about this?" Sara asks, holding up a magenta lace dress.

It's Maya's birthday next week and we're going dancing. Sara has been so busy with married life that this will be her first real outing since she's tied the knot. In celebration of her return to "girls' night," she decided a relaxing day of lunch and shopping was in order.

"I like it. But you have to try it on, see what the chest part looks like. May show too much cleavage."

"You might be right," she says, lifting the dress up in front of her and eyeing it carefully. Then she returns it to the rack.

"Well, at least try it on!" I demand, feeling bad I've deterred her from a possible outfit.

"Eh, I'm not really digging it that much. I have these things to try anyway." There are five outfits draped over the crook of her elbow. "You find anything interesting?" she asks, looking at my overflowing arms.

"Yeah, I found these," I say grinning. "Want to go try them on?"

"Yup." She follows me to the back of the store.

Once inside the changing room, I pull on the first dress. It's light blue, fitted, reaching mid-thigh. I stare at the way my curls fall across my pale chest, stark against the milky background. Tiny freckles cover my skin, creating my own personal dot-to-dot game. Ben used to drag his fingers lightly across them, creating images in their pattern. My own set of constellations. I remember it longingly.

Despite the decision to move on, I'm still hit with moments where I desperately miss lying in his arms. But we're in a good place now. Since our coffee shop discussion, we've been checking in regularly. Mostly through text messages, but a few phone calls have been sprinkled in the mix. I try to remind myself that I'm taking time to focus on me.

I decide against the washed-out tones of the fabric, making my complexion even more pasty than it already is. I move on to a deep auburn one instead, stepping out of the dressing room to show Sara.

"Hang on, I'm almost done. Let me just get this jumper on," she says, through the curtain.

"Okay."

I pivot on my heels, swaying to the sounds of Dave Matthews coming through the speakers. Observing a set of teenagers discussing the pros and cons of wearing low-rise jeans, something moves just on the other side of the department store window, catching my attention. The air rushes out of my lungs in one long whoosh as my body becomes fused to the tiles beneath my feet. My heart begins to crash frantically into my ribcage; all internal alarms are blaring.

I crane my neck to get a better view. Dark brooding eyes stare at me through the glass, interrupted continuously by the fleet of shoppers crossing in front of him.

Is that Arash?

"What do you think?" Sara says from behind me. When I don't respond, she adds, "Leyla, are you okay?" She steps up beside me, trying to find the source that's rendered me speechless.

He begins to move, hurriedly walking away from the store. His hair appears disheveled, his clothes rumpled and messy. Arash is always put together. *Maybe it isn't him.*

I have to get a better look, need to confirm that my mind's not playing tricks on me. I pull away from Sara, tearing through the store, still in the auburn dress. I race out the heavy glass doors, ignoring the employee yelling at me.

"Miss, you can't leave with that dress!" a saleswoman calls.

"Miss, miss," another urges.

There's commotion happening behind me, the tapping of multiple feet on my tail. They must think I'm stealing the outfit. I'm sure they'll call security, but if I could just get a closer look, it would be worth it.

I push through the crowd barring my way, but when I emerge on the other side, the person in question is nowhere to be found. I race up and down the walkway, searching, but there's nothing. By the time I return to the store, two employees are outside staring at me as if I've lost my mind.

"You can't leave with the dress, ma'am," a thin, petite, teenager says, stating the obvious.

"I know. I'm sorry. I just had to see..." I'm stopped short when Sara comes barreling through the doors, dressed in her own clothing again.

"What the hell happened? Have you lost your mind?" Sara yells at me. Her eyes are knit together, sporting a prominent scowl. I must look like I've gone mad.

"No, I just thought I saw someone," I say.

"What? Who?" she demands.

The two young employees stand silently, head bobbing between us like their watching a tennis match. Finally, the tall brunette finds the courage to speak.

"I'm going to have to ask you to come back inside and take off the dress, miss, before we have to call security." She stumbles over her words, surely afraid she's going to piss off the crazy lady.

"No need for that," I say. "I'll take it off." I grab Sara's hand and lead her to the dressing rooms.

"What the hell was that about?" she asks, when I pull the curtain shut.

"I don't know," I reply.

"You don't know? Are you feeling okay, Leyla?"

"I mean, I do know. But I don't know if I imagined the entire thing."

"Imagined what? You're freaking me out."

"Arash. I could have sworn he was watching me through the store window," I explain. "Can you help me with this zipper?" I huff, frustrated.

"Sure," she says, pulling it down for me. "Arash? He was here?"

"I don't know! That's the problem. I ran out, but by the time I got there, he was gone. Maybe it wasn't him. I have no idea." I slip off the dress and return to my jeans and T-shirt.

"That can't be a coincidence, right? You saw him at the coffee shop and now he's here? Doesn't make sense." I can tell her wheels are turning just like mine, making me feel like less of a nut job.

"That's exactly what I was thinking. I just wish I could have gotten a closer look. I can't be sure."

"Let's get out of here. It's giving me the creeps."

"What about our outfits?" I ask, not really in the mood for shopping any longer.

"Screw that. Let's go. We have clothes," she says, looping her arm through mine. "Let's go to my house and have a drink. Forget about your stalker." She's joking, but the apprehension is back in the pit of my stomach.

Stalker.

CHAPTER EIGHTEEN

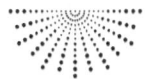

"I s Maziar home pouting that his wife has left him for the night?" I ask, winking at Sara from the passenger seat.

"No." She laughs. "He's out too."

"Are you excited? First girls' night since you said I do."

"Actually, I am. I love him, but too much together time is exhausting." She giggles. "And I'm dying to go dancing!"

We pull into The Room, a club I've never been to in Santa Monica. It appears to be crowded, the line for the valet out front long and slow. Sara uses the traffic to touch up her lipstick. As I rummage through my clutch to find my lip gloss, the phone buzzes against my fingers.

8:00 Have fun!

Ben's text fills my screen. He knows it's Maya's birthday and we're partying tonight. I slowly exhale, still having to push the sadness that fills my chest out of my body. I can't help it. There's a part of me that will always miss Ben. But I remind myself that this is good. Moving on and focusing on getting my life together. It's the mature thing to do.

We head inside, suddenly swallowed up in a dim red glow from the overhead lamps. Combined with the music thumping against the walls,

I've literally stepped into the heart of the city. Maya and Lisa are leaning on the wraparound bar, talking to the bartender, giggling as he showers them with his charm while mixing their drinks. Alexis and Jen are hovering nearby, engaged in their own conversation with two tall, dark, foreign men.

A flutter dances beneath my ribcage at the freedom the evening promises. For the first time in a long time I don't have anything to worry about. No secrets to keep, no broken relationships to mend. Just me. Whoever I want that to be for the evening.

Maya moves, exposing the bar. I spy a line of glasses seated across the top.

"Perfect timing!" she yells, when she spots us. "Trent here has given me a round of drinks for my friends on the house since it's my birthday!" She flashes a coy smile at the bartender and he winks. There's a silent exchange between them that makes me excited for her. The possibilities of the evening seem endless.

"Well, thank you, Trent," I say, as I grab a glass.

I have no idea what the clear liquid holds but as long as it's alcohol, I'm in. I take a sip, feel the cool familiar sting of gin wrapped around something lemony. It rolls slowly down my throat. The bubbles from the soda tickle my nose.

"Leyla!" Alexis shrieks excitedly.

Maya comes up beside me and wraps her arm around my waist, dragging me to the dance floor. She commands the others follow, yelling over her shoulder.

The music urges us forward, nineties tunes settling into our limbs like a familiar friend. Our bodies sway and twirl to the beats as we get lost in the memories we're creating.

Boys make their way over, grinding up against us each time they find an opening. Some we humor, others we brush off, depending on how attractive they look or how fabulously they can dance. I'm currently pushed up against a tall bronzed god with green eyes so piercing they look neon beneath the red lights.

A hand brushes my shoulder. At first, I think it's one of the girls until I notice my partner's lids scrunch up in response to the intrusion.

He stops dancing. I whip around, curious as to what has just dampened the lovely mood.

A cold chill seeps into my flesh when I see amber eyes staring back at me. I have to blink a few times to make sure I'm not hallucinating, currently three drinks in. My brain is sluggish and fuzzy. It takes me a moment to figure out that Arash is not a figment of my imagination.

He's smiling, but it doesn't reach his eyes. That familiar burn of anger is nestled deep within his irises, giving me pause. I quickly search my surroundings trying to spot my friends. They're spread out in a semi-circle, each a few feet away. The music is too loud; they won't hear me scream their names. The fear bubbles up in my throat just as my dance partner leans in to whisper in my ear.

"Who is this guy?" he asks. I don't even know his name, but the fact that his six-feet of muscle is standing behind me makes it easier to breathe in this claustrophobic crowd.

"Nobody," I say. I don't even speak to Arash, just turn and head toward Sara.

I leave my handsome dance partner eyeing my stalker as they engage in some macho battle. I feel bad for abandoning him, but my need to put distance between myself and Arash doesn't allow room for an apology. It provides me just enough time to escape into the crowd. I almost throw myself at Sara and Maya, who are spinning each other on the dance floor.

"What is it?" Maya shouts over the music.

She grabs my arm, the feel of her fingers soothing my frazzled nerves. It reminds me I'm not alone. *I'm safe.* I must look shaken up because Sara launches right in with the questions.

"Leyla, what's wrong? What's happened?" she asks, frantically searching my face for an answer.

The words are lodged in my throat. I can't speak, my body shaking from the encounter. My eyes dart back in the direction I came, searching the crowd for Arash. The bronzed god has officially moved on, now wrapped around a lanky blonde. But Arash is nowhere to be found, only setting my senses on hyperdrive. The burning acidity of bile floods my mouth.

How does he keep showing up everywhere? This can't be a coincidence, not so far away from home.

Sara is pulling me out of the crowd, toward the patio, with Maya on our heels. I'm stuck in an obedient daze as I follow their lead.

Once we're outside, the both of them turn on me, demanding an explanation.

"Talk," Sara says. Her hands are perched on her hips, reminding me of Maman when she reprimands Raha and me.

"Arash," I manage. "He's here."

"What the fuck?" Sara swears.

"Are you kidding me?" Maya says simultaneously.

Both of them are fully aware of Arash's "coincidental" pop-ups.

"I wish I were kidding. He's here. He was, anyway. Came up to me when I was dancing with that guy. But now I can't find him."

"What did he say?" Maya asks, her eyes searching the crowd outside, no doubt looking for the culprit.

"Nothing. He just tapped me on the shoulder. I was so thrown by his appearance, I couldn't even speak. I just turned and found you guys."

"I'm going to kick his ass!" Anger flushes Sara's cheeks as she takes a step toward the door.

"No," I beg. "Just leave it. I don't want to deal with him."

"Let me get the girls. We can leave," Maya says.

So what if he's here. Who cares? It's going to be fine. "No, I'm good. I'm just going to ignore him. Hopefully, he'll finally get the hint." I'm not going to let Arash ruin the night for everyone.

"Leyla, at this point the dude is in stalker status. It's no big deal. We can leave." Maya tries to reassure me.

"Please, he's harmless. We'll just steer clear. It's all good." I brush it off like it's inconsequential, despite the chill that's officially invaded my skin. Maybe if I pretend I don't care, I won't.

"Hey, can I bum a cigarette?" I ask as a guy walks by with a pack of Parliaments in his hand. I need to do something to calm down. The girls won't think anything of it. We smoke when we drink sometimes.

"Sure," he says.

There's a glint of hope in his eyes as if I've given him an invitation to hit on me. I ignore it, trying to hide my shaky fingers as he points his pack in my direction, lid open. I pull one out and put it between my lips, leaning in toward the lighter he's lit in front of me. A few deep puffs and the welcomed rush of nicotine courses through me. I sigh from the lightheadedness it brings.

He points his pack toward Sara and Maya.

"I'd love one," Maya says, smiling flirtatiously at him.

He's not her type, but she must feel sorry for him because she's throwing him a bone. He pathetically laps up her attention. When she wraps her hands around his, lighting her cigarette, he damn near passes out. Poor thing. It's almost too sad to be cute.

"Thanks," she says and turns back into our circle, shutting him out. After a moment, his morale drops and he walks away.

I try to make small talk in hopes that Sara will stop eyeing me like she's deciding if my mental health is truly stable after my most recent Arash encounter.

"Are you sure you're okay?"

"Yes!" I say. "I'm good, I promise." My voice comes off too chipper and I try not flinch at my subpar acting skills.

I throw the butt of my cigarette onto the ground and put it out with my heel. Then I grab Sara's and Maya's hands and drag them back inside. Once on the dance floor, I twirl around, moving my hips to the beat of the music. Despite the fear coursing through my veins, the girls finally relax in what I hope is a confirmation that they've let the Arash thing go.

I spend the next hour covertly searching for him—in the crowd, along the shadows of the walls, by the bar stools. But he's nowhere to be found, and after the hundredth time I scan the room, I begin to breathe easier.

The rejection must have pissed him off enough that he just left.

Maybe he expected a better response from me, or maybe he just wasn't feeling the vibe of the bar, but whatever it is, I'm thankful he's disappeared. I hope this is the last of our run-ins. I'm over it.

Lisa shows up with another round of drinks— shots this time. I gladly take a glass from her, welcoming the burn to help me disconnect from the eerie energy still claiming my body. I want to shake off the image of Arash's angry glare, dislodge it from my memory. Intoxication will help.

We proceed to take another shot on the tail of the first, then continue dancing, bouncing around for another hour. The crowd has increased in size, the heat off all the bodies making it feel like a sauna. My hair is frizzing. Wet strands kink at the base of my neck, giving my already puffy locks more volume. I must look like a shaggy dog, but I'm currently too boozed up to give a shit.

I suddenly need to pee.

Maya is dancing with the bartender, who's now finished his shift. Her arm is hooked around the back of his neck, their bodies locked together in a blur of movement, making it difficult to see where one starts and the other ends. Sara and Lisa are spinning each other on the dance floor, both laughing hysterically. They're having so much fun I don't want to interrupt them. And I have no idea where Alexis has disappeared to.

I start to bounce on the balls of my feet, very aware of my full bladder now. I scan the club quickly, one last time. When I come up empty, I head to the bathroom. *It's going to be fine.*

To my delight, there isn't a line. Matter of fact, it's empty. I run into a stall and barely make it onto the seat before the heat of my urine rushes out of me like a volcano. The relief I feel is priceless.

I hear the bathroom door swing open, but pay it little attention. I take my time, enjoying the short break from my heels. When I stand up, I sway on my feet. I reach out and steady myself against the cold metal stall. It makes me giggle, the warm buzz still making my thoughts hazy. When I exit, though, I'm stopped dead in my tracks.

Arash is leaning against the sink directly in front of me. His arms are nonchalantly crossed, his smile fixed on his face with such effort it looks painful. His calm exterior is wax-like and forced. There's something odd dancing in his pupils.

Excitement?

A boulder of dread is shoved deep into the chest and my blood runs cold.

My brain is screaming at me to move, to run out of the bathroom as fast as I can, but I can't. I'm frozen, his gaze cementing me to the tiles beneath my feet. A cold sweat breaks out across my forehead.

"Did you think you'd get away from me that easily?" he asks, tilting his head to the side in self-admiration, like he's just won a contest I hadn't realized we were in.

"What are you doing here, Arash?" I'm trying desperately to sound stronger than I feel.

"Isn't it obvious?"

"No, not really."

"I came to see you." He says it like he can't believe I'm too dense to realize it.

"What?" I can hear him talking but nothing makes sense. He acts like following me into the bathroom is standard procedure. "What are you talking about?"

He takes a step toward me and I reflexively back up. My spine hits the cool metal door, leaving me no room to escape any further.

"Now, Leyla," he says, his hands up like he's approaching a dangerous animal. Ironic, since I feel like a mouse at the moment. "Don't act like you haven't enjoyed our little game as much as I have."

It all becomes clearer as he takes another step toward me, the hunger flashing like sirens in his eyes. None of this has been a coincidence. I have no idea how he knows where I'll be, but suddenly, I'm certain he's been following me.

My heart rams into my ribcage with such force that I wonder if it may explode through my chest. My breaths ragged, all the muscles in my body tense and coiled, ready for flight. My gaze darts around the room looking for the easiest way around him.

"I wouldn't do that if I were you," he warns, only a foot away from me now. "You can't get away from me. You should know that by now. None of them can."

Them? Has he done this before?

"You've been a naughty girl, Leyla," he says, reaching out and closing the distance with his hand. His fingers wrap around a tendril of my hair, tugging at it. My stomach rolls with nausea. "I saw you with your ex. And now you're dancing with this new guy. I never told you that you could move on. Not until I'm done with you."

He's crazy. I need to get out of here. Move!

I launch my body forward, throwing my weight into him. He isn't expecting it, staggering backward against the sink. I use his imbalance as my chance to dart toward the bathroom door. I grab the handle and pull with all my force. It doesn't budge. I realize too late that it's locked. My hand flies to the deadbolt, but Arash is on me before I can turn it.

He pushes his body into mine, my head bouncing off the door. My thoughts swim as a sea of stars flash across my vision. I bite my tongue, the sharp metal tang of blood pooling in my mouth. Tears fill my eyes as the heat of his breath hits my ear.

"I told you you'd realize what a big mistake you made," he whispers.

Each word is enunciated so perfectly, like the sharp blade of a knife being pushed into my back. He wraps his hand in my hair and pulls. I scream as the burn spreads across my scalp. Before I know what's happening, he's turned me around and pinned me to the door again, one arm pushed against my wind pipe making it almost impossible to breathe. The other hand is fumbling with my clothes, now beneath my dress. I can feel his fingertips run along the skin of my stomach, teasing the elastic of my panties.

Panic devours me, a wild animal caged and desperate to escape. I swing my arms, trying to land on flesh, anywhere that would inflict enough pain to give me an opening to get away. My chest burns with the excursion as I try to get oxygen into my lungs. Black teases the edges of my vision and I pray I don't pass out.

"Stop it!" he yells. He can't restrain me, his frustration crimson paint across his skin. Anger warps his expression as he takes his arm off my neck and tries to grab my flailing hands.

I cough uncontrollably, gasping for air, but I don't stop swinging and kicking. I gather every ounce of strength I have, but he's much stronger than me. Nevertheless, I'm making it difficult as he struggles to hold me down. I'm seeing red now, in full fight mode. I don't even know what it is I'm doing exactly, but my brain is exploding with fear.

I have to get away.

He pushes his body against me again, using his weight to pin me to the door. My dress is pulled up over my hips and I feel the hot flesh of his erection against my thigh. *When did he undo his pants?*

His finger pulls on the edge of my panties and it gives. The panic sears my skin like hot acid. I can barely move now, his torso a brick wall I'm pushing against. He grabs my hair pulling my head to the side, exposing my neck.

"You need to realize that I'm stronger than you. I'm going to win. There's nothing you can do about it." To my shock, he leans in and kisses the delicate spot beneath my ear. The action is so gentle, it contradicts everything in the moment. "I've been waiting so long for this."

Images of the night in his car flood my mind; the same predatory need desperate in his eyes, but playful and sexy then. It urged my longing, propelling me forward with desire. I welcomed the feel of his lips, wanted it to become something more. Now, as I close my eyes, the betrayal is hot and furious, rolling down my cheeks in tears.

Get it together, Leyla. It's not over. Think!

The voice in my head is screaming at me.

"You're going to pay for disappointing me, Leyla." He slides his hand down my thigh, pushing his fingers against the tender flesh between my legs. I whimper, desperate to get him off of me. He's still kissing my neck.

Without thinking, my mouth clamps down on his ear, positioned stupidly close to my face. He screams in pain and I use it to push my teeth in deeper. I feel the flesh separate, and his hands fly up, trying to get me off of him.

In his momentary disorientation, he releases the force of his body on mine. I use the space to ram my knee as hard as I can into his groin. He grunts and falls back. I turn and throw open the deadbolt and rush out of the bathroom, running toward where I last left my friends. I can barely see through the blur of my tears, people gasping and staring at me as I run by. I don't look back, just pray that Arash isn't on my tail.

"Oh my God, Leyla, what happened?" Sara gasps. "You're bleeding!"

My hands fly to my face, touching the hot sticky reminder of my attacker. When I pull them away, red covers my fingers. Arash's blood. Horror takes over, as images of moments before take hold of my lungs.

I can't breathe, gasping for air. My legs buckle beneath me. Sara and Alexis grab hold of my arms, stopping me from hitting the floor. I'm crying uncontrollably now, my body wracked with sobs. My friends are surrounding me, trying to size up the damage. I must look terrifying, imagining the blood smeared across my face like a cannibal. I don't care; I can't.

All I can think of is Arash and that horrid look in his eyes. The snide smile stretched tight across his teeth like a cat in a cat and mouse game. I was his prey, his need to consume me so fierce it could be felt coming off of him in waves. I can feel his fumbling hands trying desperately to tear at my clothes, the snicker in his voice as he told me I was going to pay.

My hands run frantically over my waist, I don't find the hem of my panties, realizing they're missing from beneath my dress. I have no idea where I've lost them, but it just adds to the raw vulnerability I feel.

There's more people around us now, ones I don't recognize. A tall man, wide shoulders and bald, reaches out to me. I cringe away from him, almost breaking out in a run, if not for Maya blocking my way. She opens her arms and pulls me to her chest, affording me the safely of her embrace. I close my eyes and hide my face in her shoulder, still sobbing.

People are asking questions, but I can't even look at them to answer. They're guiding me out of the doors, my head still hidden beneath Maya's shoulder. Sara is barking orders, taking on the authoritative tone she usually does, when disaster appears.

I'm okay...I'm okay...It's over...I'm okay...

I repeat it like a mantra in my head, trying to get my bearings.

"Call the police," I hear someone say as we step out onto the sidewalk. I whip my head away from Maya. It's one of the bouncers.

"No!" I beg. Everyone stops dead in their tracks and stare at me in surprise. "I don't want to call anyone. I just want to go home." I look at Sara and Maya. "Please," I beg. "Just take me home."

I can't share the details, can't relive what just happened. I should have known he was like this, should have steered clear from the very beginning. How could I have been so stupid? If I didn't want so desperately to move on, if I'd paid closer attention, maybe I wouldn't be here right now.

"Miss, I really think we should call the police," the bouncer says, his voice gentle and fatherly. It makes me think of Baba. I cry harder.

"No," I say again. "I'm going home." I turn toward my friends. "Now."

"Can you give us a description of the perpetrator?" another bouncer asks.

Perpetrator. The word rings in my ears, claiming the air in my lungs once more. Sara jumps in, realizing I'm incapable of answering any questions, and runs off a description of Arash. It's obvious now who the guilty party is, despite my inability to voice it. My stomach clenches as his image appears in my mind. I turn toward a trashcan and throw up, retching uncontrollably, long after my insides have been wiped clean.

I suddenly remember the blood, aggressively trying to wipe it away with the back of my hand. I notice the strap of my dress is torn and part of my bra has been exposed this entire time. I feel even more naked than I did a few moments ago, my shame spread out across the sidewalk for all to see. I stare at the red swirls Arash's blood has made on my clothes and feel myself plunging into darkness, teetering on the edge of my sanity.

"Leyla, let me take you home." Sara approaches me.

It all feels like a dream. Did I really just get attacked by a psycho I dated for months? How could I have not known he was crazy? This can't be real. I have to be asleep right now. In a few minutes, my alarm will go off and I'll wake up with a sigh of relief when I realize this was all fake. Some horrible made-up nonsense in my head.

All the way to the car, and on the drive home, the alarm never comes. Desperation and guilt twist themselves around my arteries and veins, becoming one with my cells. By the time Sara pulls into my driveway, I'm sinking with hopelessness. It takes all the energy I have to get out of the car, wanting nothing more than having the world open up and swallow me whole, removing me from this new reality. I'll never be able to forget the way his arm felt, squeezing the life out of me, or the hot breath on my cheek as he mocked my weakness. I'll never be able to forget that face.

* * *

I push the door open and head inside. Sara and Maya step in behind me. I'd forgotten they were even there, turning with confusion when the door closes on its own. I don't say a word. I can't, my thoughts swimming through my mind in sluggish waves. Fear is the common undertone. And nausea. I feel like puking every few seconds when reality comes crashing back into me.

I quickly run to the bathroom, hurling into the toilet, barley making it in time. Wouldn't have really mattered. I don't have anything left in my stomach to bring up at this point, only the sour burn of bile invading my throat.

A sob escapes me as I fall back on my heels. I reach up for the hand towel, burrowing my face into the terrycloth, trying to muffle the sound. I don't want to wake my parents. Or worse, Raha. I can barely comprehend the nightmare I just lived through; how can I paint them a picture?

A soft knock comes from the door. It's barely audible. I hear it, but can't move. When I don't respond, Sara peeks in. I'm huddled in the corner, sobbing into the now-bloodstained towel. She comes up beside me, pulling me into her arms. I recoil, unable to feel anyone's hands on me. She doesn't react, understanding in her expression. Instead, she leans against the cool bathroom wall and holds my hands in hers. My body shakes with quiet sobs until my eyes give out on me. When the tears have all dried up, I resort to periodic whimpers as the image of Arash continues to haunt me.

"I'm sorry," I say.

"Why are you sorry?" she asks, her voice a kind whisper.

"Because I've ruined everyone's night."

"Are you serious? You didn't ruin anything, Leyla."

She reaches out and puts a stray curl behind my ear. Her proximity to my face suddenly reminds me of Arash's blood. I look down to find more evidence of it on my clothes. I start to frantically pull at my outfit in a state of pure panic.

"Get this off me!" I cry, not caring any longer who can hear. "I can't have this on me." I pull on my dress, trying to get it over my head, in a frenzied determination. Sara grabs the edges, helping me. I'm in such a hurry she's having difficulty, but the fabric feels as if it's been doused in gasoline and ignited against my skin.

Maya dives in, apparently hovering behind the door on high alert. My two friends help me peel off the remnants of the night and get me in the shower. Sara turns on the water, but as soon as she shuts the curtain, I turn the cold down as far as I can without burning my skin off. I need the heat. It comforts me in the way a sterilizing machine removes all the bacteria and grime from instruments. I need to be cleansed, to have all the moments of Arash's attack somehow wiped off of me.

I know it's a lost cause. I scrub my skin until it's raw, but I can still feel him up against me, feel his arms across my neck, the hard determination of his erection against my thigh.

Did I really just get attacked? By Arash? But he was so nice. Close to perfect. Yet, he almost raped me. *Can this be real?*

My thoughts are jumbled and fleeting. I'm grabbing onto straws, trying to fix myself in the moment, but I can't, everything moving at light speed but slow like molasses all at the same time. Things could have ended much worse than they did. I got lucky.

I don't feel lucky.

"Leyla, are you okay?" Maya asks.

The concern in her voice brings on another round of sobs that cause my chest muscles to cramp so badly, I can't tell if I'm crying over the memory or the pain it's causing. Oddly, I welcome the ache, reminding me I'm still here. I'm afraid that, without it, I'll fall down the rabbit hole of nothingness. A numb darkness is waiting in the corner, taunting me. It's just a matter of time until she stakes her claim.

Maya and Sara are whispering, but I'm unable to make out their words. I put my head further beneath the water, allowing the rain like sounds to fill my ears, blocking out the world.

I don't know how long I sit there, but suddenly the light brightens as someone pulls the curtain aside. I don't have the strength to turn my head and see who it is, now leaning against the cool shower tiles, my eyes closed, listening to the rhythmic whoosh of the water.

Suddenly I feel someone's hands on me and my eyes fly open in terror. *Has Arash found me?*

Raha is kneeling beside the tub, reaching out for the loofah I've dropped, now swirling toward the drain in a pool of water. She doesn't say a word. The look in her eyes is a mixture of concern and pity. It breaks my heart. Everyone who knows about what happened will look at me with that same expression now. I'll always be poor little Leyla.

She shuts off the water, plunging us into the silence of the room. I mourn the loss of the rain, something to fill my ears other than the pounding that's permanently stationed itself there.

She gently hands me a towel and stands by patiently while I dry off, then magically produces a pair of pajamas for me to pull on. The pile of my shame is still sitting in the corner of the bathroom in a rumpled mess. I imagine a can of lighter fluid and a match, as if burning my clothes will help burn Arash from my brain. Raha puts her hand on the side of my face, pulling my gaze back to her. She still doesn't speak, words not having any effect in a moment like this. But a small sad smile settles on her lips.

When I'm clean and dressed, she wraps her arm around my shoulders and guides me back out to the living room. I step into a hushed conversation, Maman seated on the couch between Maya and Sara, her head dropped in her hands, while Baba paces the floor like a wind-up doll. I falter, taking a step backward, wanting nothing more than to run and hide in my bedroom where their sad faces can't follow me. But Raha tightens her grip ever so slightly in protest.

Maman rises slowly, taking each step toward me with the utmost care. I wonder how spooked I must look, being treated with kid gloves and bubble wrap. Tears pool in Maman's eyes and her pained expression makes me feel like I'm broken. *How dare Arash take away the strong woman I am, leaving this terrified mess in her place?* She reaches out to me and pulls me into her arms, quietly crying while she strokes my hair.

"I'm so sorry, Leyla. I'm so sorry, *azizam*. This is all my fault."

"No, it's not, Maman," I reply.

My voice is monotone and dull, even to my own ears. But I can't muster up the energy in this hollow shell of mine to comfort her. I can't help absolve her of the sins she feels she's committed by putting me in Arash's path. I don't know how to.

I'm too busy searching my own mind for answers, gathering all the moments that set off my alarm system but that I chose to ignore. I should have known he was crazy. I should have known he'd do something like this. But instead, I pushed the warnings aside.

For what? The potential of making Maman happy? To have an Iranian husband? Or just because I was afraid to be alone? Either way, my lack in acknowledging all the signs is terrifying. But I can't allow myself to feel it, just like the hundred other emotions coursing through me. I bottle them all up and push them deep inside me. I find solace in the emptiness that beckons me. It's better not to feel. If I do, I'll shatter into a million tiny pieces.

"We need to call the police," Baba says. He has a determined look on his face as he grabs the phone.

"No!" All heads whip in my direction, startled by the urgency in my voice.

"We have to call them," Maman says, gently. "We have to report this." She runs her hand across my hair. I flinch.

"I can't do it," I say. My voice is a whisper, the fight having left me as quickly as it came. "I don't want to tell them what happened."

"You don't have anything to be ashamed of," Raha says. "You did nothing wrong."

"How do you know that? I spent months with him. I should have seen something, paid better attention. I wouldn't be in this mess if I had." I'm shaking as I suppress a sob fighting desperately to be set free.

"No, this is *not* your fault." Maman lifts my chin until my eyes meet hers. There's anger swimming in her expression now, not just the sad despair of before. "You did nothing wrong, do you hear me? You did nothing wrong, *azizam*. This was all him. He's a horrible piece of shit! It takes a broken type of human being to do what he did. None of it had anything to do with you. Do you hear me?" Her voice has risen in octaves, as if I need to hear it louder in order to believe. Either way, I'm having a hard time accepting I didn't have something to do with this.

"I need to call," Baba breaks into the conversation.

I want to tell him no, to put my foot down. The last thing I want to do is paint a picture to show the police how vulnerable I was. Besides, the details are becoming convoluted and confusing by the second. And a permanent brick of guilt I don't quite understand has settled in my stomach. But I don't say anything. He's grappling for some misguided control in an uncontrollable situation. I don't have the heart to take that away from him, nor the energy required to fight everyone right now. So instead, I nod, watching as he plugs the ever-dreaded numbers into the phone. 9-1-1. Our eyes lock for the few seconds it takes for the operator to pick up. Then he looks away.

My father can't even look at me now. The thought shoves a dagger deep into my chest, and I look down at my pajama top, expecting to see a ring of blood oozing out onto the fabric. I can see it, even if no one else can. How I would welcome the escape, to rid me of this flesh-eating bacteria called Arash.

A few minutes later, or eons, it's hard to tell, a knock comes from the front door. Maman has led me to the couch, now sitting beside her, in her protective embrace. She periodically asks me how I'm doing, then proceeds to apologize, struggling to stifle her tears, as she watches my reaction with that same sad expression everyone in the room wears. Everyone except Raha.

My sister has made fifty laps, the four corners of the living room her own personal track meet. She's mumbling under her breath like a crazy woman. Her cheeks are flushed, her hair a disheveled mess as she furiously runs her hand through it. She grabs her phone, searching for something, as if the internet can ping Arash's location for her. Then she curses, but nobody stops her, as she looks at my curled-up frame beside Maman.

I love how fiercely she loves me and how badly she wants to protect me. But it's useless. What's done is done. Now all we can do is hope that justice is served so he can't do it to anyone else.

Raha stops mid-step, and then instinctively moves closer to me as Baba opens the door. Maybe she's worried Arash will come back to finish what he started, just like I am. How exactly that was all meant to end sends a shudder down my spine.

Was he not worried about the repercussions? Did he not think I'd tell anyone? The look in his eyes, like a soldier given a mission, each moment planned in a calculated set of instructions from his handler. An objective that began the moment he met me.

"Come in," I hear Baba say.

This must be so difficult for him, being an Iranian man. He's raised to be the provider, the protector of his family. But he was nowhere close enough to save me from this nightmare. I can see it playing out in his mind on repeat, much like it is in mine. In the furrow of his brow, his pinched eyelids, and the perpetual state of a frown he wears on his face, he's fighting the anger that's consuming him.

"Hello, I'm Officer Scott," the officer says. His gaze runs over the length of me, assessing the damage. There's no question who the victim is.

I must be a sight. The vision in my left eye has blurred, my upper lid swollen. My head aches and the back of my skull is tender to the touch. My arms sport a zig-zag of scratches. I have no idea where bruises are visible, but I ache everywhere. I avoided looking in the mirror on purpose.

"Hi." My voice is barely a whisper.

"Leyla, I'm sorry to be meeting you under these circumstances. I understand that you were attacked tonight?"

"Yes."

"Are you okay? Do you need to go to the hospital?"

"No, I'm fine."

"Okay," he says, after staring at me for a few moments. "I need to ask you some questions. Are you comfortable doing them here?"

I have a crowd huddled around me. I want to say no, have them leave so I can explain alone, but what would be the point? They'll know eventually. There's no way I'll be able to keep the details from them. Might as well tell them all at once and get it over with, now while the numb emptiness protects me.

"It's fine. They can be here."

I try not to notice the sadness in Sara's expression or Maman's stoic posture beside me as she attempts to be my strength. I try not to see Raha's anger burning in her eyes, commingling with Baba's rage, trapping us all in this room.

Officer Scott pulls out a notepad.

"You were attacked this evening, correct?" Scott asks.

"Yes."

"What is his name? Do you know him? Can you give us a description?" Scott stops between each question, giving me time to answer.

"What did he say?"

"What did you say?"

"Then what?"

I'm staring at my hands, wringing the edge of a throw pillow between my fingers. I answer him obediently, my voice flat and quiet. All the while, the strong independent Leyla from the beginning of the night is screaming from behind the bars I've put her in. I wish I was as strong as Raha looks right now. But I'm not.

I focus on the facts. After all, that's what the officer came here to get. Those are the details that will help him find my attacker. *My attacker.* It still sounds so odd when the officer refers to Arash that way. *How do I have an attacker? How did this become part of my story?*

The details have become fuzzy now that the adrenaline isn't coursing through my veins and keeping me alert. But everyone remains patient while I sift through my mind for the answers.

Arash. Yes. No. Ex. Threat. You won't get away. No, he tried, but he didn't rape me.

Just words. One after another, I repeat them as if I wasn't even there.

They don't need to know how powerless I felt, or how violated I feel right now. I want to sleep for a million years as the details of the night fade into the background until I can't recall them any longer. I don't want to tell them that somehow, I feel this is all my fault.

Despite the full house, I am utterly alone.

The questioning ends close to three in the morning.

Somewhere within that time, a different officer arrives. She's part of the special crime scene department and is here to take the "evidence." I endure twenty minutes of grueling photographs taken of my body, tagging every bruise, scratch, swollen surface, as they build their case against my attacker. For this, I wanted to be alone.

Sharing the details of the evening is one thing, but allowing my family to see the track marks of Arash's betrayal is another. That shame I prefer to keep to myself.

I watch her pull on a pair of latex gloves as she yanks a large Ziploc bag out of her pocket. She grabs the pile of bloodstained clothing crumpled in the corner of the bathroom and puts it inside, taking with her the last bit of physical evidence I have of the nightmare I've experienced tonight.

Everyone is subdued with fatigue when the fiasco is over. Everyone except for Raha, who still appears furious. I don't have the energy to provide her any comfort. Besides, I doubt she'd believe me if I lied and told her I was okay.

Maman, though, hangs onto to my words like a lifeline, as if my ability to bounce back from this absolves her from the guilt she seems to feel. But my sister isn't out for absolution. She's out for revenge.

"Detectives will be here in the morning for more questioning," Officer Scott says as Baba walks him to the door.

"I'm tired." I rise from the couch. Maman gets up with me.

"Do you want to sleep with me tonight?" she asks. "Baba will sleep on the couch."

I look at Maman and see the worry stretched across her broken expression. I can feel the chaos brewing inside her, the energy palpable. I know she wants to keep me close, to make sure that I'm indeed okay. But I can't indulge her feelings right now. I'm too busy avoiding my own.

"No, I think I want to sleep in my own bed. You and Baba sleep together." My dad can give her the comfort she needs right now. He can help her where I can't.

"I'll sleep with Leyla," Raha says. She can read me like a book, stopping Maman before she has a chance to insist.

I look up at my sister and attempt to smile. I'm not sure if the muscles of my face are obeying my commands.

"We can stay too," Maya offers.

"No, you guys go home," I say, squeezing their hands as I walk by. "I'm so tired. I'm just going to pass out." I don't turn back around, focused on heading to my door. "Goodnight, everyone," I add, trying not to be rude. They're all worried, and I appreciate it, but I just need to get away from their questioning eyes. I can't handle all their feelings right now.

"We'll be back in the morning," I hear Sara say to my parents.

"That would be good, *aziz*," Maman replies.

The rest of the conversation is lost when I shut the door behind me. I slowly walk over to my bed, my movements drawn out and painful. I catch my reflection in the bathroom mirror, the door slightly ajar. I change course, stepping inside. I flip the switch and allow light to flood the room.

A stranger stands before me, her hair exceptionally frizzier than normal, each strand fixed in protest against the occurrence of the evening. There's a large bruise on the left side of my face, a half-moon tracing a path from my brow bone to my cheek, my eye nestled in its center. The purples and greens blend together in a patchwork quilt, sporadically decorated with bursts of reds. I run my finger gently across my swollen skin, having no clue exactly when I received this parting gift.

The rest of my face is dull and pale, my expression lifeless. The woman staring at me is no one I recognize, the best pieces of her stripped away in a matter minutes. I can't look at her anymore, shutting off the light and plunging us both back into darkness.

I make my way over to the bed and crawl beneath its protective covers, curling myself into a ball. In the solitude of its safety, I attempt to block out the memories of the evening. I feel like I'm perched in the corner of the ceiling, the moments playing out before me in broken fragments. I'm floating in an abyss, fighting to keep myself rooted in the present.

* * *

There's a moment, between sleep and awake, where the world stands still. Before the memories of Arash haunt me.

I roll over and a sharp shooting pain stabs my side, making me wince. When I open my eyes, I find the sun peeking through the crack between the curtains.

I hear the soft whistle of breathing and slowly turn over to find Raha sleeping beside me. She's taken care to lie at the edge of the bed, giving me room to be alone in her company. Her right hand is stretched out in my direction, as she reaches for me in her sleep. I smile, a small, warm comfort in the sea of frigid ice water. My sister.

I slowly push myself up on my elbow, the nagging pain in my side stating its presence again. I lift the edge of my shirt to find purple bruises spread out across my ribs. I exhale at the sight of them, constant reminders of my "attacker" left behind for my viewing pleasure.

I inch off of the bed, trying not to move the mattress too much and wake Raha. But I feel banged up and everything hurts, so I don't do such a great job. As I slowly swing my legs over the edge, she stirs.

"Hey," she says gently.

I turn to face her. "Hey."

"How are you feeling?"

"I'm okay." I try to smile. The expression hurts, reminding me of the bruise on my face. I unconsciously trace the edges, the skin inflamed and slightly lifted, making its location easily accessible.

Raha reaches out and rests her hand on my thigh. "How are you feeling?" she asks me again.

I want to be angry, to let my rage unleash its wrath on the world. I want to jump in the car, track Arash down, and take away what he's taken from me. I want him to be scared and broken, and suspicious of every woman who passes by him. But I can't. Because if I let myself feel anything other than this numb void, then all the emotions I'm trying to keep at bay will rush in with the anger, eating me alive.

"I told you I'm fine," I snap at her, annoyed that she knows me so well. I immediately regret it.

She doesn't react, just deepens her smile pushing herself up in bed until she's facing me. She scoots toward me and gently wraps her arms around me. I tense, trying desperately to fight her advances.

I don't want to feel anything.

She runs her hand across my hair. "You're okay, Leyla. You're going to be okay." She says it with such confidence that tears prickle the back of my lids. I take a deep breath, trying to keep from crying. "I know it doesn't feel like it right now, but you are one of the strongest people I know. You are going to be okay."

And just like that, my sister has forced her love into my soul, causing cracks in my armor. The floodgates are thrown open and a rush of emotion drowns me. I begin to cry against her shoulder, the weight of the night before finally breaking me into a million shard of glass. The fragility I feel infuriates and saddens me all at the same time.

"I can't get out of my head," I say, sobbing. "Every time I close my eyes I can see him, and I can hear his voice in my ear." I shudder, still crying. "I feel so broken, Raha."

My sister pulls me in closer, trying to save me from my doubts. I know if she could, she'd telepathically transfer her strength over to me. She'd take this burden in a heartbeat, save me from what it is that Arash did to me. She's always loved me more than is good for her, ready to throw herself in front of a passing train at any given moment to save me.

Just then a gentle knock comes from the door. Maman peeks her head inside. She smiles at us, but it doesn't reach her eyes, her lids crinkled with worry. The skin beneath them is kissed purple from lack of sleep. I can't imagine she or Baba got much rest last night. Her dark bob is flattened on one side.

I can see her lying in bed, curled around her pillow, eyes fixed on the wall, trying to piece together my nightmare. I wonder if what she imagined is better or worse than what actually happened.

"Can I come in?" she asks.

"Yeah," I say. I know she needs to think I'm okay, so I smile trying to convince her.

Raha and I scoot back until we are side by side making room for her to sit across from us. Maman unconsciously reaches up and touches the bruise on my face. I try not to wince. She's somewhere far away, her eyes glazed over with a memory I can't see.

"I'm so sorry, *dokhtaram*," she says. Her breath is ragged with despair. "This is all my fault."

"No, it's not, Maman," I say. "You couldn't have known."

"But I should have."

No, I should have. I was the one that was with him. You just saw what you wanted to see, a guy with his shit together who liked your daughter. A potential husband.

"This is Arash's fault and no one else's," Raha interjects. Her fury is back. "It's all that piece of shit's fault. He's a fucking psycho! And good at hiding it. No one could have known. Not you, Maman. Or you, Leyla."

I wrap my fingers around Raha's confidence and hold on tight, praying it will get me through the next few weeks of doubt that I'm already experiencing.

"Do you hear me?" she says, grabbing my hand. "This is not your fault." Her eyes are fixed on mine, trying to push her words into me.

I can't help the tears that spring up, and before I know it, I'm crying again. The emotional roller coaster ride I'm suddenly on is exhausting and I want off, but I can't seem to find the exit sign. Up and down I go, one minute trying to console my mom, the other sobbing on my sister's shoulder.

I lie down between Maman and Raha, pulling my knees to my chest, hiding my face. The mere act of sitting up requires more effort than I possess. Maman rubs my head; Raha places her hand on my ankle, letting me know I'm not alone. My soldiers flanking me when the battle has already been lost. I try to find comfort in their presence, but I come up short. Despite the fact that they're sitting right next to me, I still feel alone.

"I should never have pushed you to go out with him. I should have let you live your life the way you wanted to and be with whoever your heart told you to be with. Even if I didn't agree."

She's talking about Ben, his image coming into view. It makes my heart constrict and I cry harder. What I would give to go back six months, to feel his arms wrapped around me. He'd never hurt me like this.

"I won't ever do that again. *Ghasam mekhoram!*" *I swear.*

She makes a vow, as if her pledge to God can somehow hit a rewind button, to take us back to before. Sadly, it's too late. I don't point that out, though. This isn't her fault. She couldn't have known, and if she had, I know she'd never have let me near him.

Baba makes his way into the room and sits beside Maman. My entire family is on this bed, a life raft supporting us. He reaches out and places his hand on my face, brushing away my tears. The weight of his fingers is soothing, despite the soreness of my bruise. He gently touches my chin, pulling my gaze up to his deep brown eyes. He smiles, warm and weary, as he looks at me.

"Do you know how much I love you?" he asks. "You are my *donyah*." *My world.* His words make me sob more fiercely. "This boy hasn't ruined you," he says. "The world isn't an ugly place like you feel it is right now. He's just one person. And you're still my amazing Leyla. You remember that, *eshgham*." *My love.* He leans down and kisses my cheek.

I scoot toward him and place my head on his lap, wanting desperately to feel the strength of his arms to protect me. When I was a little girl, I always thought my dad was a superhero, that if he just held me, I'd be protected in a shield where no monsters could get me. As if he's reading my mind, he wraps his big arms around me and murmurs soothingly as I cry.

"I know, *dokhtaram*. I know."

I let Baba comfort me, let him breathe his strength into me until I'm sure that Arash won't win.

* * *

Later that morning, the detectives arrive. They are dressed in plain clothes, which I find comforting. I wonder to myself if that's why they don't have uniforms like regular officers. The victims they talk to have no desire to put their weaknesses out on display while being intimidated by dark blue outfits.

They each have a badge. Detective Gomez wears his on a chain around his neck, but Detective Pearson has hers clipped to her black belt. She's wearing a pair of black slacks and a white blouse. Her caramel skin stands out stark against the pale background. Detective Gomez has on navy pants and a white polo. Despite their not having matching uniforms, there seems to be a general consensus among their fashion decisions.

"Hi, Leyla," Detective Pearson says. She follows it up with her name as she slowly inches closer to me. There's a warmth in the chocolate pools of her eyes. She shakes my hand.

Detective Gomez has a kind face too, but when he introduces himself and tries to shake my hand as well, I flinch, instinctively recoiling into the couch cushions. I can't let him touch me, and I have no idea why. He's not Arash. But he doesn't mention my response, just pulls his arm back letting it drop to his side, in one slow swoop, without batting an eye.

I'm safe.

I find myself repeating this phrase continuously as they take seats across from me on two chairs Baba has dragged over from the dining room table. The previous night plays out in my head as they ask me to divulge all the details again, like a movie reel on repeat for all my audience to see.

"May we record this?" Detective Pearson says.

I nod my consent.

Another forty-five minutes of grueling questions take place. I'm forced to repeat much of what I'd already told the police officer the night before.

"Why didn't you leave?" Detective Pearson asks.

The one question that no one has mentioned, yet I've asked myself a million times already. Because I didn't want to ruin the night for my friends. Because I still thought running into him was coincidence. Because I had no idea what he was actually capable of.

"I don't know."

"Did you feel threatened when he approached you on the dance floor?" Detective Gomez says.

"Yes."

"But not enough to leave?" he asks.

"Wait. Surely, detectives, you aren't suggesting this was my daughter's fault?" Baba voice sharply cuts through the room. His nostrils flare with anger, his breaths becoming more labored.

Maman reaches out and grabs his hand, in a calming effort.

"They aren't, Ali *jan*," she says.

"No, of course not, Mr. Amini. I apologize if that's how it sounded," Detective Gomez confirms. "Leyla, I wasn't suggesting anything of that nature."

"I know." I blame myself whether or not that's what the detectives meant.

"We've viewed the camera footage from the club. We've confirmed that Arash was there last night, and that he followed you into the bathroom," Detective Gomez says. "We're just trying to establish Arash's character and get a better understanding of the night's events. That's all."

I nod.

"I think we have enough for now," Detective Pearson adds. "Is there anything else you can remember that you want to tell us?" The motherly look in her eyes is so natural I find myself wondering if she has any children or if this line of business has convinced her the world is too ugly.

"No."

"Okay." She smiles. "We will be in touch."

The detectives rise in unison and Baba walks them to the door. They are halfway through the doorway when I suddenly remember the missing panties.

"Oh, wait!"

The detectives turn and face me, expectantly. Baba and Maman are both watching closely. Oddly, the idea that I lost my underwear somewhere in the struggle feels horribly embarrassing. You'd think after all the information I've shared thus far, this would be a minor blip in the plethora of humiliating details.

"I lost my panties." I drop my gaze.

"At the club?" Detective Pearson asks.

"Yes," I whisper.

"Okay, thank you for letting us know. We'll look into it."

I nod, my gaze fixed on the floor. I can't look at her. My throat burns with shame and I'm not even sure why. *Damn roller coaster ride.*

Baba shuts the door behind them. Before he or Maman has a chance to say anything else, I beat them to it.

"I'm going to go lie down," I say, heading to my room. I'm spent. And I have no desire for further questioning today.

* * *

I sit on a lounge chair, trying to read a book for an hour. Instead, I end up staring at the petals of Maman's Gerber daisies hypnotically swaying in the breeze, like little feet tap-dancing in the wind. I just like the quiet. All the questioning and recalling has left me winded. The heaviness of my family's gaze is more than I can bear. Out here, lost in the sounds of nature, I can turn my mind off, if only for a little while.

I tense when I hear the back door open; my new response to the unexpected.

"Hey," Sara says as she comes around and sits on the chair beside me.

"Hi," I reply. I smile warily, the effort sending a wave of achiness across my cheek.

Maziar steps around her and sits on the arm of her chair. I have to resist the urge to turn away, embarrassed by the way I look. Bruised and battered, accented by a lovely pair of worn out Victoria Secret sweats.

"Hey," he says. His smile is stretched across his face, but his expression is apprehensive. For a moment, I wonder if he feels the urge to flinch as well. "How are you feeling?"

"Well, I've seen better days," I reply, with a half chuckle. My attempt at lightening the mood sounds strained and awkward.

Maziar gives me a sad courtesy laugh, and worry crinkles the edges of Sara's eyes. I have to look away, the pity in their expressions all too familiar this week.

"Is there anything we can do?" Maziar asks, reaching out and squeezing my arm.

I breathe in sharply, shutting my eyes. My first instinct is to pull away, physical contact making me uncomfortable. Maziar retracts his hand.

"I'm sorry," I say as I exhale. "I've just been having a tough time. It's not you."

I leave out the explanation that each time someone touches me I'm reminded of Arash's fingers on my body.

"No, don't be sorry," Maziar says, his voice low and soothing, mimicking his understanding.

"Thanks." I shake my head side to side, trying to physically expel thoughts of Arash. "So, what are you guys up to today?" I ask, with a perkier tone.

"Just some errands. We're going to lunch and wanted to see if you want to come along?" Sara says, hopeful.

"Thanks, but I think I'm going to stay in. Not in the going out mood, if you know what I mean." I sweep my hand across the front of my face as if it's artwork on exhibit. "Too many questions, you know?"

"Yeah," Sara replies. "So in a few days then?"

"Sure." I have no real intention of going out with anyone. But it's easier to be compliant.

They hang out for another hour, making small talk, trying to avoid the hovering monster on the patio. No questions or comments that could remind me of Arash. What they don't know is that no matter what they try to distract me with, he weasels his way into each moment. The undercurrent of fear is continuously interrupted by surges of anger when I think about his ability to make me feel helpless, despite his absence. He's taken my right to feel safe. And I hate him for it.

It will get better; I must believe that. I pray the memory of his touch fades until I can't remember every detail of his face while he taunted me. I hope for a night when he isn't reflected in my dreams.

I indulge my friends, plastering on a smile despite the pain it brings, acting as though there's nothing more interesting than their most recent Crate and Barrel excursion. Focusing on creating the perfect apartment is easier than focusing on the muscles that ache each time I move.

Once they leave, I'm exhausted, making my way back to my

bedroom. I pull the shades, the sunlight a contradiction to the heaviness I feel. I crawl beneath the covers, the weight of the comforter providing a false sense of security. When I was little, it created a shield against the demons of the night, much like it's doing now. I pull them up over my head, allowing myself to drift into a fitful sleep.

When the darkness comes for me, I go willingly.

CHAPTER NINETEEN

Three days. That's how long it takes. Seventy-two hours until my story has made Iranian headlines amongst the community. Although my camp tries to keep it quiet, spectators at the scene created their own stories around my blood-stained face and torn clothing, like a bad game of telephone.

The phone rings nonstop, my parents having to thwart off inquiries from concerned friends. Everyone seems to be out for the scoop, like persistent reporters trying to get an exclusive. All types of explanations evolve. I was attacked in the women's bathroom. A fistfight with a girl over a guy I barely knew. Committing murder and currently being smuggled into Canada. That one is my favorite.

I just hole myself up in the house, a prison of my own making. Maman tries to coerce me into going to the store with her; Baba tries to get me to go on a walk. The furthest I make it is my backyard. Surrounded by an eight-foot cinder block wall, I don't have to worry about an attacker finding me here.

I know I'll need to face the real world soon. I've requested a week off from work, stating a "family emergency" with little else in the arena of details. It's a bit sticky, considering I just started, but I refuse to give my boss the gory play-by-play. The fewer people I need to share my story with, the better.

The detectives are still looking for Arash. His apartment is empty; his parents' home is as well. He hasn't been to work. He's left his cell phone and credit cards behind, making it difficult to track him. At least that's what they tell Baba, who stands vigilant at the phone, waiting on news that he's been captured. Not sure our incident justifies life without parole, but Baba sure hopes so.

My dad looks ragged and aged in just a few days. His eyebrows are pulled in tight and the wrinkles at the edges of his eyes are deeper now. There's a permanent scowl on his face. He rarely leaves the living room, constantly glancing at the phone every few minutes, as if it will ring out of sheer will. Maman says he's been having nightmares. Graphic ones, which include murder and Arash.

Until he's in police custody, I don't think any of us will be able to exhale. It's like we're all holding our breath, just waiting. I know he won't stay locked up, not initially, but just to know his location has been established will make me less anxious. Arash has the uncanny way of finding me. I won't leave my house. I can't risk it. Plus, there's the issue of how I look.

The remnants of Arash's attack became evident within the first twenty-four hours, popping up in the form of bruises. With the amount of adrenaline pumping, I hadn't felt any of them at the time they occurred, but by the next morning, I felt, and looked, like I'd been run over by a truck.

The bruise on my face has deepened, making it hard to show my expressions without flinching from the pain. In addition, I have bruises across my ribs, my right shoulder, and lower spine. It's tough to move. Turning to my right has become damn near impossible, knocking the wind out of me each time I try. My neck is sore and tender too, but thankfully devoid of any evidence of our struggle.

"You can't stay locked in the house forever, *azizam*," Maman says.

"I know that, Maman." I try desperately not to roll my eyes at her. "It's only been a few days! And have you missed my face? It's black and blue. I can barely walk from all the bruises. It's embarrassing!"

"Is that the only reason?" Maman doesn't look convinced.

No, he's still out there and he can find me. "Yes," I say.

Maman continues to blame herself for setting me up with Arash, despite how much we all tell her it isn't her fault. She sees the repercussions of that one act displayed all over me, and I know it's killing her. Her emotions teeter between despair and rage on a momentary basis.

I can hear her murmuring with Baba in the living room, at night when they think I've gone to bed. Her sobs carry through the walls, muffled but identifiable. I imagine Baba pulling her close as he wraps her up in his big, strong embrace, reminding her that I'm okay. It makes me happy to know they have each other.

Maman wants to believe me when I tell her it's just vanity keeping me locked up inside. But Baba sees right through me.

"*Dokhtaram*, everything is going to be okay," he says.

Tears suddenly spring to my eyes. My dad has a way of saying just the right things to open the floodgates I fight to keep closed.

I turn so Maman can't see my expression, unable to hold up the façade while Baba tears holes through my defenses with his keen ability to read me. He's aware I have more scars than just the black and blue patches that mark my skin.

I stride over to the door, trying to make a point, as I reach out and grab its handle. I allow myself a fraction of a second to hesitate, then pull it open, gliding out onto the steps.

It's just the front yard. I'm safe.

There are a pair of Adirondack chairs, in matching green, with a small table to my left. I nonchalantly sashay over to them and take a seat, turning to flash my parents a big smile.

"See, I'm fine," I say. "I'll be good as new as soon as these bruises fade, okay?"

Maman exhales a sigh of relief. The short distance I've made it into public is apparently a small win. She grins in response.

"I'll get some *chayee* and join you." She turns and heads back into the house.

Baba eyes me for another moment before heading in behind her. There's an air of sadness about him, despite his best attempt at covering it up. It's been permanently etched in his features for days. I wish he'd believe my act along with Maman because I hate seeing him this way.

I watch his back disappear into the house and find myself alone, out in the open, for the first time in days. Panic begins to settle in, creeping slowly up my sides until I can feel its fingers wrapped around my throat. I inhale, filling my lungs with oxygen as I count to five, then push the air meticulously through my lips, slowing it down even further on the exit. A few breaths later, my muscles respond as they loosen down my limbs.

I lean my head back on the seat, feeling the hard wood against my tender skull. I close my eyes and focus on the smooth solid surface digging into my neck. I try to shut out the noise around me. The birds chirping, the kids playing, all too much for my frayed senses. It actually seems to be working, until I hear the familiar rumble of an engine. It gets louder, nearing the house.

My eyes snap open, my body hitching forward, perched on the balls of my feet, ready to bolt to the door. I whip my head left then right trying to find the source of the noise. Suddenly, a silver mustang comes into view. The smooth sleek exterior reminds me of a model car I bought once for my cousin from Toys-R-Us for his birthday.

The sun is bouncing off of the hood, making it hard to see the driver behind its glare. I hold my breath as it gets closer, craning my neck to watch. I'm stuck in some sort of cruel mirage as the car pulls up in front of my house. I don't move, stuck to my seat, staring in disbelief.

The door swings open and Ben steps out. His blue eyes are locked on my face and I unconsciously move my hand up trying to hide my bruises. He approaches me in three quick strides, more like he's gliding on water than walking. I don't believe it; I must have conjured him up in my desperation to feel something other than the cold numbness that's been embedded in my veins for days.

He drops down onto the grass in front of me, looking deep into my eyes. Silently, he strips me of my armor, taking me apart piece by piece. Once he's done, there's nothing left but the raw truth.

"Oh, baby," he says, as he reaches out and gently moves my hand, running his thumb across my cheek. He traces the bruise that's marred my face.

His voice feels like a fingers clenched tightly around my heart. It rips me open, breaking the dam inside of me, the one I've built to trap Arash behind. A flood of emotions comes pouring to the surface and the fear and devastation I've struggled to lock away, rushes through me. I drop my head in my hands.

He reaches out and pulls me into him, trying to save me from a war he wasn't there for with a demon he barely knows. I let him hold me, allowing myself to grab hold of the comfort he provides. I know he can't fix this. He doesn't have the magic needed to erase the horrid memories of the other night, or to put my pieces back together again. I only have the power to do that. And I know I will. It'll just take some time.

Maman clears her throat, letting us know she's standing behind us. Ben tries to pull away, but I knot my fists into his shirt, silently begging him to stay close to me. His familiar scent, the feel of his hand on the small of my back, the way his chin brushes across the crown of my head, are all reminders of a better time. I'm desperate to recall those moments.

He leaves one arm wrapped around me as he pulls us both up together. I don't let go, still nuzzled against his shoulder, when he reaches out and greets Maman.

"Hi, Simeen, *khanoom*," he says.

His broken Farsi makes me happy. I know he learned it from Sara, but none of that matters anymore. He's here, holding *me*, when I need him the most. Their past is no longer important.

"Hello, Ben," Maman replies.

I pull my head away from him so I can see her expression. I'm expecting irritation, but instead, I find wonderment. She's eyeing me quizzically, and I just smile, linking my arm around Ben's waist.

I don't know what any of this means. I don't know if Ben's sudden appearance or show of affection is anything more than friendly concern. What I do know, is that for the first time in days, there's a warmth replacing the frigid cold that's claimed me. And I don't want it to end.

"Would you like some *chayee*, Ben?" Maman asks politely.

"I'd love some," he replies, flashing her his dimples.

She approaches us with a tray balanced expertly on one hand. She places both cups down on the small round table between the chairs, along with a box of chocolate-covered almonds she'd brought out to share with me. She smiles, a strange relief taking over her features. It seems foreign in contrast to the constant worry she's worn all week.

"Enjoy," she says. "The weather out here is beautiful today." She softly cups my cheek before heading back inside, leaving Ben and me on the lawn. Her reaction is baffling. Maman seemed comforted that I was wrapped up in Ben's arms, happy almost.

"Let's sit down," he says, breaking me from my thoughts.

He guides us closer to the chairs and takes a seat. A cold breeze replaces his body and disappointment invades my heart at his departure. I hug my chest, sheltering myself from the sudden temperature change. But when I sit down beside him, he reaches out and gently pries my arm away, nestling my hand in his.

He's staring at me, his blue eyes fierce as he fights to keep his expression steady. I feel the weight of his words balancing on the edge of his tongue, trying to find a voice. They don't come; his turmoil plainly visible.

"How are you even here?" I ask. Coincidence seems impossible, and I wonder if news has spread further than I'd realized. I become nauseous with the possibility that my nightmare has spread through various zip codes.

"Maziar called me," he says.

I stare at him, wondering if I've heard him correctly. Maziar, his archnemesis, called him? That doesn't make any sense.

"What?" I reply. "He called you?"

"Yeah," Ben says.

He smiles at my confusion. The edges of his eyes crinkle, creating a familiar web of lines. It feels like a lifetime ago, he and I together, tangled beneath the sheets as I reached out and ran my fingers over the tiny wrinkles.

"What did he say?"

"He told me what happened and that I needed to come see you. He was worried about you. Said you seemed pretty shook up."

"Oh." I suddenly feel despondent, realizing that his visit is only at Maziar's insistence.

I look away, unable to hold his gaze any longer. I want to hide the tears that have filled my eyes at his admission. *Damn these emotions and their horrible timing!*

"Hey," he says, resting his fingers beneath my chin and gently forcing me to face him. "Do you really think he needed to tell me to come see you? I would have come either way," he says, reading my mind.

I fight to pinched back the tears, but a lone droplet rolls slowly down my cheek. He reaches out and brushes it away.

"You okay, Leyla?" he asks.

"Yeah, I'm fine," I say. "I have my moments." I smile shakily. "But overall I'm good."

I can tell he doesn't believe me, but he won't push. He leans back in his chair, still holding my hand.

We sit in the quiet of the morning, listening to the breeze gently rustling the leaves overhead and the birds chirping their songs. The distant sound of children playing makes me smile. My world has turned upside down, but the world itself hasn't. It's business as usual around me and I find it reassuring. Despite not feeling normal at the moment, I can see it hovering in the horizon, waiting until I'm ready. It gives me hope.

"What happened?" he asks. His voice is quiet but it cuts through the silence like a blade.

My stomach rolls with his question, knowing I need to answer, but desperate not to. I don't want to relive it, can't hash out the details and watch as Ben's expression changes, despite his best efforts. I don't want to see him feel sorry for me, see that hint of pity in his eyes that's visible in the eyes of my family. But when I turn to look at him, the familiarity in his features reminds me of the safe haven he once was.

I find myself searching for the right words as the story of my attack flows out of me like the waves of the ocean, both smooth and calm, but rough and choppy. He doesn't say anything, just listens until I'm finished.

"That stupid son of a bitch! I'm going to fucking kill him," he says. His face is flushed with anger.

"They haven't found him," I add, my voice low. I scan the street, searching for Arash, realizing I've been sitting here too long, distracted. He could be lurking in a corner watching us. A shiver rolls down my spine.

"It doesn't matter. I'm not going to let him get near you," Ben says. The confidence in his voice gives me pause. It's so big, it stretches across the length of the lawn. I almost believe him. "I mean it, Leyla. He isn't going to get near you."

I love his need to protect me. It's ferocious and uncompromising. It reminds me of Raha. The only two people who have been able to make me feel safe, in the past few days.

The attack has left me weary and doubtful of men, worried something is wrong with my radar. I blame myself for what happened. I've heard it all: something is wrong with Arash, not you. This isn't your fault, how could you have known? But the truth is, there was a part of me that did know. Maybe I didn't realize how messed up he really was, but I knew something was off. I chose to push it aside, believing I was being dramatic. I completely disregarded the blaring alarms, morphing into his prey. Who knows what would have happened if I'd paid closer attention to my intuition? Maybe if I'd broken it off earlier, he wouldn't have become so obsessed with me.

With Ben, though, the fear of the unknown, or the idea that I've missed something terribly critical, doesn't exist. I find it surprising that I don't feel the need to question my certainty about him. In fact, his confidence and calm demeanor helps me find my own peace. I'm comfortable in my skin—the bruised pieces of me that are visible to the eye, as well as those that are not. For one fleeting second, I allow myself to believe that even in the ugliest of moments, something beautiful can still emerge.

"Why are you here?" I ask him again.

"What do you mean? I wanted to make sure you were okay," he answers.

"Is that all?" I don't have time for misplaced hopes and unanswered questions. Not today. Not when I'm still trying to piece myself together.

"No," he says. "I needed to see you."

Five little words crack open the door letting light into the dark. I exhale at the budding hope blooming in my chest.

"Why?" I ask.

He doesn't answer right away. But the lines deepen across his forehead and my heart picks up pace. I feel like we're balancing on the edge of a cliff.

"What do you want me to say?" he finally says.

He looks flustered and slightly frustrated. Not the reaction I was hoping for. In an attempt to preserve the moment, I decide I need to be honest. He looks away, flicking a small piece of fuzz off his pant leg.

"I made a mistake," I begin, "when I let my insecurities get in the way of what we had."

"Leyla, we don't need to do this right now," he says.

"Yes, we do. I've realized in the last few days that some things shouldn't go unsaid. Some feelings demand attention, even if we don't want to give it to them. I made a mistake," I repeat. "I should never have doubted you. And because I did, I lost you."

He's still staring at his pants.

"Ben, look at me. Please," I urge. When our eyes meet, a soft current of nostalgia flows through me. "I know I messed up. I just need you to know that I'm sorry. I really wish I could take it all back."

I try to swallow down the knot lodged in my throat. I can't cry, can't make him feel sorry for me. I don't want his pity.

"A lot has happened to you," he says. "And I don't really know where we're heading. But we don't need to figure it all out at this very second. I need to make sure you're okay, Leyla. That's all that matters to me right now."

As I stare into Ben's beautiful blue eyes, I know it would be easy to lose myself in him. He could erase the past week from my mind, if only for the moment. But what would that help? I can't ignore what's happened to me. I know I need to deal with it so I can truly mend.

Maybe how I feel about Ben right now is because of the attack or maybe it has nothing to do with the aftermath. Maybe the hope I feel for a future between us precedes anything that has to do with Arash. But if I'm honest with myself, I won't know the truth of it until I face this experience head on.

"Okay," I say, giving Ben a smile.

"Good." He grins, his dimples defined marvelously, as usual. He reaches over and hands me a cup of *chayee* and takes one for himself, leaning back in his seat. Then, with his free hand, he reaches out and grabs mine again. We sit side by side for a long time, quietly enjoying the sounds of life bustling around us. I absorb the warmth of the sun, allowing it to thaw my frozen limbs, taking with it the tiny icicles lodged in my heart.

* * *

"You're not mad?" Sara asks. Her eyes are scrunched together like she's bracing herself for a beating. I laugh.

"No, I'm not. I've told you that a million times already!" I'm leaning back on the couch, watching Baba plant a small lemon tree through the window. He seems calm and at ease from this distance.

"Maziar was just trying to help," Sara adds.

"I know," I reply, hoping it eases the tension out of her shoulders.

Despite my continuous protests about being okay, everyone tiptoes around like I'm made of glass, about to break at the slightest pressure. Arash still haunts me in my dreams, but he's losing his hold on my waking hours. I've realized I'm surrounded by people that love me. He can't get to me in here. He'd be an idiot if he tried. Between Baba, Raha, and Ben, he doesn't stand a chance, no matter how crazy he is.

"I can't believe Maziar is the one who called Ben," I say.

I'm still staring at my father crouched over in the dirt. The past week has taken its toll on him, his frame appearing smaller somehow. Arash has aged him.

"I know. He was worried you'd be so pissed. But after we came over and you didn't want to leave the house, Maziar was really worried about you. I know he seems like an ass sometimes, but he cares. He saw how shook up you were. And the bruises didn't help."

I unconsciously touch my face. The purple has faded into a lavender with a dull yellow border. A lot less noticeable if I put makeup over it.

"We debated all day on whether we should try to get a hold of Ben. I said no, but it was Maziar who insisted. He thought that if the tables were turned, he'd want someone to let him know. He finally convinced me, so I got Ben's number from Setie," Sara explains.

"Poor Setie," I say, laughing. "She must think we're all stalkers, constantly asking for information about Ben."

"She wasn't easy to convince," Sara says. She looks down at the couch and pulls on the edge of a frayed string, falling silent.

"What is it, Sara?" I ask, my stomach twisting in knots.

"We had to tell her what happened before she agreed to give us his number. She's really protective of Ben," she whispers. "I'm so sorry, Leyla. I know you didn't want anyone to know, but we weren't sure what else to do." She gnaws on her bottom lip.

I reach out and put my hand on her knee.

"It's okay, Sara. Judging from the phone ringing off the hook, I doubt we'll be able to keep a lid on this very long. It's almost better we tell everyone the truth. Some of the stories people are hearing are pretty ridiculous."

Despite the fact that my news is being broadcast throughout the community, I feel peaceful today. Maybe it's the fact that I'm surrounded by the people who matter the most, the ones who would do anything to help me. Or maybe it's just time. Either way, I feel okay right now. All I can do is focus on the present. Too much worrying about the future causes a panic attack.

As if the anxiety gods hear me, the phone rings. The sound fills the room like a blaring fire alarm. Raha picks it up from the kitchen, where she's helping Maman with lunch.

"Yes, she's here. Please hold." She's walking toward me her eyebrows knit tightly together, her lips stretched down in a frown. She pushes the receiver into my hand. "It's the detective."

"Hello?" My voice comes out shaky.

"Hi, Miss Amini, this is Detective Pearson."

"Hi, Detective," I say.

"The suspect is in custody." She pauses, letting her words sink in. *Suspect. Custody.* "We need you to come down to the station for some further questioning."

Questioning? Didn't I already explain the night in more details than I cared to relive?

"I told you guys everything already," I say in protest.

"New details have been brought to light, and we just have a few more questions for you."

I'm frozen silent as I listen to the words so readily leaving the detective's lips. *New development?* They come with ease, as if they don't hold the weight of my world in them. I feel an irrational fear that maybe Arash has somehow convinced them that this entire situation is my fault. The air catches in my throat at the prospect of being found guilty somehow.

"Miss Amini, are you still there?"

"Yes...yes, I'm here."

"Leyla," she says, using my first name. Her tone has dropped; it's more soothing and empathetic than the all-business one she started off with. "There's nothing for you to be worried about. We just have some questions, nothing more."

I don't want to go, don't want to deal with Arash and the other night any longer. For the first time in days, I haven't felt like crawling out of my skin every second.

I finish the call and hang up. My hands are shaking so bad, Raha has to pry the receiver out from between my fingers. She gives it to Maman, who is now standing beside her. A worried expression is painted on both their faces. I try, but can't get any words out. They're caught in my throat, disappearing between my vocal cords. I thought I'd be happy to know he'd been caught.

Deep inside, there's a part of me that's so sad for the role I'm playing in ruining his life. He's a monster and deserves what's coming to him, I know that. But I can't help think I've somehow propelled the inevitable by coming forward. It's almost as if I feel guilty. The emotion is so contradictory to the situation. It makes little sense.

Our silent powwow has alerted Baba that something is wrong, because I can hear the backdoor swing shut and his long purposeful strides as he makes his way into the room. He's frantically wiping dirt across the front of his gardening pants, leaving smeared mud stain patterns along the fabric. It reminds me of the blood swirled across my dress. My stomach lurches.

"What's happened?" Baba asks, stepping up beside Maman. She turns to him, her expression a complicated web of lines and I wonder if she's dealing with a conundrum of emotions too.

"They found him," I say. "They want me to go down there. They have more questions. Something about a new development in the case." My voice is as uncertain as I feel.

"Okay," Baba says. "Let me change and we'll go."

"I'll come with you," Maman adds.

"No," I blurt out, gaining a wince from her in return. "I love you and I appreciate that you want to come with me. But I'll be too worried about how you're feeling. I can't focus on both of us when I have to deal with this. I'm sorry. But Sara will stay here with you so you're not alone." I look at Sara for confirmation.

"Of course I will." She walks up to Maman and puts her arm around her. "We'll wait together."

"Maybe you should call Ben and have him go with you too," Maman suddenly says.

The room falls silent, stunned by Maman's suggestion. Did she willingly tell me to include Ben? I whip my head toward Baba, waiting for him to protest, but instead he just smiles.

"Ben is a good man," he says.

My mouth drops open in disbelief. I'm certain I'm stuck in some alternate universe.

"You know what I've realized this past week?" Baba continues. "Everyone's past has something in it. What happened to you isn't going to define you, *dokhtaram*. And just like your past doesn't define you, his shouldn't either. We shouldn't have judged him just because he was with Sara before. She wasn't for him."

"*Har kesi ghestmaty dareh, ghesmatesh ba toh bood*," Maman adds. *Everyone has a destiny and his destiny led him to you.*

"We're just friends," I say.

"I don't think so." Baba smiles knowingly. "I can see how he feels about you when he looks at you. I was a young man once; I remember what it means to be that in love. I'm glad you have him. Especially right now."

"He's a good support for you, *azizam*," Maman adds.

I always believed that things happened for a reason. Maybe I've endured the unimaginable as a pathway used by the universe to bring Ben and me together again. A tool to clear the veil of social standards from my parents' eyes.

It would be so easy to allow Ben to shoulder some of this burden, walking beside me on the path that appears to have no end. But I can't. I need be certain that what we have is based on a past before all of this. That what we feel for one another is not fabricated by the fibers of this cataclysmic event. When he looks at me, I don't see the reflection of a victim in his eyes like I do with everyone else. I just see me. So I can't let him be my strength, I need to find my own. I need to battle my demon without his help.

"No," I say. "I need to do this by myself."

I smile up at Maman, grateful that she's found a way to accept Ben. I wish the circumstances were different for the change in her, but regardless, it makes me happy. I turn to Raha.

"You want to go for a ride?" I ask. I can do this without Ben, but I can't do this without her.

"Absolutely," she says. Her fierceness emanates off of her like the hot rays of the sun. I absorb it, hoping it provides me with force of my own.

"Let's go," Baba adds, grabbing his keys and kissing Maman on the head. Like the Tazmanian Devil, he's already changed and ready to leave. She reaches out and squeezes his arm. A loving exchange occurs in the words they don't speak. Their consistency makes my pulse slow.

"Come on," Raha says, coming up beside me. She grabs my hand in hers and looks me straight in the eye. "You can do this."

My limbs shake and my nerves are unhinged. But despite my body's betrayal, I believe her.

I can do this.

* * *

I walk toward the double doors of the police station with lead in place of my legs. I feel like I'm dragging my body to a guillotine, except I'm not the one getting my head cut off. I'm the executioner. The thought weighs heavily on my mind, pushing me into the concrete beneath the soles of my feet.

Baba reaches out and grabs the metal handle, swinging the door open. He holds it, standing aside for Raha and I to pass through. My sister squeezes my hand, still held firmly between hers, and whispers, "You can do this." *Keep it coming, I need it.*

I try to hang onto her words, using them as a shield to protect me from my own fear. It's not working, my body vibrating with apprehension. Raha and Baba flank me, two soldiers in this war, blindly moving forward, propelled by their need to protect me.

As we walk down the hall toward the front desk, I can see three blue-clad men behind the counter, busily going about their business. The closer to them we get, the harder it feels to breathe. *I can do this. I'm safe. I can do this.* I repeat my mantra, a life vest as the sea crashes around me. *I can do this.*

There are dark brown chairs lining the wall directly across from the front desk. Their leather is worn and faded, no doubt from years of sitting idly by while observing the lives that have changed in here. Baba leads me over to them and I take a seat, waiting. Raha sits beside me. Her foot immediately begins to tap in quick succession against the linoleum floor. The only indication of the fury she wants to unleash on an Arash she can't see. Baba walks up to the officers.

"Leyla Amini is here to see Detectives Pearson and Gomez," he says.

"Okay, sir. Have a seat and they will be with you shortly."

A door to an office directly behind the front desk swings open and out steps Detective Gomez. He's accompanied by a young woman, close in age to myself. She has long black hair extending down to her waist. Its thick and glossy coat shines beneath the halogen lights. Her eyes are dark obsidian gems with amber accents, nestled inside her smooth olive skin. Worry lines fan out from their edges, and what I imagine are normally full, exotic lips, are pursed together in a dissatisfied pucker. Detective Gomez is speaking to her in hushed tones, his hand resting gently on the side of her arm. Her gaze is set on the floor as she nods every few seconds at his words. He wears a serene expression, his calm demeanor clashing against hers.

I have the irrational urge to grab her arm as he walks her toward the exit, but I'm stopped short when our eyes meet. The room goes still, all the voices hushed into oblivion. We lock gazes and an expression of understanding crosses her features, leaving me confused. I can feel a deep-rooted sadness in her that makes my heart clench in response. Before I have a chance to say anything, to ask her if I know her, the moment is gone. She redirects her path to the door, taking quick strides to get out of the station. She appears to feel as trapped within its four walls as I do.

"Leyla?" Detective Gomez says, breaking me away from my thoughts.

"Who was that?" I ask.

"I'm not at liberty to say," he answers, smiling kindly at me. "But if you're ready?" He points toward the door he just came out of with the mystery girl.

"Okay."

I stand hesitantly, wanting nothing more than to run back to the car. I feel Baba's hand resting on the small of my back as he gently pushes me alongside him toward the office. Raha is a few steps in front of me, walking beside the detective. She glances over her shoulder and gives me a reassuring nod. I just try to put one foot in front of the other.

Detective Gomez pushes the door to the office open and I hold my breath. Despite its being impossible, I expect to find Arash inside. Instead, a small room with two desks appears. Detective Pearson is standing beside one.

"Hello, Mr. Amini. Miss Amini," she says. "Are you ready?"

"For what? What am I doing here?"

Detective Pearson doesn't answer me. Instead, she looks at my family and says, "I'm sorry, but we're going to need you guys to wait outside, if that's okay?" The inflection of her voice lifts at the end of her sentence like she's posing a question, but there's no mistaking it's a demand.

Baba goes to protest, but I place my hand on his arm.

"It's okay. I'll be fine," I urge. "I promise."

His brow furrows and the wrinkles around his eyes deepen, but he nods and steps toward the door.

"We'll be outside if you need us," Raha says, eyeing the detectives to let them know she won't be far. As if I need to fear the two officers standing before me. The real monster is in custody somewhere nearby. That thought is what makes me shiver.

Once they've left the room, Detective Gomez points to one of the chairs. "Have a seat, Leyla."

I sit down, fidgeting as I try to get comfortable. I finally give up, knowing it won't happen. My nerves are firing off, the adrenaline coursing through my veins. I'm on the defensive, despite being in for questioning on a crime I didn't commit.

"What is this all about?" I ask. "I told you everything that happened that night."

A silent exchange occurs between the detectives, making me even more uneasy.

"What is this new development?" I demand.

"We just need to ask you a few more questions regarding your time with Arash, including prior to the attack. Is that okay?"

I nod, obvious they won't be answering me. *What the hell is going on?*

Thoughts are reeling through my mind. A part of me is so terrified I'll find out that Arash is an even bigger monster than I had previously thought.

A barrage of questions commences. When did we meet? Was there any strange behavior I noticed? Did Arash ever say anything that would indicate that he could be dangerous? Were there any evenings that he'd disappear for long periods of time without me being able to get a hold of him? If so, when?

"During the incident, did the suspect seem agitated or at ease? Did he apologize?" Detective Pearson asks.

"No, he didn't apologize. Matter of fact, he seemed excited and very comfortable." The image of Arash pressed against me makes my insides clench and I get queasy.

"Is there anything else you can remember? Something he may have said that stands out or seems odd?" Detective Gomez says.

Suddenly I'm back in the bathroom, pushing against the weight of Arash's body, as I pray for an opening to get away. I remember the heat of his breath as he leans in and whispers in my ear.

"You're going to realize you made a big mistake."

"Is that something he said?" Detective Gomez asks.

"Yes. He said it to me the night we broke up and then again in the bathroom." A shiver runs the length of me. Goosebumps accompany the nausea.

I can see Arash clearly in my mind. The smirk he wore tore the strength from my hands, making me feel helpless. Suddenly, the next words that left his mouth, crash into me.

"He also mentioned them." I stare at the detectives wide-eyed, feeling the blood drain from my face. *Are there more? How did I not remember this before?*

"Them?" Detective Pearson says.

"Yes, he kept referring to 'them.' That they all realized their mistakes like I would."

Another covert expression passes between the two detectives.

"Are there other victims?" I ask. If I were standing, I'd be swaying on my feet with desperation. I grasp the arm of my chair, my knuckles white with the force.

"We aren't at liberty to discuss any further details at the moment. Thank you for coming in, Leyla. The information you provided has been very useful. We'll be in touch."

The detectives reach out to shake my hand, shutting me down. It's very clear they won't be divulging any further details today. Detective Gomez strolls alongside me as he takes me to the brown leather seats where Baba and Raha are sitting, heads bent close, speaking in hushed tones.

My mind is flooded with images of Arash. Bits and pieces of conversations fly at me like ninja stars, narrowly missing my head. Nothing has been confirmed, but my gut is confident there's more to this "case" than the detectives are willing to let on.

"You okay?" Raha asks. The concern is written in lines across her forehead.

"I'm fine," I say. "Can we go home?"

"Of course."

I look at Baba as he watches me over Raha's shoulder. He smiles, a gentleness in his expression that makes my heart ache to be near him. I step around her and into my father's arms. He holds me, kissing the crown of my head.

"*Bereem khooneh,* Baba," I beg. *Let's go home.*

"Okay, *dokhtaram,*" he says. "Are we done here, detectives?"

"Yes, we are," Detective Gomez says. "Thanks for coming in. We'll be in touch."

Baba leads me to the exit with Raha falling in step beside us.

My two protectors stand on either side of me, their heads whipping back and forth, searching for a predator. There aren't any left out here looking for me. Not today. I've only been prey once, and the commander of that nightmare is sitting behind a row of steel bars. For today anyway.

CHAPTER TWENTY

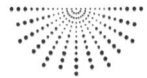

I sit in my office, staring blankly out the glass wall facing into the law firm. The staff moves about in rhythmic waves, choreographed in their day to day tasks. Some are making their way from one end of the hall to the other, arms piled high with files. Others sit at their cubicles, eyes focused on their computer screens, intently tapping away on their keyboards.

The hustle and bustle usually reminds me of a symphony, the muted sounds carried into the room like instruments playing in harmony. On normal days, it motivates me, giving me the encouragement I need to keep up with the music. But today, it's the source of panic and a splitting head ache. I lean back in the plush leather seat massaging the bridge of my nose, trying to push away the pressure settled there.

It's my official first day back to work. A little over a week since the "incident." That's what I'm calling it now because it sounds better in my head. "Attack" or "attempted sexual assault" seem too life-altering and less manageable.

The bruises on my face have faded enough that a good bottle of full-coverage makeup has melted them away into the background of my skin. From a close distance their outlines are still discernible, but I have no desire to allow anyone that far into my personal space. My battered body still shows more obvious remnants of Arash's betrayal, but they are conveniently covered by the mint green blouse and black trousers I put on this morning. Nonetheless, I've checked myself in the full length mirror of the bathroom and reapplied makeup twice already, and it's not even noon.

My gaze turns toward the files piled on my desk. I run my finger across the edge, the accordion of manila paper caressing my fingertips. I know I should open one up and get something done, but I have zero motivation in the arena of work. I can't read through the details of other people's "incidents" right now. Despite not being exactly like my own, they've been wronged somehow too, some betrayed by people they trusted.

Suddenly my door swings open, whipping my head up from the desk. James, a senior attorney who's assigned himself as a mentor of sorts, comes strolling in.

"Hey, kid. How you doing?" he asks.

He's in his fifties, not old enough to be my father, but yet he molds into the role nicely. There's a kindness about him that reminds me so much of Baba it creates a lump in my throat. The wrinkles that fan across the edges of his eyes and the worry lines on his forehead make it tough to speak. I cough in a futile attempt to clear my throat and push back the tears.

"I'm good," I answer. I smile, trying to sell it. "How are you, James?"

"How's everything with your family? Is everything okay?" he says, completely ignoring my attempt at redirecting the focus of the conversation.

I took time off under the pretense of a family emergency, the details ambiguous. I've been asked questions by those I've run into when I dare to leave my office, but I've kept the responses vague and indirect. Rumors have already formed in my absence, much like in any office scenario. I've avoided investigating the stories, uninterested in what they all might think. However, James is different.

"Yeah, everything is okay," I say.

He eyes me carefully from the door and judging from the way his brows pinch tightly together, he doesn't believe me. "What happened?" he finally asks.

I stare at him dumbfounded, my brain unable to come up with a viable response fast enough. I should be better at this acting thing, putting on a happy face and seeming like I'm okay. I've been doing it all week. But in this moment, I can't. So instead, I fumble through my mind, attempting to find the words that have escaped me.

James takes three long strides in my direction, quickly closing the distance between us, but before he can make his way around to me, I push my seat back and raise my hand to stop him. Hurt flashes across his features and my chest clenches, fearing the barrage of questions I'm certain are coming my way. But they don't. Instead, he plops down in the seat set up in front of the large oak desk and leans forward on his knees. The hurt is replaced by concern pooling in his fatherly eyes.

"That bad, kid?" he says. His voice is soft and thoughtful.

"Yeah," I whisper.

"But you're okay, right?" he asks again.

"I'm getting there."

"Good." He smiles at me, considering me for a moment before he continues. "You know what I've learned in life?"

"What?" I reply. The edges of my lips curl up in a sad smile. His efforts are appreciated and the fact that he isn't hounding me with questions allows the tension to seep out of my shoulders.

"That the saying 'What doesn't kill you makes you stronger' really is true. I know it sounds corny but whatever this is," he says, nodding in my general direction, "is only going to give you strength, because it's obvious it hasn't broken you. You're here. You're still standing, kid. That's all that matters." He smiles and gets up. Before he leaves, he turns and faces me. "Just so you know, I'm a hell of a good listener. My door's always open if you need me." With that, he turns and leaves, gently shutting the door behind him.

I drop my head into my hands. The breath seeps out of me slowly, as I rub my temples, trying to make the pounding subside. My heart is rattling in my chest and it's getting harder to breathe. I contemplate calling Raha to come pick me up, throwing the towel in on this "first day back" thing.

"You're okay. You're safe. You can do this," I mumble out loud to myself. Then I grab the top file and force myself to read it. I need a distraction.

An hour later, I've made some progress. It's not billable-hours worthy, but it's something. And I haven't yet run for the hills, so there's that too. I decide I need some sustenance, but since my stomach still feels all knotted up and twisted, I settle on the idea of a cup of coffee, heading to the employee lounge to make one.

I take the pot off of the base and rinse out the morning's brew. I meticulously fill a new filter with eight scoops of grains, in case anyone else needs an afternoon pick-me-up. The simplicity of the action helps sooth my nerves, making me feel closer to normal. Then I lean against the counter, watching it drip in a slow stream from the nozzle. The familiar splashing sounds as it hits the bottom of the pot are both hypnotic and calming.

I'm lost in thought when suddenly a pair of hands grab my waist. I jump a foot in the air and scream, wrapping my arms tightly around me, trying to shelter my body from the perpetrator. I turn ready to dash out of the door, sure Arash has finally found me.

I find Isabelle staring at me wide-eyed and petrified. Her normally tanned skin looks paled with surprise.

"Oh my God, I'm sorry! I didn't mean to scare you," she apologizes. "I was just playing around. I've been meaning to come into your office all day to say hi but I've been swamped."

I feel the heat of blood flush my skin crimson with embarrassment. I run my hand through my hair, smoothing it down, worried my fright has it standing on end.

"It's okay. I'm sorry. I just wasn't expecting it, that's all."

She smiles, laugh lines hugging the corners of her lips as she steps in and wraps her arms around me.

"I've missed you," she says. "It's no fun without my lunch date. I think I've had my fix of fishing stories from James." She giggles.

I count slowly to ten in my head, trying to keep my body loose when all it wants to do is stiffen beneath her touch.

"Are you okay, Leyla?" she asks, when she finally lets go.

I don't know how many times I've been asked that today. I should feel special with everyone's concern, but I'd rather just be left alone. As Isabelle stares at me, waiting, I struggle to find my words. The sudden departure of the adrenaline rush has my thoughts fuzzy.

"Yes, I'm good. Sorry. I'm just tired. First day back and all," I answer. Just then the coffee maker beeps, signaling its completion. "It's ready!" I say, brightening my tone. I try to smile, pretending it's just any other Monday. "Want some?" I hold up two white coffee mugs in Isabelle's direction.

"Sure," she says. I fill them up and hand her one as we make our way over to the cream and sugar further down on the counter.

"How's it going with that guy?" I ask, desperate to take the focus off of myself.

Isabelle is another of the junior attorneys in the office. We started a week apart, and therefore became fast friends as we navigated through the newness of our roles in the firm. James took us both under his wing, solidifying our little triangle.

Isabelle loves to talk, especially about herself. Asking about her newest love interest works like a charm as she begins rambling on about how gorgeous he is. One cup of coffee, and ten long minutes later, I think I've learned everything there is to know about him.

When I finally break free, I head straight toward the bathrooms, hiding inside one of the large stalls. I lean my back against the door and swallow in the silence. So much stimulation. My brain hurts. I'm exhausted. Pretending everything is okay and dodging inquisitions has depleted my energy. I'm not in the mood for all of this socializing. I wish people would mind their own business and just go away.

I afford myself only a few minutes to dance in my pity party, then I head back out, ready to take on some more work. But just as I do, my boss walks in.

"Oh, hey, Leyla, nice to have you back," she says.

"Thanks, Linda. It's great to be back." I'm tired of the forced enthusiasm, so my chipper tone comes out subpar.

When she asks, "Is everything okay?" I can't pretend anymore.

"No," I reply, dropping my head and closing my eyes. I force the air in and out of my lungs as it burns inside my chest, bracing myself for the next question.

"What's wrong?" she asks, reaching out and gently placing her hand on my arm.

The truth sits heavily on the tip of my tongue, wanting nothing more than to be set free so I can be done with this charade. But I wonder if I'm ready to see yet again, another person stare at me with pity in their eyes and confusion in their words as they search for the right things to say. Sadly, there are no right things, and their attempts are futile. But they try anyway, and I humor them, because it's the thought that counts.

Part of me wants to tell her what's happened. Maybe the pity wouldn't be so bad in this situation. It could win me another week off from work where I don't have to overexert myself trying to play the part and avoid the questions. But as I stare at Linda's kind eyes watching me, I realize that I don't want to run and hide any longer. The days of staying cooped up in my room beneath the comforter need to be over. I won't let Arash take anything more from me. Including living. James is right; he didn't break me.

"It's just been a rough week," I finally reply.

"Anything I can do?" she asks.

I wrap my fingers around the strength I feel and use it to release the tight hold on my lungs. The air begins to flow more freely, making each intake of breath easier to bear.

"Thanks, Linda. I really appreciate it. But I'm okay," I say.

I squeeze her hand, still resting on my arm, and return her smile. Then I head out of the bathroom and back to my office, grabbing another file off of my desk, taking my life back.

* * *

"Hey," Raha says, plopping down on my bed beside me.

"Hi."

I'm finally in a pair of sweats, my work clothes draped over the back of my chair. My hair's pulled up in a loose bun on the top of my head and I have a throw blanket wrapped around me. The television is on in the background, a Geico commercial playing. Raha snuggles up beside me, pulling the blanket over until we're sharing it.

"How was it? Was it hard?" she asks.

"Was what hard?"

"Being at work."

"Yeah, it was, I guess. It was hard having to answer people's questions without actually telling them anything. I felt like I was dodging everyone most of the day. But I managed," I say.

"Good, Sissy. I knew you could do it," Raha encourages. "Going back tomorrow?"

"Yup," I answer.

"Fantastic," Raha adds, leaning her head against mine and draping her foot over my leg. "Want to watch the latest episode of Gray's Anatomy?" she asks.

"Of course," I answer, smiling as she winks at me.

My sister has no idea what an intricate role she's played in my healing. She's held my hand when necessary, been furious when called for, and now that I'm trying to put the pieces back together, to go back to feeling more like myself and less like the broken version of me, she eases into the normalcy of our relationship magnificently.

CHAPTER TWENTY-ONE

"Hi, *aziz*," Zandayee says.

My aunt pushes me away from her, trying to get a better look as she turns me left, then right. Her gaze searches my skin, looking for the remnants of my attack. But it's been two weeks and the bruises have faded. The only scars left are those that no one can see.

"I'm fine," I say, leaning in and kissing both her cheeks. Customary Iranian greeting.

"*Khodara shokr.*" *Thank God.* She shakes her head in disbelief.

It's not every day she hears about a Persian girl almost getting raped in a club bathroom. Especially when it's her niece. And the attacker is the boy she set her up with. Sadly, it probably happens more frequently than we know.

I give her a quick smile, uncomfortable with the worry in her eyes. I move onto Dayee. He pulls me into his arms and kisses the crown of my head. He makes no references to the elephant in the room, looking down at me knowingly. He doesn't appear to want to acknowledge it, and I don't want to be reminded.

Maman comes in from the kitchen, tray of *chayee* in hand, setting it down on the coffee table. Baba and Dayee grab their glasses and head over to the dining room, where Maman has set up an array of *sheerini*, *sweets*, along with *tokhmeh*, *roasted watermelon seeds*, and cut up fruit. Maman and Zandayee follow. This is their monthly Hokm battle. I use their distraction as a way to escape.

Hokm, a trick-playing card game of two teams is the most popular card game in Iran. Each team has two members that must sit across from each other at the table, with the objective of reaching seven points to win the round. Hokm translates into "command or order," but in card game jargon, it's Persian for trumping the other team's hand.

Maman wanted to cancel it, but I've finally agreed to let Ben take me out, so I urged her to enjoy herself. She's spent the last two weeks fighting her own battles, dealing with war wounds that have evolved as a result of my own. We both need a mental break.

I head into my room to grab my jacket and purse, leaving the grown-ups to their own devices. Ben is taking me out to dinner. He's been coming over after work a few nights this week, hanging out with me at the house. We watch movies, or just sit in the backyard. He's suggested we go to a theater or out for a bite to eat, but I haven't felt up to it. However, I've officially gotten through my first week back at work without any meltdowns. This is cause to celebrate. Plus, I'm tired of being a prisoner of my own making.

As I make my way back to the living room, I bump into Raha, eavesdropping in the hallway. I'm reminded of when we were little and Baba and Maman would have huge arguments. We were too young to understand that couples disagree, sometimes very loudly, so we'd huddle together in the hallway on high alert, waiting. I'm not sure if we thought Baba would storm out the front door never to return, or that Maman would vanish into thin air, leaving her daughters behind, but we'd hold onto each other tightly as we pressed our backs into the wall, eyes shut, waiting for some horrible fate we were sure would come.

"What's going on?" I ask.

"Shh!" she urges. She points to her ear, signaling I should listen.

I move in closer to her and she instinctively holds my hand. I'm transported into the past immediately, a warm rush of nostalgia for my youth running through my fingertips. I stifle a giggle until Raha pins me to my spot with her eyes. That's when I pay attention to the conversation going on in the other room.

"His sister is the one that turned him in," Zandayee says. "His parents were so angry with her. They've pretty much disowned her." Her voice is low and concealing.

His sister turned him in? The image of the dark-haired girl from the police station floods my mind. *Of course!* How did I not see the resemblance before? That's why she looked so familiar, because she looked like her brother.

"*Beechareh*," Maman says, empathetically. *Poor thing.* "It's not her fault! Ali, can you believe this?"

"No. I thought when they asked Leyla to come back for more questions, it was standard procedure. I never imagined this."

The fear flooding my arteries propels me forward. Raha tries to stop me, no doubt sure the parental units will stop talking once they see we're in ear shot, but I push past her.

"Imagined what?" I demand, startling my family. Their heads all whip in my direction. "What's happened?"

Maman and Zandayee exchange worried glances, and Dayee leans forward in his seat. But it's Baba who speaks.

"Nothing has been confirmed yet, *dokhtaram*," he says. "Let's not rush to any conclusions."

I take a step toward him, ready to launch into my argument, when the doorbell rings, distracting me from my mission. I'm frozen in the moment, suspended between the need to hear the rest of their story and the fear of what they have to say. I can't move, can't think behind the sound of my heart pounding in my ears. Maman has gone pale, almost green, as if the *chayee* she's drinking has somehow gone sour. The unreadable look on Baba's face only makes me more nervous.

"Hi, everyone." Ben glances around the room. It's obvious in the energy that something is wrong.

"Hello, Ben," Baba replies, pulling his gaze away from me. He stands as Ben carefully makes his way over to shake his hand.

"Hi," Maman says, as Ben leans down to hug her.

She looks momentarily uncomfortable beneath Zandayee's gaze, but quickly shakes it off. There's no room left within these walls to be concerned with how things appear to others. She squeezes his arm, a silent declaration to her sister-in-law that this non-Iranian from Sara's past has been accepted into the Amini family. Zandayee turns away.

I want to be angry, feel appalled at my aunt's blatant judgment, but I can't find the fury. Not now, not when there's something huge hanging in the balance. I have the distinct feeling it's going to crush me.

"Tell me," I demand.

I haven't even greeted Ben as he lingers behind Maman, waiting. His posture is sharp and alert. His intuition on point. Four strides. That's all it takes for him to make it to my side. He doesn't say a word, or even touch me. He stands ready to catch me if it all comes tumbling down.

"There's talk that this may not be Arash's first time."

I hear Raha gasp from behind me.

My pulse accelerates and I feel like my heart may explode. But I'm not happy with that explanation, so I force my voice up through my chest, wrapping it around my words.

"What does that mean?"

"We aren't sure. But I don't want you to worry about anything else right now, *azizam*. You've been through a lot and we don't know anything for sure. It's all just talk. You know how people are. It could be nothing," Maman says.

Nothing. If only it were that simple.

"Just tell me! Stop being cryptic. It only makes it worse!" I yell, my words echoing off the walls in the silence, making it clear I'm no longer asking.

Baba looks like he's about to answer me, but he stops, unable to deal the last blow. It's Dayee who steps forward in his place. The empathetic expression he wears is one more dagger twisting deep into my chest. I've grown weary and tired of everyone's concern. I'm not the broken little bird they all seem to believe.

"Like your Baba said, nothing has been confirmed, but we've heard of one other family that has brought their daughter forward."

"Forward?" I ask.

"Yes. She's saying Arash raped her."

All the words are lost to the enormous shock this new information provides, leaving me speechless. I don't know what to say or how to react. What Arash did to me was horrible, unforgivable. But I had thought it was his first time, a moment gone terribly wrong. He'd made choices I was sure he regretted, ruining a life he'd barely begun. A dangerous, aggressive boy with a fractured ego and overwhelming insecurities. Surely that was it?

But now there's confirmation that he's done this before. I wasn't his only prey. Maybe it wasn't me that brought this on myself.

Maybe the truth is that Arash is a monster in the body of a man.

* * *

"Talk to me, Leyla," Ben says.

He's sitting across from me, trying to appear as if he's enjoying his food, but I can see it's a façade. He squints every time he swallows, like the food is painful as it moves down his throat.

He insisted we still go to dinner, despite the fact that all I wanted to do was crawl back into my oversize sweats and lie beneath my comforter. Sleep would be impossible, but the protection of the down feather cocoon seemed necessary. I know those days were supposed to be over, but the current information I've just received feels like an exception to the rule.

He wouldn't have it though, nearly dragging me out the front door with my parents as his cheering squad. Moments like this, I'm both grateful and annoyed at their change of heart.

As a result, I've been pushing *albaloo polo, cherry rice*, around my plate for the past hour. A new Persian food restaurant opened near Ben's apartment; he thought it would be nice to give it a try.

He'd heard their *albaloo polo* was worth the visit and he knew it was my favorite. It's good, the perfect combination of sour cherries and cherry syrup, the right amount of tart to offset the sweet. But each bite I try to consume feels like I'm eating Styrofoam, lodging in my throat as I struggle to swallow it. I've given up, resorting to sorting out the cherries from the rice. I currently have two impressive piles on my plate.

I meet Ben's gaze, see the concern in his eyes. *Will he ever stop looking at me like that?* Always so worried about me. It makes me feel weak when I'm not, further dampening my mood.

"I'm fine," I say. My tone is sharper than I'd expected and I have to keep from rolling my eyes at him.

"I know you are," he replies. He's staring at me, his eyes sweeping over the features of my face. I feel exposed, unraveling with the frustration I feel.

I don't want this.

I don't want Arash and his malicious past to be part of my story. I don't want everyone to keep looking at me like I'm going to shatter at any moment. I want to rewind back to the night I met him, ignoring Maman's excitement over the potential of a "good Iranian boy" dating her daughter. I want to erase the night I let him touch me in his car, finding his aggression a hot turn-on rather than what it truly was. The beginning of our cat and mouse game; the monster sizing up his unsuspecting prey. Imagining the thoughts going through his head makes me want to vomit. *How could I be so stupid?*

I think that's the worst part. Feeling as if I don't even know myself. I thought I was intuitive, a good judge of character, but Arash stripped away any confidence I had. I feel as though I can't trust myself anymore, second-guessing every move I make. I'm at a loss, struggling to figure out who I am if I'm not all the things I thought I was before.

"I want to fucking kill him," Ben says. He's been watching me, always aware of the war waging inside my mind. "I want to wrap my fingers around his neck and squeeze the life out him." His anger is buried deep within the furrow of his brow. His normally clear blue eyes are mottled with the darkness he feels, dulled yet burning at the same time. Even in his uncharacteristic fury, he's beautiful.

A flutter stirs beneath my ribcage, my body responding to the force of his gaze. He wears his protective nature like armor, my personal soldier, ready to kill my predator. It's constant and unwavering, this need to make things right in my world. I find it endearing and thoroughly breathtaking.

I'm suddenly yearning to be closer to him. It's odd to feel this way, in a moment like this, where we're discussing the man that's changed my life in more ways than I care to think about. But nonetheless, I can feel the yearning taking hold.

"When I think about what could have happened..." He stops before he finishes his sentence, shaking his head.

"Ben," I say, "I'm okay. It could have been worse, but it wasn't." I don't know if he believes me, but he gives me a half-smile. His left dimple flashes, reminding me of a time when things were simpler.

"I know you are. I'm just not sure I am," he says. "I can't sleep, thinking of what he did to you. It haunts my dreams. I know this isn't supposed to be about me, and it's not." He tries to reassure me, wide-eyed and supportive. "It's just, I'm driving myself nuts. I can't help thinking that if things had gone differently between us, then maybe this would never have happened."

Everyone constantly blaming themselves for a situation that nobody could have controlled. None of us could have guessed Arash would have done this. If anyone should have been onto him, it's me. Ben is the least to blame.

"Hey," I say, rubbing my thumb across his palm. "No one could have stopped this, least of all you. Shit just happens sometimes. It sucks and it's hard, but it's over now. I can't go back no matter how badly I want to. I don't want Arash to control how I feel anymore. There are other women who had it much worse than I did, and I just want to be thankful that things didn't cross that line for me. I won't let him win. I want to move forward. And I want to do that with you."

Even in the upside down that has become my life, one thing is certain. I want Ben.

He moves his hand up to the side of my face, running his thumb gently down my cheek. I lean into it, taking in the feel of him. In that moment, nothing exists other than him and me.

The waitress interrupts us, asking if we'd be interested in tea and Persian pastries. Ben politely declines, requesting our check. I try to reach for it, a futile attempt. Ben just looks at me, causing me to withdraw my fingers away from the black leather folder. I wait patiently while he pays then let him lead me to his car.

I turn to take my seat, but am stopped short when he pulls on my arm. As I face him, he steps toward me, pulling my body into his. His gaze is weighted with emotion. I can see his desire, feel his need to lean in and kiss me, but he hesitates.

He doesn't know that my body is currently on fire. Or that I can hardly breathe from how close he's standing to me. I want nothing more than to feel his lips on mine.

I don't wait for him to wade through his indecisiveness. I understand that he's unsure of whether I'm ready. So instead, I silently give him permission to kiss me by pressing my lips gently to his. Hot, wanting sparks rain down around us.

I inhale the familiarity of his intoxication. My tongue finds his, losing myself in the feel of his mouth. My fingers intertwine in his hair, the soft strands melting into my fingertips. The definition of his muscles press hard against my breast; I wish we were naked, tangled in his bedsheets.

We stay wrapped around each other, until a crowd from the restaurant walks past us, whistling at our public display of affection. We pull away, breathless and giggling.

As he drives me home, Ben holds my hand, his thumb instinctively rubbing the skin of my palm. For the first time, in what feels like forever, the calm I feel isn't fleeting. And when I finally crawl into bed, the demons of the night don't come to haunt me.

CHAPTER TWENTY-TWO

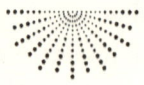

"What do you want to watch?" Ben asks.

He's in the kitchen, opening a bottle of wine. The light overhead throws a shadow behind him, defining the outline of his body. The rounded slopes of his shoulders, leading to the curve of his back, ending at the indent of his tight waist. His jeans sit comfortably on his hips, exposing the bronze of his skin as he reaches into the cabinet above him for two glasses. He grabs the wine opener from the counter, flashing his dimples at me as he catches me staring. I can feel a flush warm my cheeks, but I can't turn my eyes away.

As he opens the bottle, twisting the cork, the definition of his forearm and the distinct road map of his veins makes something unexpected stir inside me. Goosebumps rise to my skin, and I squirm beneath the throw blanket on the couch. I unconsciously run my hand through my curls, suddenly insecure about my presentation.

I'm in a pair of black leggings and an oversize gray sweater. Plans were for a low-key evening of movie rentals and junk food. I haven't given any thought to how I look these past few weeks, too preoccupied with other emotions to worry about my vanity. Now, I suddenly wish I'd taken time to put on some makeup. A little lipstick or mascara would make me feel less frumpy in comparison to Ben's Guess model appearance. The worst part is he's gorgeous without trying.

He doesn't seem to sense my discomfort when he strides over to me, wine glasses and a bucket of popcorn balanced strategically against his chest. He hands me a glass and plops down beside me, placing the bucket between us. I steady my gaze on the television screen as he fiddles with the remote, trying to get the Blu-ray to play.

I steal small glances at him when he isn't looking, noticing the furrow of concentration creasing his forehead, the way he's biting his lower lip while he tries to figure out why the television isn't cooperating. The heat on my skin intensifies as my eyes trace the outline of his face, memorizing the magnificent chisel of his jaw. I instinctively lean toward him, but stop short, pulling back.

I want so badly to be near him, his naked body pressed against mine, but I'm hesitant. There's a part of me that feels like something's wrong. Shouldn't I be sickened by the thought of someone else's touch? Isn't that how I'm supposed to react? Just two months after I've been assaulted, I'm ready to jump into bed with another man. But the other man is Ben, and I've been in love with him for the better part of a year.

I'm plagued with the question of what my family would think or my friends would say. Would it rid them of the pity in their eyes to see me move on? Or would I be judged for throwing myself into another man's arms in such a short time?

What if Ben realizes I'm damaged? Perhaps he deserves better, someone who doesn't carry a horrid experience like a satchel on a camel's hump, my burden to bear as it winds into my DNA. Despite how far along I come, the memories of that dreadful night will always be somewhere in the darkest crevices of my mind.

And what if I try to have sex with him and realize I can't? Till now, I've only daydreamed about what it would mean to be that close to Ben, skin on skin, fingers running across my body. What if he tries to touch me and I can't keep Arash locked away? Another rejection for Ben could quite possibly be the last straw. Yet something inside me urges me forward, despite the risk.

Life is barely starting to revert back to normal. I'm back to work and in the swing of things. I'm also no longer holding myself prisoner at home, forcing myself to venture out more. I prefer not to be alone, though. Arash posted bail as expected, and although he's legally not allowed near me, I still can't help but be nervous.

Nonetheless, I'm not as much of a wreck as I was weeks ago. I'm starting to feel more like myself. It helps that the physical evidence of Arash's obsession is no longer visible when I look at myself in the mirror. It's easier to see who I used to be when I'm not hidden behind a patchwork of bruises.

Ben's hand brushes against mine as he grabs the spare remote, mumbling obscenities under his breath. A surge of electricity burns up my arm pulling my attention back to him. When the result of his effort lights up the television screen, I giggle, earning me a wink and a dimple in return.

"There we go," he says, leaning back against the couch.

He lifts the wine glass to his lips and a sigh escapes me. Worry lines suddenly crease Ben's forehead.

"Are you okay?"

"Yes, I am," I stutter. "I'm fine. Sorry."

I quickly pat his hand, returning my attention to the television screen. Disappointment dampens my mood. Every reaction now is connected to the trauma I've experienced. I can't even sigh without it triggering worry. The idea that I want him isn't even on his radar.

Scenes are flashing across the TV, but I'm not paying attention. Instead, I'm distinctly aware of the heat rising off Ben's body as he sits close to me. He drags his fingers through his hair and I can't help but imagine what they'd feel like running across my skin.

The couch shakes as he chuckles, the deep rumble starting at the pit of his stomach, fanning outward like a burst of sunshine. He instinctively moves closer to me, lifting his arm so I can scoot beneath it. I feel safe here, wrapped up in the way he feels about me. His fierce need to protect me has made its way to the forefront these past few weeks. I've fed off of his strength, as I've rediscovered my own.

I lean into him, his heart beating methodically against my cheek. It's soothing, lulling me into a peaceful bubble of content. The thumps of my heart seem to sync with his, two perfect pairs in a drum circle. I sigh again as I feel him kiss the top of my head.

I deserve to be happy, this much I'm sure of. And despite tainting a part of my past, I refuse to allow Arash the power to ruin anything further for me. He doesn't get to restrain me any longer.

We stay intertwined on the couch, sharing the bucket of popcorn now resting on my lap. I feel Ben's fingers twist around one of my curls. His signature move; he does it unconsciously, but I always notice.

Desire rises further inside me, so fierce it demands my attention. I can't ignore it any longer, can't worry about what things will look like in the morning, or who will care. All I know is that my body craves him, needs to feel connected in a way I can only imagine with him.

Before I have a chance to complicate the situation with my unyielding doubts, I turn beneath his arm. He meets my gaze, confusion lingering momentarily before understanding settles in. I twist my fingers in his hair as I push my body into his lap, straddling him. I'm vaguely aware of the popcorn now scattered all over the floor beneath his feet.

I press into him until I can feel the quickening pace of his heart beneath the taut outline of his chest. I'm kissing him now, our lips and tongues twisting around each other, blurring into one. There are so many layers between us. So much past. So many memories. I yearn with the need to erase them, to begin somewhere new, where nothing other than the two of us exists.

I frantically pull at his shirt, ripping it up over his head and flinging it to the floor. I need the feel of his skin beneath my fingertips, the rise and fall of his breath, to remind me that I'm not dreaming. He follows suit, undressing me until I sit on his lap bare chested.

His movements are slow while he stares deep into my eyes. His fingers rise to the tender flesh of my breast, running circles across it until my nipple is between his fingertips. He applies a gentle pressure causing me to moan with pleasure. The sensation so overwhelming, I almost lose myself.

My eyes flutter shut, my head falls back, exposing my nakedness to him further. I feel the warmth of his mouth lay kisses across my skin, a flutter of lips and tongue tracing shapes along my body. He takes in one nipple, then the other, teasing them between his teeth until I think I may shatter into a million pieces. The sensation builds and intensifies, causing me to lose my inhibitions, low moans escaping me before I can contain them.

I'm unraveling beneath his touch, the burden of the past two months shedding like snake skin. He kisses my forehead, replacing the memory of my head crashing into the door. When his hand grazes my chest, he removes the feeling of my dress strap being torn. And when he gently finds the tender flesh between my legs, he eradicates the image of Arash trying to press his fingers into me and the realization of the nightmare to come. With every caress, he erases a bruise or scar left behind by my attacker. Ben frees me in that moment, in more ways than he could imagine, creating a world around me that is filled with love and wanting, one that pushes my demon back into the depths of where he came.

Hours later, when I lie naked and wrapped around his body, I no longer feel the constriction in my chest, the inability to breathe from dread. The assault, despite the terrible recollection haunting me, isn't the part I feared the most. It's the loss of trust in myself and my inability to see the truth in people. The fact that I'd disregarded so many warning signs Arash had so readily displayed, pretending that my intuition was playing tricks on me, terrifies me the most.

How do you build trust again with your own self? How do you prove to yourself that you aren't naïve and that the world isn't a dangerous place you can't seem to see? I really don't know. But in this moment, as I lie with my head against Ben's beating heart while he plays nonchalantly with my curls, I know one thing to be true: I am not wrong about Ben.

He's strong and protective when I need him to be, and he's loving and gentle in our cherished moments. He's the kind of person I can depend on, reminding me that I'm stronger than I think. Ben will always look at me like I'm the only person in his world who matters, despite the scars I now bear. I chose him, which means my ability to see people isn't as skewed as I think it is.

Maybe Arash was the exception. Maybe my ability to judge was blindsided by his "perfect Iranian boy" exterior and my need to see

Maman happy. Maybe there isn't anything wrong with me, and the flaw really was in the details surrounding my decisions.

It's going to be a long road until I'm completely healed. It will take some time before I can go out into public without feeling the need to constantly look over my shoulder. It may take even longer before I can fully trust my own judgment again. But, with Ben's love surrounding me, I can see the light where I once felt darkness. He helps remind me that there's still good in the world around me. I see my strength reflected in his eyes, and I know it's just a matter of time.

EPILOGUE

The heat of the sand beneath my toes reminds me that summer is on its way. The sun bounces off the horizon, turning the ocean into glass. Seaweed floats across the water's edge, forming dark patches that break up the mirror-like appearance.

The cool breeze creates a subtle whistle as it runs across my skin, and the crashing waves provide the background music. I'm content with silently staring as I listen to Nature's symphony playing around me.

Ben grabs my hand and kisses the soft skin of my wrist, pulling my attention to him. The sun catches the diamond on my finger, the light almost blinding. It makes me smile. The engagement still hasn't fully settled in, making me giddy and breathless each time I notice my ring. I'm certain this is just some exquisite dream.

It's been a year and a half since Arash and the night that turned my world upside down.

Since then, much has changed.

"When is your appointment?" Ben asks.

"It's at four. We have time," I say. I have three hours until my therapy session.

The need to discuss the aftermath of fear and pain that Arash created became a necessity. But as the days stretched on, it became abundantly clear that my family had their own war wounds to deal with. I needed to find a way to heal myself, so I found outside help.

"When are we supposed to be at the shelter tomorrow?" Ben asks.

"I think ten, but I'll ask Dr. Jane today."

Since Ben and I have started volunteering our time helping Dr. Jane at the local charity, I've found peace. The camaraderie, albeit sad, that I feel with women who have had experiences similar to mine lets me know I'm not alone. It's helped me slowly piece myself together again. Now, the links in my chain are much stronger than I could have imagined.

Arash is currently serving time.

In the weeks following the attack, two other victims came forward with rape charges of their own. Months of grueling court cases, taking the stand as he glared me down from behind the defendant table, and sleepless nights, led to a jury finding him guilty. I no longer have to look over my shoulder, the demon of my nightmares tucked safely inside a cage of steel bars.

Ghesmat. Destiny.

Although we hope what fate has in store for us is a plethora of amazing things, life doesn't always go as we planned. Sometimes, the trials we face are so big that we fear we may be crushed beneath its repercussions. But we face them, despite feeling like we can't, because life doesn't leave us another choice. It isn't equipped with a rewind button.

If I could go back into the past and make different choices, erasing Arash from my life entirely, I would. If I could clear my mind of the images that still find ways to haunt me in the deepest moments of my sleep, I would. But I don't have the magic to do that.

What I do have the power to do is learn and grow as I evolve from this experience. In my weakest moments, I use it to prove to myself that I am truly strong. I wield it as evidence that there's always light at the end of the tunnel. And I remind myself how lucky I am to have so many people rooting for me.

This life I've created around me is truly beautiful.

THE END

Thank you for reading! Did you enjoy?

Please Add Your Review! And turn the page for a sneak peek of book three, FORBIDDEN BY TIME, available now!

SNEAK PEEK OF FORBIDDEN BY TIME

If there were pictures in the dictionary, Mom's face would be next to the word *swoon*. The giddy expression she wears every time Maziar and Sara are around, resembles that of a love sick teenager. It wouldn't be so annoying, if it wasn't always peppered with pitying glances in my direction and covert comments about how I'm not married as well. *Not as hidden as you think, Mom.*

The older sibling left behind in the marital race is an Iranian nightmare. Now add the fact that I'm a girl and you have the perfect recipe for disaster. I should get used to it. I can only assume if Mom looks at me this way, everyone else is probably saying worse. The lack of a husband when currently of child bearing age is not a cute accessory.

You'd think at twenty-eight, I still have lots of time, but Persian girl years resemble that of dogs, for every one we get older, we actually age a decade. I'm officially approaching old maid status. Ridiculous, but sadly the truth of it. I'm not vying to get married or anything. Or maybe I am, but that's just what I tell myself. I honestly don't know anymore. I definitely don't need a man; I just think dying alone may be depressing.

My need to oppose the unfair Iranian girl conundrum is why I'm currently sitting in the passenger seat of Maziar's BMW as he drives us over to the coffee shop where we will meet my new realtor. Or at least, potential new realtor. He still has to pass the good old fashioned father-brother test.

I stare out the window, watching the trees breeze by as the leaves blur into a wave of green. I try to block out the chatter between Dad and Maziar. They talk too much, and I have a headache.

My mind wanders to the dinner that set the wheels in motion on my newest endeavor: buying a house. Despite the need for freedom, as it provides me a way to shake the chains my family has bound me with but are too oblivious to see, there's a part of me that's terrified of the magnitude of this commitment.

"I can't wait until you're sitting here with your husband too, Bita, and my grandchildren are surrounding me," Mom had said dreamily. "Wouldn't that be nice?" She turned her lovesick gaze toward me then, and all I wanted to do was roll my eyes.

As if that wasn't bad enough, Maziar thought he'd be the "good" brother that he thinks he is, and jump in for the rescue. I don't need saving, but no one seems to realize that.

"Oh, leave her alone, Mom. She has plenty of time to get married," he'd replied, smiling at me. "Not all of us can be as lucky as me." Could he be any more annoying. "Plus, no one is thinking babies yet. Just practicing." He winked at Sara who turned the color of a cherry.

"Seriously, you guys are bordering intolerable right now." I'd finally allowed myself the eye roll I'd been suppressing. "There's more to life than just getting married."

"Of course there is," Mom agreed. "But you've finished school and passed your exams. Now you're officially a dentist and we couldn't be prouder. What else is there for you to accomplish, though? You're getting older, *azizam.*" *My dearest.*

Now, just a few minutes out from our destination, I wish I hadn't let her get to me.

But the cultural expectations placed on young Iranian women are damn near impossible, really. We're encouraged to "stand on our own two feet," studying for careers that can support us without the help of a partner. But at the same time, we're urged to be on the prowl for a suitable husband. Suitable means hot, established, goal driven, and loving. Like that's easy. When was I supposed to be on this husband hunt anyway? I spent half my life studying my ass off. In a library. Alone.

"You're right, Mom. I'm getting older and it's time I take the next step." Her eyes had lit up momentarily as I'd hoped they would. Then, I delivered the blow. I'm such a bitch. "I'm going to buy my own place."

I cringe in the passenger seat as I recall my impulsive, and very emotionally charged, reaction. Dad being the open-minded, rational man he is, seemed to think this was a good idea. After giving me his lecture on all the expenses owning a house would require, and all the responsibilities I'd have, he gave in, taking Mom with him.

I hope I can make this work. Not so much because I'm afraid of failing. But more so, because coming back home after failing would give my brother enough ammunition to make me feel stupid until I'm on my death bed, and Mom exactly what she needs to control me forever. Not making it at this one thing, will tighten my chains to the point of suffocation.

I'm jarred from my thoughts when Maziar squeezes my wrist. I look around, realizing he's parked. It's go time.

"You ready?" The worry nestled in my brother's eyes makes the knot in my stomach multiply in size.

"Yup. I'm good," I lie. I slap on a winning smile and follow my family through the parking lot. I refuse to let my anxiety ruin this for me. I'm a grown ass woman, I can do this.

"He comes highly recommended," Dad says, as we make our way toward the entrance to the coffee shop. "Shahram just used him to buy Banoo's first condo and they loved him."

"Okay, Dad, whatever you think is best. We just need to get the process stared. It takes a while to find something," I reply.

"I don't know about using an Iranian realtor," Maziar teases. "I mean, you know how Iranians can be. He may screw us." He winks at me.

"Oh, Maziar, don't be so negative." Dad rolls his eyes. "And don't generalize people like that. We should support our community when we can. Let's talk to the poor guy before we decide on his intentions. That's the whole point of this meeting anyway."

My brother loves messing with Dad, pushing his buttons when he can. A playful camaraderie is ever present between the two of them. Sometimes, I feel like I've been left out of an inside joke that only they understand. Makes me wish I were a boy. Iranian men and their sons. Legacies to their names and reminders of who they used to be. Despite being Daddy's girl, there's a bond there I can't compete with.

I head toward the coffee shop doors with Maziar and Dad flanking me, two soldiers in an unnecessary battle. This business of buying a house has proven tedious. First, with their lack of confidence in me, and now, stuck between the walls of their opinions. It's been a tennis match of locations, style, and budget. I just want my own place. I've grown weary of Mom's constant intrusion and Dad's never ending guidance. I love my parents, but I'd prefer to love them from a distance.

The cold air rushes into our faces as Dad pulls open the door. It's a nice distraction from the heat bearing down on us as it bounces off the parking lot asphalt. The California summer sun is vicious, with little regard for sunburns and skin cancer.

A gentleman, possibly in his late thirties, looks up at us as we walk through the door. Recognition crosses his face and he stands, reaching out toward Dad when we approach his table.

"*Aghah* Parviz?" His brows rise in question and he smiles. His perfectly etched arches catch my attention. Full yet tamed. The new fad among trendy Iranian men. They give women a run for their money when it comes to getting their eyebrows primped.

"*Salom* Ramtin, *khan*," Dad greets him.

His smile broadens further as he reaches over to take my hand. "Bita *khanoom*, I presume?"

Despite the tiny flutter beneath my ribcage, his attention doesn't linger on me too long, turning it back toward the men accompanying me. I can only guess he presumes the deciding factor of whether he gets signed on as my realtor lies with them. A single Iranian woman, regardless of her age, is always viewed as some sort of damsel in distress when her father or brother are around. Stereotypical for sure, but something in the way he flashes me a tiny grin before turning toward the men, softens the blow. Almost like he's humoring them and it's our little secret. It pulls at me, unexpectedly.

"Can I get you some coffee?" Ramtin asks, looking around the table.

Dad stands. "I'll get it," he says.

"No, Parviz *aghah. Khayesh meekonam. It's my pleasure.* I have this."

Taarof, the art of hospitality in the Iranian culture. It would be considered rude if Dad doesn't offer to pay for his own family's drinks, as well as if Ramtin doesn't take the initiative to pay for it himself. Complicated and drawn out at times, but a popular Iranian social norm.

"*Merci* Ramtin. I would love a cappuccino," Dad says, taking his seat.

Ramtin turns toward my brother and I. "And for you?"

"Thanks. I'll have one too," Maziar adds. "And Bita will have a regular coffee."

As Ramtin walks up to the counter, I elbow my brother in the side.

"What?" Maziar asks, innocently.

"I can speak for myself." I scowl at him. "You seem to forget who's the older sibling around here."

"Dude, relax. I just know you like regular coffee. I'm not taking away your womanhood or anything." He chuckles, arms raised in surrender.

"You're so damn annoying."

"Okay, okay. I won't order coffee for you anymore. Jeez, I was trying to be nice."

I glare at him. But when my brother leans in and pecks me on the cheek, I can't help but giggle. I'm such a sucker when it comes to him. Definitely a downfall.

Ramtin returns with our drinks and takes his seat. He immediately launches into questions, focused on his mission to get our business. We discuss desirable locations, town houses versus traditional homes, number of beds and baths. He's very smooth, the perfect combination of business class and down home roots.

I lean back in my chair, the conversation barreling forward. Each question I answer is accompanied by both Maziar and Dad throwing in their opinions as well, giving me a moment to stare at Ramtin.

He's much older than me, but there's a childlike quality to him. Something in the deep set of his rich brown eyes feels adventurous. When he smiles, his plump lips stretch across his perfect teeth, exuding a charm that takes my breath away. I wouldn't say he's gorgeous, but nonetheless, there's something about him that makes me curious and has me intrigued.

"So we want to mainly focus on single family dwellings, and possibly town houses?" he asks.

"Yeah, that sounds good," I answer.

"Do you really want a town house?" Maziar interjects. "You share a wall and it could get loud if your neighbor isn't considerate." He turns toward Ramtin and starts listing pros and cons.

My attention is drawn to a tiny scar below Ramtin's left eye. It's small and oval, possibly from a bad bout of chicken pox. A tiny imperfection that somehow adds to his sex appeal.

"Does Saturday work for you?" he suddenly says.

"Huh, what?" I realize he's directing the question at me. I feel my cheeks burn and pray I don't appear red and blotchy.

Maziar and Dad just wait for me to respond, neither privy to the fact that I've been checking this guy out for the past hour. He isn't really my type, older than the guys I usually date, so it would make sense they'd be oblivious.

"Saturday," I mumble.

"Yes, does that work for you to go look at some houses?" Ramtin repeats. He smiles, and there's that twinkle again. It makes my skin prickle.

"Uhm, yeah. That should be fine."

He watches me for a moment longer than he should, making my stomach knot, then he looks away as he gathers his papers.

"Then I'll see you all this weekend."

He stands and I take in his long, lean frame. The cobra shape of his upper body and the way his shirt is pulled tight over his biceps puts my generation to shame. He's not buff by industry standards, just sharply defined.

How old is he? Sadly, the conversation never progresses to more personal terrain, and I leave the coffee shop under a barrage of commentary from Dad and Maziar, ruining my daydream buzz.

* * *

"The bedroom is kind of small." I make a slow lap within its four walls.

"Okay, that's good to know," Ramtin says.

He's leaning against the door frame, arms across his chest. His six-foot frame, slim and runner-like, only takes up half the space. The light from the window down the hall outlines his body in a luminescent glow, accentuating the rise and fall of his chest beneath his shirt.

The crisp white button up he wears amplifies his olive-toned skin, complimented further by the opposing dark shade of his jeans. His eyes are framed by long lashes and his eyebrows are in pristine condition, as usual. A grin subtly plays at the corner of his full lips.

For a moment I'm transported into an alternate universe, one I've been popping in and out of in my head the past few weeks while house hunting. Where Ramtin is mine and we're out browsing locations for our first home together. I imagine he'd lean against the wall like so, waiting for me to fully absorb the feel of our potential dwelling place.

He's old enough to be my dad. Okay, maybe not that old, but still. I was able to discover he's forty- three, so I guess he could technically have fathered me, if he knocked someone up at fourteen.

Mom and Dad make it down the hallway, their conversation pulling me out of my daydream. *Why am I even thinking about this guy that way? Is he my type?*

I really don't know what my type is. With very little experience in the arena of relationships, I still haven't figured it out. I usually go for the typical Iranian guys, the ones my friends drool over because they're hot, driven, and my age, but they are always too cocky and full of themselves to think about being anything other than the good time guy. Those guys don't work out well for me. Their immaturity causes me to lose interest quickly. *Why haven't I ever dated an older man?*

I turn to face the window, busying myself by taking in the view of the neighborhood. Honestly, I'm just no longer able to stare at Ramtin as he watches me with little interest further than the current possibility of a sale. I'm over here planning out futures that don't seem to be near his radar.

Three houses in, I realized I needed to downsize my idea of what I could afford. Dad's helping me with the down payment, but I'm determined to do this "adulting" business on my own. I need to stand on my own two feet, show myself that I can really do this grown up thing. We can't all be Peter Pan.

"It's cute, isn't it Bita?" Mom says, as Ramtin steps aside to let her pass. "The bedrooms are slightly small, but it's quaint and in such a fabulous neighborhood. It'll be easy to rent once you get married."

I have to consciously keep myself from flinching. She discusses my future as if marriage is the only outcome. What if I never find a guy I love enough to marry? Because, let's be honest here, being single indefinitely is a real possibility. But I don't say that to Mom. It would only spark a debate I really don't feel like engaging in. Plus, for some odd reason I don't yet understand, the idea of discussing my inability to find a mate while Ramtin is in earshot, is humiliating.

"I agree with your mom, this is good for you, *dokhtaram*. You don't need too much space right now when it's just you," Dad joins in.

And there it is, reference two, albeit subtly, to the lack of a husband.

"Well, I personally love this neighborhood and think it's a great little place where Bita could set down her own roots," Ramtin suddenly says.

My parents fall silent, exchanging wide-eyed expressions. I spare a quick glance in Ramtin's direction and he winks at me, flashing his perfect smile, making my stomach drop into my toes. *He doesn't think my only outcome to success is through a husband.* I try to hide the smirk curling the edges of my lips.

"We have a few more houses to look at before you need to make a decision, Bita," Ramtin adds. "If you're ready, we can head to the next one."

"Yeah, I'm ready." I follow Ramtin down the hall, wondering how this stranger somehow managed to leave my parents speechless. I'm not entirely sure, but the warmth growing in the pit of my stomach is a sure indication that he has my attention.

We make it to three more houses before we part ways.

"I really liked that first one," Mom says, as we drive home.

"Yes, it was the best location. Your mom's right, it will be easy to rent with its proximity to the beach."

I'm glad my parents have their priorities straight. Always hovering in the back of each conversation: when will she get married? Add a younger brother that just tied the knot, and the pressure is on.

I turn and lean my head against the backseat window, feeling the warmth from the sun. I stare out onto the streets of Santa Monica, watching couples walking hand in hand along the sidewalk. A sigh escapes me, a longing I try to deny, pushing to the surface. Despite my protests, I do dream of finding "the one." Maybe that makes me weak, or maybe it's just human nature. But a life of solitude scares me a little.

As we stop at a red light, a couple embraces. He leans down and kisses the crown of her head, and I'm oddly reminded of Ramtin. What would it feel like to have his strong arms wrapped around my waist, and the afternoon stubble on his face playfully scratch my skin as he kisses me?

We drive on, and as the image of the couple embracing, shrinks in my line of vision, so does the possibilities I've let run rampant in my mind all afternoon. Daydreams of Ramtin evaporate with the summer heat, taking with them the little bubbles of hope that have begun to form.

Grab your copy of FORBIDDEN BY TIME available now. Sign up for the City Owl Press newsletter to receive notice of all book releases!

Don't miss the book 3 of the Forbidden Love series with FORBIDDEN BY TIME available now and find more from Negeen Papehn at www.negeenpapehn.com

* * *

When love blossoms from the unexpected will the years between separate them forever?

On the outside, Bita appears to have it all under control. She's a no-nonsense, strong-willed, force to be reckoned with. On the inside, though, she's spent most of her life dealing with her pushy Iranian mother, ever concerned father, and overbearing younger brother.

But that's all about to change.

Bita is determined to stand on her own two feet. She's purchasing her first home, and ultimately, her independence. When Bita meets Ramtin, the sexy, older real estate agent, she gets more than she ever imagined. What was meant to be a simple property transaction, blooms into a fierce desire that leaves her breathless.

Now they must make their relationship work despite their fifteen-year age gap, and interference from their traditional families. Ramtin is everything she never knew she wanted, that is, until something unexpected becomes an all-or-nothing deal-breaker, and Ramtin may not be all in. Bita must decide what's worth fighting for and if Ramtin is worth the final risk...losing her heart.

* * *

All reviews are **welcome** and **appreciated**. Please consider leaving one on your favorite social media and book buying sites.

For books in the world of romance and speculative fiction that embody Innovation, Creativity, and Affordability, check out City Owl Press at www.cityowlpress.com.

ACKNOWLEDGMENTS

I've discovered that being a writer is not as solitary as I once believed. In the past few years, I've found myself surrounded by a group of amazing women that have each played an intricate role in the creations that I put down on paper. They are my tribe, my support system, and my dear friends. Without them, I couldn't have made it through the struggle of publishing, with its constant ups-and-downs, and the relentless ego beatings. And without their continuous motivation, encouragement, and confidence, the Forbidden Love series would never have come to be.

Ann, I can't begin to put into words what a fierce inspiration you have been for me. Your constant encouragement when the outlook seemed dim, and your devotion to plotting, editing, revising every word I write, has truly given me the courage to embark on this crazy roller coaster ride. I could not, and will not, do it without you. You are now and forever my writing guru. I thank you from the bottom of my heart.

Leslie, your friendship means the world to me. Despite never actually being in the same room together (although that is the goal for the new year), I feel as though I've known you all my life. Your ability to be rational when I'm freaking out, and your constant confidence in me, keeps me going. I love our plot calls, and even our shoot the shit calls, when we discuss how amazing Polynesian sauce might be. I cherish this friendship and depend on it more than you know.

Michele, you deserve an entire page of this acknowledgment dedicated to you. Thank you for entrusting me with your story. Despite becoming fast-friends, you opened up to me when we were mere acquaintances, and gave me the details of a nightmare no one should have to live through. Thank you for thinking that I deserved it and know that I will carry it with me forever. Without you, and your tireless rereads of Leyla's story, I couldn't have made her reactions and emotions as true to life as I did. She is who she became with your help and nurturing. You are the best sensitivity reader a girl could ask for. I hope I've made you proud.

Melissa, what can I say other than I absolutely adore you. We have become amazing friends and confidants through this City Owl adventure, and I couldn't be happier. Thanks for always pushing me forward, and coming to my aid whenever needed, whether that be when I'm beyond lost on the marketing front, or making me fabulous graphics, or reading through Forbidden by Destiny because I couldn't trust my grammarly skills. Anytime within this process, when I've doubted my abilities or my story, I hear your voice telling me you couldn't put it down as your tore through all two-hundred plus pages in three days. Here's to hoping we have writing retreats and bountiful wine sessions on the horizon.

Amanda Skenandore, thank you for being so willing to play middle-man when I tried to plot out the series of events that would occur after the assault. And also for passing me along to your fabulous husband, Steven, who tirelessly answered my text messages, and even spent time on the phone with me until I got it right. The time you guys volunteered is truly appreciated. Thank you so much for being a part of this book.

To my entire City Owl family, I could not ask for a better tribe to be a part of. Tina and Yelena, thank you for all your tireless efforts to bring our stories to life. You two are amazing. Amanda, thank you for going on this last run with me. Your insight and opinions helped shape this story into what we have sitting before us today. And to all my City

Owl sisters, there are too many of you to list, but you know who you are and I thank you for always being so helpful and supportive. Couldn't ask for a better group of soul sisters.

Mibl Art, my cover is fabulous and I'm totally obsessed.

Maryam, you are the best Iranian name genie. None of the characters would be who they are if you weren't the one naming them, and always making sure the names fit the side of the culture they're on. Your enthusiasm is infectious. I love you *dokhtar khaleh*.

Mom and Dad, you guys have always been my loudest cheering squad. I love having you both in my corner on this, and all things in life. You two have always encouraged me to be the best version of myself and for that I'm grateful. Also, Mom, thanks for giving me every Iranian saying you could think of each time I called asking if you could come up with one that fit the situation I was trying to convey. You both already know how much I love you.

Mike, thanks for supporting my version of a cross-fit obsession. I know the stress of deadlines and the worry of writer's block was tedious at times, but every chess game and monopoly competition you played with the boys to keep them busy so I could write, did not go unnoticed. I love you.

And to my beautiful not-so-little boys. Dreams are possible, so make them big and give it all you've got. You never know what can happen. This, and all things I do in my life, are for you. I hope when you look at my name scrawled across the cover, that the pride you feel is something you carry with you always. I live and breathe for you. Love you more than you will ever know.

ABOUT THE AUTHOR

NEGEEN PAPEHN was born and raised in southern California, where she currently lives with her husband and two rambunctious boys. She wasn't always a writer. A graduate of USC dental school, Negeen spends half of her week with patients and the other half in front of her laptop. In the little time she finds in between, she loves to play with her boys, go wine tasting with her friends, throw parties, and relax with her family.

Website: www.negeenpapehn.com

Twitter: twitter.com/NegeenPapehn

Facebook: www.facebook.com/NegeenPapehn/

Instagram: www.instagram.com/NegeenPapehn/

ABOUT THE PUBLISHER

City Owl Press is a cutting edge indie publishing company, bringing the world of romance and speculative fiction to discerning readers.

www.cityowlpress.com

www.ingramcontent.com/pod-product-compliance
Lightning Source LLC
Chambersburg PA
CBHW031218020726
47499CB00002B/640